Hadley

Sarra Manning

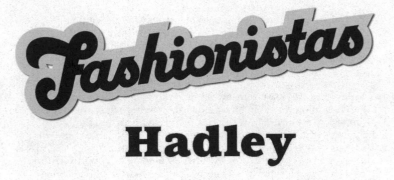

Hadley

Hodder
Children's
Books

A DIVISION OF HACHETTE CHILDREN'S BOOKS

A Catalogue record for this book is available from the British Library

ISBN-13: 978 0 340 93221 6

Typeset in Bembo by Avon DataSet Ltd, Bidford on Avon, Warwickshire

Printed and bound in China by Imago

The paper and board used in this paperback by Hodder Children's Books
are natural recyclable products made from wood grown in sustainable
forests. The manufacturing processes conform to the environmental
regulations of the country of origin.

Hodder Children's Books
a division of Hachette Children's Books
338 Euston Road, London NW1 3BH
An Hachette Livre UK company

Acknowledgements

Thanks to Chris Hemblade, Lorraine Candy and all at British *ELLE* for paying me to go to LA to hobnob with celebrities 'who don't have a mean bone in their bodies'. This book could not have happened without you.

Thanks also to my wonderful agent, Kate Jones and Laura Sampson and Karolina Sutton at ICM Books. Props as well to my editor Emily Thomas and Hachette Children's Books.

There are so many celebrities who were a source of continual delight and wonder as I read about their antics on the *ohnotheydidn't* LJ blog. To mention them by name would result in several lawsuits. But hey, ladies, thanks for the inspiration.

http://sarramanning.blogspot.com

BOOK TWO:
Hadley

'Your star is descending round here blindly . . .'
– Bailed Out by the Auteurs

Previously on

Laura, a TV model contest winner; Irina, a newly
discovered Russian model; Candy, a reality TV star
with punk icon parents, and Hadley, an ex-child
star, all move into a model agency flat in London.
After years of being the prettiest girl in town,
Laura gets a rude awakening when she realises that
she needs to lose her attitude and her excess weight
to make it in the world of modelling. But Laura
never imagined that she might have to lose Tom,
her devoted boyfriend back home, or that he
might not be quite as devoted as she thought.
And now, hard-nosed Irina has already
decided that the flat only has room
for one potential supermodel . . .
Read all about it in *Fashionistas:*

Laura

Prologue

'Mark Harlow, you have been found guilty of five counts of theft, two counts of fraud and one count of insider trading.'

Hadley tried hard not to fidget with the collar of her black wool dress. It looked demure, which was entirely the image she wanted to project. But even with the air con going full blast, April in LA wasn't really the right temperature for black wool dresses – even if they were from Marc Jacobs and a stunning contrast to her freshly streaked blonde hair.

Her father refused to show the merest flicker of emotion as he was convicted. Hadley's own face was equally expressionless as she watched the court artist sketching furiously. She made a mental note to get her publicist to have a word, because the picture that had turned up on the KTLA news last night had made her look about thirty.

Hadley adjusted her Chanel sunglasses and listened intently as the Judge elaborated on her father's list of crimes before sentencing him.

There was the new casino in Vegas that had never happened. The dodgy investment deals. The off-shore accounts in the Dominican Republic, that he swore blind had been emptied by his business associates, which meant that . . .

'You've stolen seventeen million dollars from your daughter, who entrusted you to safeguard the earnings that she's amassed since the age of three. It's a pity, Mr Harlow, that I can't punish you for betraying your own flesh and blood but that's not the duty of this court. It's the duty of your conscience. As you have no means to pay financial reconstitution to your daughter, I have no choice but to sentence you to three years in state custody.'

Her father was sweating now; little beads of perspiration peppering his forehead, as he swayed in the dock. Hadley heard her mother Amber release a frantic whimper, but Hadley sat still with her hands folded in her lap as her father was led away in handcuffs.

Outside the court there was a scrum of reporters and bulbs flashing. Amber leaned heavily on their lawyer's arm as she and Hadley stood at the top of the courthouse steps.

'Can we have a quote?'

'Hadley, how do you feel about the sentence?'

'Is it true you're moving to the UK?'

'The Harlow family will be issuing a statement,' their lawyer snapped. 'Until that time, no comment.'

He started to clear a path through the crowd with the help of two cops, but Hadley paused.

'I just want to say thank you to my fans for supporting me through such a tough time.' Her voice quivered slightly at the end of the sentence. Just a fraction, but it spoke volumes of quiet dignity, unlike Amber, who was sobbing hysterically into a ratty tissue. 'But I hope you'll understand that my family needs time and space to come to terms with this tragedy.'

'But Hadley, aren't you angry with . . . ?' A reporter shoved his mic right in her face, almost dislodging her shades. These people were so *rude*.

'No further questions,' the lawyer said firmly and they were on the move again, heads down as they hustled to the safety of the car.

Thank God for tinted windows. Hadley took off her shades as the door shut behind her and shook out her hair. Just as well she'd had time for a blow dry this morning.

'You're unbelievable!' Amber hissed, turning off the waterworks in an instant. Miraculously, her mascara was still intact. 'How could you have sued your father? After all we've done for you!'

Hadley put a hand on her heart, which was still beating steadily. 'I told you it wasn't my fault,' she gasped. 'It was, like, this whole lawyer thing. I'm totally devastated.'

Devastated was like a total understatement. Her loving papa had stolen $17 million from her and all he got was a lousy three years in jail. What was up with *that*? At least he was being sent to the Big House, and Hadley hoped with every fibre of her being that he'd have to wear a polyester jumpsuit in some gross shade. Totally serve him right.

'Well, I'm glad you're moving to London – I can hardly bear to look at you any more.' Amber rummaged in her clutch for a packet of gum.

'You have to stop stressing out,' Hadley advised, trying to tamp down the little flicker of hurt at Amber's words. It had to be the hormones. 'It's bad for the baby, Mom.'

Amber patted her aerobicised stomach and smiled for the first time. 'Bab*ies*.'

OK, as attention grabbers went, that was a good one. 'Huh? You mean, there's . . .?'

'More than one of them. Guess that fertility treatment paid off,' Amber said smugly. 'Face facts, sweetie, you're washed up. And this time round, I'm doubling my odds. I've already got a business manager lined up.'

'You're having *twins*?' It was, like, obscene to the power of one million. Especially as there wasn't enough money left for a nanny. Now Hadley couldn't get to London quick enough. 'Well, congratulations, I guess.'

'Thanks, honey.' Amber moved closer so that she could squeeze her daughter's hand tightly. Hadley knew exactly what was coming next. 'You know, the medical bills are mounting up and that crummy apartment complex doesn't even have a pool.'

Just for a second, the lack of pool tugged at Hadley's heartstrings but then she remembered the heart-shaped swimming pool with the ten-bedroom mansion attached to it, which had been repossessed. 'I'm sorry, Mom. I'm flat out broke. That's why I'm going to London. I can't even get an audition here.'

'Oh, c'mon, Hadley, I know you've got something tucked away for a rainy day. If you won't do it for me, then you can do it for your little sisters or brothers. Though I'm hoping for one of each, just to cover all the bases.'

'This limo took the last of my money,' Hadley confessed. 'I have to fly coach. If I can get some work in London, I'll see if I can help you.'

Amber pursed her lips. Probably in annoyance but it was hard to tell through the Botox. 'You're so ungrateful,' she said through clenched teeth. 'When I think of the sacrifices I made for you. I didn't eat for a week so you could have a new—'

'. . . dress for my *Starr Family* audition,' Hadley finished for her. 'I know, and I'm sorry, but we're both going to have to adjust to being poor now.'

The P-word finally shut Amber up. Usually it took a couple of Xanax. Maybe she was busy pondering life as a pauper or thinking of another way to touch up Hadley for a cash advance on the twins' earnings.

It wasn't until the car pulled up by the Virgin check-in desk at LAX that Amber spoke again.

'You're really not going to get much modelling work, sweetie,' she advised casually. 'You have a short bottom lip and your arms have no muscle definition. I'd aim for TV, if I were you.'

'Thanks, Mom.' Hadley slid out of the car, shades on in preparation for the paparazzi – but they seemed to have got lost en route from the courthouse. 'I know it will work out. You gotta have a dream in order for it to come true, right?'

'Yup, that's the spirit,' Amber drawled in a monotone. 'Shut the door, you're letting the heat in.'

The door slammed in Hadley's face and she stared at the two cases that the driver had just hauled out of the boot. What was she meant to do with them? Where was the studio lackey to carry them for her?

Newsflash; there wasn't one. She was going to have to do it for herself. She was going to have to do a lot of things for herself that she'd never done before. Like, check in her luggage and not lose her passport.

But how difficult could it be? Normal people managed to do it all the time.

Hadley grabbed the suitcase handles and started dragging them towards the entrance. It was just as well that she worked out so much.

'Miss? Excuse me, miss?'

She turned round to find two overweight women in matching 'California Dreamin'' T-shirts, staring at her. At least she could still rustle up a couple of fans, even if they were middle-aged and had bad dye jobs.

'Hi,' she said brightly, turning on her Hadley smile. 'How you guys doing?'

'Miss, you might find it easier if you roll your case on its wheels.'

Suitcases had wheels? Since when? Hadley shoved her sunglasses further up her nose and smiled at them. 'Oh, I know, but I prefer to drag them so I can work on my upper arms,' she lied. 'Gotta keep toned.'

Now they were both staring her, getting that glazed look that never led to anything good. She could predict the next words out of their mouths. Something along the lines of, 'You used to be so cute/It's such a shame you had to grow up/When are you going to make another movie?' (delete where applicable).

'Oh! My! God!' one of them squealed and Hadley braced herself for the inevitable.

'It's Hadley Harlow! We thought you were dead!'

Chapter One

London was majorly depressing. Like, all grey and damp – and that was before Hadley had even left the airport.

But on the plus side, because her therapist always told her to maximize the positive, she'd totally got upgraded. Gotta love her ever-faithful gay fanbase and how they always seemed to work the check-in desk.

And when Hadley hauled her cases off the carousel, she actually remembered to wheel them. Now it was just the complete lack of a driver holding up a sign with her name on it that was clouding her horizon.

Hadley scanned the crowd with rising panic. Everyone seemed to know where they were going or had people to meet them; all hugging and shedding tears of joy, like in that scene from *Love, Actually*. She had no one. Just two cases that weighed, like, a ton.

Then, out of the corner of her eye, she spotted it. A sign that said, 'Taxis' with an arrow and everything. It was so thoughtful of the people at Heathrow.

Once she was settled in the back of a black cab, Hadley decided to enjoy some moments of quiet reflection. Compared to the endless sunlight of LA, where the wide streets were lined with palm trees and squat white buildings, London was way different. There were patches of green everywhere and tiny houses and people; so many people walking about. No one walked in LA, unless it was from their car to the entrance of the Coffee Bean and Tea Leaf.

Not like she was a London virgin or anything. *Little Girl Lost II* had been set in London. OK, it had actually been shot in Toronto, but she'd been flown over for the premiere. Though mostly she'd been cooped up in a junior suite at the Dorchester, doing interviews. But she'd been filmed for a kid's programme on the open-top deck of one of those cute, red buses. They'd gone past the Palace of Buckingham and lots of really old buildings and statues and stuff.

Hadley peered out of the window and wondered what the Fierce Talent Management apartment would look like and how big the pool would be. Though it would probably have to be indoors, 'cause it rained all the time here.

She still wasn't sure how she felt about sharing with three other girls – it would either be awesome or awful. Other girls were a total unknown quantity. But she'd watched *Friends* as part of her research, and it looked like it could be fun. Though she couldn't live somewhere painted purple – it was bad for her chi.

The driver asked for the street address and Hadley tentatively pressed some buttons on her Sidekick.

'Flat three, forty-seven Bay-ham Street, Camden. Hey, is that near the Palace of Buckingham?'

The cab driver barked out a laugh as if he was coughing up a lung. 'You new in town, love?'

'Is it that obvious?'

What was obvious was that the sixty seven thousand dollars she'd managed to claw back from one of her father's off-shore accounts wasn't going to last long. The cab bill came to eighty pounds, plus tip, and even if Hadley wasn't familiar with the current rate of exchange, she knew that this was still way more than a mani/pedi at the chichi place she used to go to on Sunset.

Hadley stood on the doorstep of 37 Bayham Street, trying to get a feel for the nabe. It was so ghetto. There were a few straggly trees and a man walking a pit bull with a muzzle strapped over its jaws of death, but apart from that there were no signs of nature; just a cab office across the road, which was strewn with graffiti tags, and a little shop with metal grilles over the windows. Welcome to the war zone, Hadley.

And the cab driver hadn't been planning to help her with her luggage, even though she'd tipped him far more than he deserved. Hadley was still fuming as she followed him up the stairs of this tiny little house. It smelled really funky too. Of paint and something else that made her want to dry heave.

They came to a door at the top of the stairs and the cab driver dropped her cases with no respect for their Louis Vuitton-ness. 'There you are. Unless you want me to ring the bell for you as well.'

Hadley put down her vanity case. 'I think I can manage.'

He cursed all the way down the stairs. Obviously he wasn't cut out for a customer-orientated industry, Hadley thought as she pressed the bell. Her manicure was looking decidedly ragged.

The door swung open and there was a micro-sized little person standing there, wearing a T-shirt that looked as if it had been put through a shredder. Oh, but . . .

'Candy!'

She didn't actually know Candy that well, though they'd hung out a bit at LA Fashion Week, but still, at least, Candy spoke American.

'Hadley?' Candy grabbed a case and tried to yank it through the door. 'What the hell have you got in here?'

'Oh my God! I am so pysched to be here!' Psyched wasn't the word. The lobby or whatever was so small that Hadley felt claustrophobic. She turned back to Candy and forced herself to hug her. They hugged all the time in *Friends*. 'Who'd a thunk it?'

Candy squeezed her back. 'Had . . . Great to see you too . . . get off me, please!'

Yeah, the hugging thing was definitely overrated, but if she was interacting with Candy then she didn't have to deal with the tall, pretty girl with a majorly cranky face who'd emerged from another room.

'Hey there!' Hadley tried to sound bright and chirpy.

Jeez, everyone in this country was so standoffish. The girl just stared at her for a bit longer.

'I'm Laura.' She was British; that explained it all. Hadley ixnayed on the hugging when Laura stuck out a hand to be shook, like she was the Queen or something. 'So . . . um, you're a new model too?'

Did she look like a new anything? Hello! She'd been in the public eye since she was three. 'I'm not just a model,' Hadley informed her, because they needed to get that squared up right away. 'I'm, like, an actress and a singer and I do a lot of charity work too. I'm an all-round entertainer.' Look me up on the fricking IMDB! she longed to scream.

'Hadley, sweetie, no one remembers who you are in Britain,' Candy drawled. Which wasn't true. She used to be really massive in Britain. Also, the whole of Europe, and parts of Southeast Asia too. 'I thought that was the whole point of you coming to London, to relaunch your career.'

'Hey, my career does so *not* need relaunching.' Hadley whirled round so she could spin this situation herself, before it spun completely out of control. She wasn't washed up; she was rethinking her options. Why was that so hard for people to understand? 'I just had to get away from LA because of, like, the constant press attention. I had the highest rated entertainment show three years in a row

13

and I was the fifth biggest ranking draw at the box office in 1997 . . .'

'I'm going to put the kettle on.' That Lauren girl was so British that she should have her own show on BBC America. Oh, but now she was getting The Look too. 'Hey, were you in *Hadley's House*? God, I loved that show when I was a kid.'

It was best just to get it out of the way as quickly and painfully as possible. Like having collagen filler without a local anaesthetic.

'I was. I'm Hadley!' Hadley steeled herself to give Lauren a hug too. 'It's so adorable that you're a fan.'

Her personal space bubble was done with being invaded, and Lauren didn't seem that down with the hugging either. Hadley rested her hands on the other girls' shoulders so they could still have a connection. 'But y'know, Lauren . . .'

'It's Laura,' she said flatly.

Laura, Lauren. Potato, Potarto.

'. . . I'm a normal girl,' Hadley tried to explain. 'Just like you. Well, almost like you. And it's really important that where I live is, like, this comfort zone. I can't be in a negative space right now.'

'Well, I'll try not to,' Laura said doubtfully. 'Make the space negative, that is.'

Hadley's sunglasses were inching down her nose. She should have probably taken them off but after an eleven-hour flight, her eyes were itching like mad. 'I'm meant to be incognito so please don't tell anyone I'm here. The paparazzi . . .' She tailed off meaningfully.

'But who would I tell?'

Candy patted Laura on the shoulder; she really was a regular people person.

'She won't tell anyone, Had. Now, why don't we get you settled in?' Candy said, walking out of the room and throwing open a door. 'This is our bathroom.'

Muy problemo. *Our* bathroom?

'You mean, we *share* a bathroom? Candy, is this the actual apartment 'cause I was expecting a complex with a gym and a pool and a twenty-four-hour concierge and I thought that other room was just a really crummy lobby. I didn't realize it was an actual room room and that this was an actual, like, apartment . . .'

'Breathe,' Candy advised. 'Yeah, it's small, but I'm used to a fifth floor walk-up so it's not much different. You must have visited real apartments when you stayed in New York.'

'We always stayed at the Plaza.' Hadley sagged against the wall. 'Is my room habitable?'

There was a definite twitch from Candy. 'Well, I guess you could call it *bijou*. That's French for no room to swing a cat.' She gestured to a door across the hall that was practically on top of the kitchen – not that Hadley had any plans to go in *there*. 'Best to get it over with quickly.'

Hadley peered around the door and almost banged her

15

nose on the far wall. She'd never actually seen a broom closet but she imagined that it would be about five times bigger than this. There was a single bed, a fitted wardrobe, and that was it.

'I didn't know rooms came so small,' she said weakly.

'Sorry.' Candy shrugged. 'First come, first served.' She lowered her voice. 'This Russian girl stole the room I picked out. She's all cheekbones and Slavic attitude.'

Four of them were meant to share this chicken coop? 'Maybe I could book into a hotel?' Hadley suggested. 'Because I had certain specifics when it came to living here and these Fierce people have totally ignored them. My old agent would never have pulled a trick like this.'

'It's not so bad,' Candy said, peeping over Hadley's shoulder. 'Face it, neither of us are going to spend much downtime here anyway. We'll be out all the time. London is a real party town. C'mon, it's gonna rock.'

'I guess,' Hadley sighed. At least she'd be getting down with the normal folk, which would be an important life lesson. 'If this is how people in London live, then I can live like this too.'

'Hell, yeah, that's the spirit.' Candy punched the air with her fist. 'Well, I'd better unpack. Maybe we can go and get some food later. British supermarkets are so cool.'

Supermarkets were another unknown quantity. Hadley suspected that she might have been in one when they were filming an episode of *The Starr Family*.

16

'Do they sell sushi?'

'Well, I don't know, but maybe we can get British food, like, ah, custard and Yorkshire puddings.' Candy didn't sound completely enthralled with the supermarket expedition any more. 'Anyway, unpacking.'

Hadley nodded. Unpacking would keep her busy, not that she had anything much to actually unpack into. But Candy was already drifting towards her own room.

'Hey, I was sorry to hear about your dad,' she called over her shoulder. 'That really sucked.'

Finally, Candy and her agreed on something.

Chapter Two

Yesterday had been a blip. A temporary malfunction on the Hadley radar screen.

After a trip to Sainsbury's (and yay, they *had* sold sushi, even if had been really gross sushi) they'd trailed back to the apartment – or *flat*, as that Lauren/Laura/Lara, whatever her name was kept calling it.

They'd met Irina, who was really funny looking; way too thin and with these great blotchy freckles that she should have lasered off like years ago. Sides, she didn't even talk American or British, but this Ghetto Rap/Russian hybrid thing. And she'd stared at Hadley as if she was in a cage at the zoo.

Hadley had been forced to retreat to her room and practise her deep breathing exercises so she could dial down the hysteria. It hadn't really worked because Laura had spent hours yapping on the phone in her monotone accent and Hadley now knew far more than she'd ever wanted to about some guy named Tom and exactly what he and Laura had got up to behind something called a cricket pavilion.

The walls had felt like they were closing in on her for real and she should have been bone tired, but even with her eye mask on and ear plugs in, Hadley hadn't been able to get to sleep. Every time she'd tried to thump the pillow into shape or make sure the scratchy quilt was covering her properly, some new annoyance kicked in. Her brain had been buzzing like an angry bee and trying to make her think about stuff that she just couldn't deal with.

She'd dozed off for a couple of hours, but at 7am Hadley admitted defeat and headed for the bathroom. Even though Britain seemed pretty Third World there was plenty of hot water and a high maintenance hair and beauty regime was what she needed to turn her frown upside down, banish her demons and make her ready to take on the world.

Even Laura banging on the door when Hadley was in the middle of an extremely finesse operation with a pair of tweezers couldn't hold her back.

Thanks to some drops and a couple of cans of Diet Coke, her eyes were restored to their usual sparkly blue as she wriggled into her white Armani trouser suit, which said, 'I'm sexy and hot but I'm also the mistress of my own destiny.' The good folks at Fierce weren't going to know what had hit them.

Her little team for Operation Stardust, as Hadley liked to call it, were waiting for her when she was ushered into a conference room at the Fierce offices.

'Hey guys,' she trilled, coming into the room with her

phasers set on stun. 'I'm really pleased to meet you all.'

She walked around the table, dispensing handshakes and smiles that showed off her expensive dental work.

There was Derek, the director of Fierce's talent division, who she'd been speaking to on the phone. He was six foot, four inches of ebony-skinned handsome. A twitchy little girl who was a junior something or other – Hadley racked her brains for a name. Tegan – Yeah, Tegan. And finally a scruffy looking guy in a crumpled suit who must be Mervyn, the independent publicist that she'd hired. Hadley hoped he worked the press better than he worked his clothes, otherwise they were in trouble.

Hadley had done her homework. She knew all their names, had a little comment about how much she loved their clothes or their hair or their latest campaign, and by the time she sat down, they were all leaning eagerly forward.

Being polite and charming got way more results than the business end of a hissy fit.

'Tegan, did you have a chance to prepare the biography?' she asked, forcing down a sip of the water Derek had poured for her. It had better be filtered or she'd be breaking out before lunchtime.

The biogs were duly distributed but before anyone could read them, Hadley clapped her hands. 'I think it would be easier if I just took you through the high spots myself. OK, guys?'

Before anyone could disagree, and disagreement was not part of the deal, Hadley started.

'I've been in the public eye since I was eighteen months old, when I appeared in my first commercial for Tater Tots. When I was three I got a role as Judy, the youngest daughter in *The Starr Family*, which was the highest rated sitcom in the US for five years. When that got cancelled, I starred in my own show, *Hadley's House*, for four years. I was the youngest ever winner of an Emmy; the show was syndicated in forty-five different countries; and the Hadley fashion figure was the bestselling toy for Christmas 1998. But I also took the lead in the *Little Girl Lost* film franchise. *Little Girl Lost II*, which was set in London, fyi, was the biggest grossing movie at the US box office in 1997. And then do you know what happened?'

Derek coughed. 'Well, *Hadley's House* was cancelled . . .'

Off-message. Hadley folded her arms and smiled thinly. '*I* grew up,' she said. 'Puberty kicked in and it was not kind to me. By the time I was over it, it was all *The OC* and the Olsen twins. Then there was that, like, um, that unpleasant business with my family and I can't even get a good table at The Ivy any more. So, London, here I am, make the most of me!'

Derek smiled encouragingly; he had beautiful teeth, considering he was British. 'It's always better to hear these things in person, rather than just a dry handful of facts,' he noted. 'So, why don't you tell us what Fierce can do for you?'

'Two objectives, people.' Hadley fixed each person in turn with an intense look. 'We have to make me famous again and we have to make me lots and lots of money. And we have to do it really fast. Actually, would that make it three objectives?'

'Well, we've already discussed a three-pronged attack to reintroduce you to the public as a new, exciting adult talent,' Derek interjected smoothly. 'Acting, modelling and a few guest-presenter TV spots on—'

'I'm not chasing after crumbs. I'm a *brand*. I'm a creative artiste. That doesn't mean I'm going to appear on some late-night satellite show, introducing a video from some band that nobody's heard of,' Hadley growled, while smiling at the same time, a tip she'd picked up from Amber who used it when she was dealing with uppity studio execs. 'I can sing, so let's get me into the studio to work with some really rad hip-hop guys. It worked for Paris. Tegan, honey, maybe you should be taking notes?'

Tegan dutifully started scribbling on a pad of paper, while Derek stared at Hadley thoughtfully. 'We're looking into the possibility of a few celebrity endorsements,' he said.

'Looking isn't good enough, we need to make this *happen*,' Hadley said firmly. Jeez, what did these people expect to get paid for? 'I want a really big bucks Japanese TV-ad campaign. Tegan, Gwyneth Paltrow and Nicole Kidman have both done them. Can you get us the 411?'

Derek opened his mouth but Hadley held up her hand because she was nowhere near finished. 'Remember, people, I'm so over that former-child-star shtick, so no *Where Are They Now?* VH1 specials.'

Hadley decided it was time to let Derek speak. 'OK, we want to shoot a new set of pictures to send out to casting directors and the press. So maybe we can coordinate schedules?'

That was more like it. Hadley flicked on her Sidekick and whizzed through several blank dates. 'I'm sure we can find a window next week. I'll need photographer approval so have them send over their books. And Tegan, I'll email you my sizes. I'm wearing a lot of Marc Jacobs and Marni these days.' She gave Tegan and Derek a dismissive smile.

Neither of them even twitched an eyelash. Hadley tried again. 'Mervyn and I need some serious face-time so, y'know, vamoose.'

Hadley beamed brightly to soften the blow. She hadn't meant to sound so harsh, but at least they were slowly getting to their feet. British peeps obviously weren't as thrusting and dynamic as their US cousins, which meant she'd regularly have to light a fire under their asses. Like, she didn't already have enough to do.

The door shut behind Derek and Tegan and Hadley turned to Mervyn eagerly.

'So, what have you got for me?'

He pulled a crumpled, A4 manila envelope from his battered leather briefcase and slid it across the table. 'I heard on the vine that Orlando Bloom might be on the market but it was misinformation so I came up with a plan B.'

Hadley sighed. Orlando was super-cute and high-profile enough to kick-start her career with just a few well-placed phone calls to the right gossip columnists. Still, plan B was probably almost as cute.

She eased the glossy headshot out and flipped it over before thrusting the photo away with an anguished shriek. 'Ewwwww! No way! I'd, like, rather do porn than be seen out with *him*!'

Mervyn shuffled excitedly. 'I've got a friend who does some glamour stuff. Tasteful like, just the odd nipple shot.'

Hadley felt the nagging throb of a tension headache. 'I was being ironic or something.' She jabbed a fingernail in the direction of the photo. 'Anyway, he's strictly Z-list.'

'His sitcom is doing really well over here and there's a buzz that he's going to be in the next Harry Potter movie.'

For one teeny second, Hadley's interest piqued. Just for a second. 'Really? How much . . . No! What am I saying? It would be like selling my soul to the devil. End of discussion. Now let's talk about my publicity strategy.'

Chapter Three

Apart from his completely insane troll idea, Mervyn had come up with the goods. Hadley was on every VIP guest list and in possession of a clutch of glossy invites to nightclub openings, film premieres and product launches.

Tonight she was going to a party for a new cellphone. Except they called them mobile phones over here. She was going to have to remember these little things.

'Treat it like a dress rehearsal,' Mervyn had advised. 'Look, learn, listen. And don't wear anything too flashy, you're strictly flying under the radar tonight.'

Regretfully Hadley ran her hand over a pink Betsey Johnson number that really made her highlights pop and took down a sedate little black dress with some subtle beading round the hem. Flying under the radar really wasn't her forte.

'Elegant,' Merv decided when she finally managed to find him on an upstairs balcony of some, like, *dive* in Mayfair, which was meant to be the Beverly Hills of London. Like, *au contraire.* There was flock wallpaper, little gilt chairs and these ornate chandeliers, but Hadley had black gunk on her arm from where she'd brushed against the wall and she could actually feel it penetrating through five layers of fake tan. 'You're a real class act.'

Hadley smiled weakly. Mervyn was OK. He seemed to mean well. And he'd be all right looking, for an old guy, if he got someone to iron his clothes, had his hair cut and rethought the gag-making aftershave.

'Thanks,' she murmured, surveying the shuffling masses on the dance floor. 'So, are you going to give me a guided tour to the London scene?'

Mervyn leaned over the balcony. 'See that guy with the white suit on? He runs a production company; you should get to know him. Her in the rubber dress? She's in a girl band, right slag too. Footballers – soccer players to you Yanks – should be avoided at all costs, unless they're on the England squad.'

Hadley's eyes glazed over. She was still jet lagged and Mervyn wasn't really making any kind of sense. 'Cute famous boys,' she reminded him. 'Really cute, really famous boys. Or, like, film directors.'

'Red T-shirt at three o'clock. He's an up and coming comedian, going to be in the new Johnny Depp movie.' Hadley followed Mervyn's outstretched hand and peered at a gawky youth with gangling limbs and ginger hair.

'He clashes with my tan,' she backtracked. 'We wouldn't look good in photos. Are you sure that Orlando's not single?'

Mervyn sighed, but a girl had to have some standards.

'Well, early days yet. 'Let's go down and mingle.' He snagged a couple of glasses from a passing waiter. 'Get that down you.'

Hadley stared at the proffered glass of champagne. 'I don't drink,' she said flatly. 'I'm not old enough.'

'You can drink over here at eighteen.' Mervyn squinted and leaned in closer. 'So, those rumours about you being in rehab were . . . ?'

'No!' Hadley was aghast. If she wasn't dead, then she was a drug addict. Why did people make up stuff? 'Where did you hear that? I've never even had a liqueur chocolate. Alcohol is bad for the skin.' And she'd seen too many actors high on heck knows what. No one believed the stories their publicists released about 'nervous exhaustion'. It was just Hollywood code for strung out substance abuser. She wasn't going to become *that* kind of cliché.

'Pity, we could have worked that angle. Maybe got you in *OK*, revealing exclusively your heart-breaking battle back to recovery. Triumph over adversity. Tears and traumas. They bloody love that stuff.'

Hadley took the glass of champagne; curling her fingers around the slender stem. She was an actress; it was a prop, simple as that. 'People already think I'm a flake, without them thinking that I'm a flake with an addiction.'

She walked away, Mervyn hot on her heels. 'We could always play the Daddy card,' he suggested, as they made their way down the stairs, fighting against the crowd who were heading towards the balconies. 'There's a story waiting to be told.'

'No,' she said sharply, reaching the bottom step and yanking Mervyn into an alcove by grabbing a handful of his shirt. 'Let's get one thing clear. We leave my family out of this. Your job is to find me some tabloid-friendly piece of arm candy to have my picture taken with on a regular basis. Is that going to be a problem, 'cause I can get another publicist . . .' Hadley let the threat hang in the air.

'No need to get your knickers in a twist,' Mervyn assured her. His smile was as shop-soiled as his clothes. 'I'm just spit-balling a few ideas.'

Hadley forced herself to relax. Or to relax *slightly*. 'OK, let's go see if we can find any likely candidates,' she chirped, shooting a dazzling smile at Mervyn, who was looking at her warily. 'It's just really important to establish some ground rules.'

Holding her champagne glass in front of her like a protective talisman, Hadley followed Mervyn to the bar and dutifully giggled and chatted with a series of total dweebs. The air in the club was muggy and thick enough to curl up her bangs and make her skin glisten in a way that wasn't entirely attractive.

Hadley took a tiny sip of her drink to get rid of the cotton-mouth. All these new people talking about stuff she didn't know (what was a 'chav'? And why did everyone keep saying 'am I bothered?' and shaking with laughter?)

was an ordeal. Not that she was shy, but she did have intimacy issues in social situations.

'Let me get you a top-up,' someone said in her ear and Hadley realized she was holding an empty glass while Mervyn smiled knowingly at her.

'So what do you think of London?' asked this stubbly dude who was something in TV.

'I love it,' she announced decisively, because, dissing their city of choice? Not cool. 'Your buses are so cute and everywhere is, like, really old. But what's a TopShop?'

The champagne did make everything easier. Hadley forgot that the balls of her feet felt as if they were on fire in her Christian Loboutin limo shoes. She forgot that she was meant to be flying under the radar and smiled happily for the photographer who asked to take her picture with the ginger geek that Mervyn had pointed out earlier. And she totally forgot that she didn't drink alcohol.

'I had such a good night,' she announced hours later when Irina opened the door to the apartment. 'I feel so chilled.'

Irina looked distinctly unimpressed. 'Keys,' she intoned darkly. 'Use them.'

Hadley pulled a face behind Irina's retreating back. She had a very negative energy.

'Keys are so low-tech,' she grumbled. 'I can't believe the door doesn't have an electronic touch pad. Security is really important.'

She toed off her shoes and tiptoed into the lounge, where Candy was curled up on the sofa with a dark, dangerous-looking hunk of man-flesh. They both stared at her as she flopped into the empty armchair and displayed a large expanse of thigh.

'How many fat units are in champagne?' Hadley tugged down the hem of her dress because Candy's date was totally checking out her legs. Not that they weren't worth checking out, because they *so* were, but it was rude.

Candy rolled her eyes. 'Don't destroy my entire belief system and tell me that you're pissed,' she drawled, before turning to her smirking companion, who was still looking at Hadley's legs. 'Hadders is a total control freak. She weighs all her food and she doesn't even swear.'

Hadley tried to tuck her legs under her and almost fell out of the chair. 'Swearing's not cool.'

'This is Hadley, Reed,' Candy informed her companion. 'Hadders, this is Reed, my brother.' Well, that explained the wandering eyes, which were exactly the same pale blue as Candy's. Though Hadley had a feeling that his thick, tufty black hair didn't owe anything to a bottle of dye, unlike his sister's.

Hadley waggled her fingers and tried to remember what she knew about him. She was sure that she knew something. It was slowly and muddily coming back to her. Reed, actually Candy's half-brother, had only had a couple of cameo roles on the family's reality show *At Home With The*

Careless. The official line was that he was too busy working as a music video director. But the unofficial line was that he wanted nothing to do with 'that trainwreck of a show' and hadn't spoken to his mother in five years anyway.

He was also rumoured to be a notorious modelizer. Word was that he'd worked his way through an entire model apartment in New York and left all six of the girls with broken hearts. But, hey, music video director was kind of all right.

'I liked that video you did for The Hormones with the water bottles . . .'

'Milk cartons,' Candy and Reed supplied in unison.

'Whatever. And you did the TV ads for American Outfitters . . .' Suddenly Hadley felt remarkably sober. She sat up and leaned forward eagerly. She'd never consider Reed as a pretend boyfriend. He wasn't high profile enough, but he was going places.

Currently, he was shrugging modestly. 'They gave me free rein to do what I wanted,' he said in a transatlantic purr. 'It was the right move at the right time.'

'And now he's going to make a movie!' Candy had abandoned her jaded NYC-kid cool and was bursting with sisterly pride. It was sweet, not an adjective that Hadley would normally have used to describe Candy. 'He's got the money and he's going to be shooting in London.'

'I've got *some* of the money, Lemonhead,' Reed interjected, shooting his half-sis a lazy smile.

'Don't fricking call me that, Bonehead.'

Before Candy and Reed could descend into swapping insults, Hadley stretched out her legs and, just like that, Reed's head swivelled in their direction. 'What's your movie about?' she husked.

Reed had a really beautiful mouth. Firm lips saved from being too pretty by a downward droop to them, like he didn't smile that often. 'It's about these two kids, childhood sweethearts, who run away to England because their parents don't approve of their relationship. And they get corrupted by the big city and lose sight of their dreams,' Reed explained, then screwed up his face. 'But it's funnier than that, and darker. I want to shoot it as this modern noir, like Douglas Sirk meets Larry Clark, y'know?'

Hadley didn't know. It was possible that Reed was speaking Martian. But she understood the important points. 'I'd love to audition for you. Not that I audition, but maybe I could do a read-through of the script. I'm really jonesing for a challenging role to get my teeth into.' She angled her head so Reed could see how telegenic her right profile was and continued. 'I think that there'd be a real shock value having my name attached to the project, which would be great publicity but then when people saw what I did with the part they'd . . .'

Candy was mouthing something at her and looking extremely pained and Reed was folding his arms and not looking at her legs any more, but straight in her eyes with

34

a flinty look. 'I already have someone in mind,' he said tersely. 'Don't take this the wrong way, but I'm looking for a girl who's very raw. You're a little too LA.'

She wasn't a little too anything, Hadley thought as she felt herself go cold under the weight of Reed's chilly disregard. Almost through sheer force of will, she prevented the goosebumps from popping up and pinned on a smile. 'Nila problemo,' she said lightly. 'Can't blame a girl for trying.'

'Course.' Reed smiled back, with absolute zero warmth. 'So, what were you saying about your iPod?' He turned back to Candy who almost missed her cue before rambling on that all her songs had disappeared after she yanked out her firewire cable.

Hadley stifled a yawn. *She* never missed a cue, and right now it was coming over loud and clear that she'd outstayed her welcome. Besides, like some low budget, underground movie about two disaffected teens was going to be a viable star vehicle for her!

'I'm going to bed,' she said to no one in particular, getting to her feet and slowly sauntering out of the room, with just the slightest hint of an ass wiggle to show Mr Hotshot Movie Director that she was way out of his league.

Hadley pondered the situation further as she waited in the hall for Laura to get out of the bathroom. She wasn't going to get angry about it, because she didn't do angry.

But for someone who only dated models, Reed sure did think a lot of himself.

'Bathroom's free.'

Hadley looked up to see Laura staring down at her. 'Huh?'

'I just need to brush my teeth then the bathroom's all yours,' Laura repeated, leaving the door open.

'Your hair's rocking,' Hadley cooed encouragingly, as she took down her jar of specially blended cold cream. Laura was super-hard to talk to, but maybe her recent bad haircut could be a bonding thing. 'It really suits you.'

Laura stared balefully at her reflection in the mirror. 'I'm so getting hair extensions.'

The bathroom reeked of at least ten different brands of perfume, hairspray and body lotion. Hadley tried not to breathe in as she began to remove her make-up.

'Candy's bro is quite a fox,' Laura suddenly said through a mouthful of toothpaste. 'He couldn't take his eyes off my boobs.'

Laura's breasts were quite gaze-worthy, though Hadley hadn't yet plucked up the courage to ask her if they were real. 'He's a modelizer,' she said shortly. 'He's one of those guys who only dates models.'

'Well, I'm not really in the market,' Laura said, as if guys who only dated models weren't anything to be phased about. 'Tom is fifty times better looking than him anyway.'

Hadley had seen several pictures of Tom the boyfriend on Laura's notice-board and though he was passably cute for a jock, he didn't even exist in the same sphere as men like Reed.

'How did you and Tom hook up?' Hadley asked, not just because it was a great conversational gambit but also because she genuinely wanted to know.

She hadn't genuinely wanted to know every single word, inconsequential gesture and yearning look that had taken place during Laura's two-year crush on Tom. By the time they finally kissed, Hadley's cheek muscles ached with the strain of all the encouraging smiles.

'So, like, how did you know what to say to him?'

Laura spat out a mouthful of toothpaste. 'I don't know,' she said unhelpfully. 'I just did. We went to the same school and we knew the same people and we're into the same music. We have tons in common.'

'But how did you know that you had tons in common?'

'It just happened. C'mon, Hads, you know what it's like when you're going out with someone.' Laura stuffed her toothbrush back into the holder and picked up her towel. 'I've got to go to bed. I've got my big cover shoot tomorrow.'

'Cool,' Hadley mumbled vaguely, her beauty regime temporarily forgotten. She eased herself into the tub and stared at her red-tipped toes through the milky water.

Hadley'd had her first screen kiss aged nine, when she'd

got her very own boyfriend on *Hadley's House*. Mostly they'd just held hands and had televisual adventures, which always finished with them sharing a plate of Oreos and a glass of milk together. And she'd even had a love interest in the last *Little Girl Lost* movie (and she was still bugged that it had gone straight to DVD) but they'd had a stunt double to do the kissing scenes because she'd been wearing her braces by then and his agent had been concerned about potential facial injuries.

No way would Amber and her dad let her date for real, because then she'd have lost her family-friendly appeal. And during the two years that she was 'resting', Amber had barely let her leave the house until the braces came off and she'd had her nose job and Stairmastered away any faint traces of puppy fat. Hadley had to face facts; she was practically a nun. But, like, a really pretty nun with a matching set of Louis Vuitton luggage.

There was a knock on the door and before Hadley could call out, Candy was bursting in.

'Oh my God!' Hadley squeaked, wrapping her arms around every inch of flesh she could. 'I didn't say you could come in.'

'Don't hit on Reed,' Candy spat out, hands clenching into fists. 'He's not available and he's not going to give you a part in his movie so back the hell off!'

'But I wasn't—'

'You're not his type, Hadley. And you and I are going to

38

have serious problems if you don't get that into the three brain cells that you have.'

Hadley was still reeling with shock and light years away from a retort as Candy swept out and slammed the door behind her.

Next time she'd make sure that Candy knew she was a fully-trained kickboxer who could roundhouse small, mouthy girls into the next town if she put her mind to it. Hadley hauled herself out of the bath so she could find the acupressure points at the base of her spine and do some deep breathing exercises until she was calm again.

She didn't know what hurt most. Candy thinking she was at all interested in her sneery brother or Candy thinking that she was dumb. They'd lived together for four whole days, surely Candy knew her better than that by now?

'Serve her right if I kickboxed some sense into her,' she muttered to herself and held that thought.

Disco!

She hadn't known how to kickbox until they decided to go down the action adventure route for *Little Girl Lost III*. But she'd learned. Hadley had had lessons from Chuck Diver, America's foremost kickboxing instructor. And she hadn't been able to dance the tango for the closing credits of *Hadley's House* until she'd had lessons.

Those that knew, did. Those that didn't, paid someone else to teach them. When it came to boys, she was as clueless as an Amish chick at her first dance, so she needed help. Professional help.

Besides, how could she hope to market herself as an exciting, mature talent if she'd never even been on a date?

Hadley scurried to her room and pulled out her Sidekick.

'Hey Mervyn,' she trilled, when he picked up the phone. 'I hope I didn't wake you.'

'I was asle—'

'Yeah, whatever, sorry about that. I've been thinking about our secret project and it couldn't do any harm to meet up with plan B. I figure I can dump him after a couple of weeks. Can you make the call and get his people to set up a meeting ASAP?'

'Hadley, love, I thought you said that—'

'I changed my mind 'cause I'm so flaky and stuff.' Hadley didn't wait to hear if Mervyn could pick up on the huge amounts of irony in that statement. 'Let's talk first thing tomorrow.'

Operation Stardust had just got a third objective. Or was that a fourth objective? Hadley made a mental note to get to the bottom of that the next day.

Chapter Four

His people gave her people (that would be Mervyn) this whole power trip. Meetings were set up. Meetings were cancelled at an hour's notice, all blamed on sudden changes to his shooting schedule, even though he was playing third male lead in a British sitcom; not filming an action trilogy for a major Hollywood studio. Like, in his dreams.

Hadley was not amused. She'd told Mervyn to call the meeting off. Cancelled. Not going to happen. Finito. And five minutes later they'd rung back, all gushing apologies and promised faithfully that it would happen the next morning.

Which was just as well, as Hadley had a photo shoot scheduled for later that afternoon and she had a rule about being punctual.

'We have to be done by one,' she told Mervyn for the fifth time, as he paid the taxi driver.

'Doubt we'll get anything settled today.' Mervyn winced as the sun made contact with his red-rimmed eyes. Daylight really did not become him. 'I'm not taking any crap from—'

'Can I ask you a personal question?' Hadley didn't wait

for his reply because really, it had to be said. 'Do you possess an iron or, like, a washing machine? 'Cause you need to think about what impression you're sending out.'

She looked meaningfully at the tired old suit that was all he ever wore. Quite frankly, with what she was paying him, he could afford to have something made by one of those spiffy British tailors.

'I'm a busy man – don't have time to iron.'

'Well, make time,' Hadley suggested sweetly, adjusting the collar of her Gucci leather jacket so her hair spilled down her back in a silken curtain of gold. Note to self: She really needed to get her roots done. 'Like, today I want to give off a cool vibe that's young and funky and a million years away from the—'

'The horrible pastel twin-sets you used to wear on *Hadley's House*,' Mervyn interrupted slyly. 'More modern, less Mormon?'

Hadley and her skinny jeans made an executive decision to ignore their press agent. Instead, she gave a dazzling smile to the doorman, because Mervyn certainly wasn't getting one.

She'd been slightly alarmed that they were having the meeting in a hotel room. It seemed way sleazy, but the minimalist lobby of the boutique hotel in Notting Hill went some way to calming her nerves. She could still feel the sweat clinging to her palms as she rode up in the elevator with Mervyn, who'd taken her pep talk to heart and buttoned up his jacket to hide the small stain (possibly ketchup?) on his shirt.

'You nervous?' Mervyn enquired, as they reached the fifth floor. 'It'll be OK. I'll do the talking, like we agreed.'

'I am so *not* nervous,' Hadley insisted, giving the door an imperious rap. 'Why should I be nervous?'

The door was opened by a hatchet-faced flunkie, and behind the woman's head she caught a glimpse of hair almost as blonde and shiny as her own.

It took ten steps to get to the sofa and a Herculean effort to actually sit down and look George in the eye. *George*. Her absolute arch nemesis. Her love interest for the last three seasons of *Hadley's House*, who'd made each of those seasons a living hell with his snide remarks, scene stealing and annoying practical jokes, like swapping her pimple cream for toothpaste.

On paper, George should have been good-looking. He'd done the fake and bake, had enviably swingy blond hair and a fairly clean jawline, but all the separate, fairly handsome pieces of George, when added together, were not that hot. He was just another easy-on-the-eye Hollywood blond with nothing striking to lift him above the best friend, or the rebound boyfriend, or all those other parts, which meant he wasn't star material.

He was never going to have his moment in the sun, so why the heck was George smirking like he was better than her?

'George,' Hadley said thinly, tipping her head a scant five degrees in his direction and resisting the urge to shuffle down the couch.

George narrowed his eyes and showed off a blinding white smile. 'Hey, Hadley, how does it feel to be a has-been?'

Oh, the nerve of him! 'I don't know. How does it feel to *still* be third on the bill?'

'I must admit I'm surprised to see you here,' George confessed in a low tone. ' 'Cause I read this story on defamer.com that you died of a heroin OD in a room at the Chateau Marmont. I'm so glad that you managed to clean up.'

'And I read somewhere that you're totally gay and got caught doing something I'm not even going to repeat with a married man which is why you need me to be your fake girlfriend, so you can wipe that silly smile off your face, George. It's not impressing anyone.' Hadley crossed her legs and fixed George with her most unimpressed stare until he was forced to back down. It was good to know that she still had the power to bust his balls, pardon her French.

'He wasn't married, and I am not gay,' he burst out furiously, before straightening up so he could smirk all over again. 'You haven't changed. As ever, the sweetness and light routine is still only skin deep, and, by the way, honey, glad those zits have finally cleared up.'

Hadley wasn't going to dignify that with a response.

Except . . . 'Sticks and stones may break my bones, but words will never hurt me,' she sing-songed.

'At least I'm *working*,' George snorted. 'And at least my father didn't steal all my money.'

She'd vowed not to let George get a rise out of her. But he was so darn good at it. 'What? You mean the lousy twenty thousand dollars you got per season, while I was making, what was it? Oh yeah, that's right, a cool half a million.'

'It's a pity that you didn't manage to spend some of it on getting your boobs done before . . .'

Hadley looked up, mid eye-roll, to see Mervyn and George's publicist sitting on the sofa opposite, their heads going back and forth like they were at a tennis match.

'This isn't going to work, is it?' Mervyn said, shaking his head. 'Delia and I thought you could put the past behind you.'

'What are you talking about?' Hadley asked crossly. 'Of course it's going to work out, right, George?'

'Why the hell wouldn't it?' George huffed. 'Better the devil you know. Sides, if I can help out an old friend who may never get another paid job, then it's just my way of giving something back.'

'Whatever! There isn't a single girl in the country who'd put up with you.' Hadley turned to Mervyn. 'It's really simple, Merv. We'll get some carefully coordinated outfits, have our photos taken together, get a few quotes ready about how we lost touch, met up again and fell in love. We don't have to actually like each other.'

'And as long as Hadley doesn't try to slip me some tongue when we're kissing, we'll be fine,' George added sweetly.

To which she could only hiss: 'As if! And I want a sliding scale of cash bonuses depending on how much coverage we get. Hey, we could even get engaged!'

'Yeah, as long as you buy the ring.'

George was the most revolting snake to ever slither across the face of the earth. Hadley took out her Sidekick and typed in a reminder that when the time came, *she'd* be the one to dump *him*.

'I think we're done here,' she announced decisively, standing up. 'Mervyn, you can coordinate schedules with Delia. George, you might want to go easy on those highlights. People will begin to suspect that you're not a natural blond.'

It wasn't even lunchtime and Hadley had already managed to score a pretend boyfriend, give Mervyn some much-needed style advice and kick George to the kerb where he totally belonged. Her multi-tasking skills were formidable.

Chapter Five

H adley was still coasting a wave of invincibility as she strolled into the photo studio.

Derek was talking to someone who was probably the photographer. It was the camera he was holding that gave it away. Not that Hadley had seen his book. Plus, the studio was a little on the small side. Nothing like the Smashbox complex in LA, which would have been her location of choice. But she wasn't in LA any more and so she just had to suffer, mostly in silence.

'Hi, I'm Hadley,' she said to the photographer, making sure her handshake was firm. 'Who have you shot for?'

'Vince, pleased to meet you.' He was Cockney; like he came from that show that Laura watched, *EastEnders* or something. 'I've done a bit of fashion for *Polka Dot* and I shoot a lot of celeb stuff for the Sunday sups.'

Why did she never understand English people? 'Vince shot Elektra for the cover of the *Observer Music Monthly*,' Derek supplied, one hand on her shoulder as if she should start moving away. Hadley dug her heels in.

'I want the pictures to be edgy, but not too edgy,' she informed Vince, digging her notebook out of her Louis Vuitton tote. 'We'll do a couple of rolls of black and white and I prefer to be shot slightly from above. Don't even bother with my left profile, OK? And I brought some tear sheets so you can get an idea of the mood I want.'

Hadley whisked Christina Aguilera's recent *Vogue* shoot under Vince's nose and watched him bite his lip. It didn't exactly inspire confidence. 'It's all about the lighting,' she said gently. 'And I look better against a slightly off-white backdrop.'

Vince nodded vigorously. 'OK, I'll get right on that.' He was already scurrying off to bark instructions at his assistants. Life was so much easier when she simply told people what to do and then they did it.

'Hadley, we need . . .'

Now that was a lesson that Derek could benefit from. 'Hey, how are you doing?' She patted him gently on the arm. 'Any jobs for me yet?'

'I've got several leads. Y'know, there's a really great TV-presenter gig coming up.' Derek had great big brown eyes, which were staring at her soulfully – but Hadley was immune.

'I told you, no TV work, unless I'm a guest on a top-rated chat show. What about ad campaigns? It's been nearly two weeks!' Her voice was definitely hitting the upper register, which was so not good. 'Derek, I need you on board the good ship *Hadley*. You have to try harder than this.'

His hand was back on her shoulder, trying to steer her

left. 'Hadley, you have to trust *me* to manage your career, and *you* need to manage your expectations,' Derek said calmly. 'This isn't going to happen overnight.'

Like, she was that unreasonable! 'I know, but you've had way longer than overnight. I can't just sit around waiting for fame to come knocking.'

She'd never admit it out loud, but sometimes she missed Amber. At least when *she* told people to jump, they didn't even ask 'How high?', they simply leaped into the air without a murmur.

'Look, we'll get some great pictures today,' Derek said in a more conciliatory tone. 'I've got some lunches lined up and we'll start a buzz.'

Hadley held up her hands in defeat. 'Fine, but I want some good news by the end of the week. With a nice, fat cheque attached to it. Can you get me some water, with ice and lemon, please?'

Once Derek was dispatched to do something that even he couldn't mess up, Hadley then had to do battle with Gill, the stylist, who had a distinct lack of designer dresses for her to wear. 'None of them would lend,' she bleated. 'But we got some great stuff from the high street.'

Chain-store clothes brought Hadley out in a rash. She gave Gill her house keys and told her to take a taxi to the apartment so she could pick up her own designer clothes.

Once she was dispatched, Hadley took out her bottle of lavender essential oil and inhaled great calming whiffs of it as she bonded with Kerry, the make-up girl, about the new range of glittery eye-shadow from MAC. It was always good to get the little people on-side.

'The blue would look great with your lovely red hair,' Hadley simpered. 'Anyway, I was thinking we should do a smoky eye thing. I'll do my own base and then I want really neutral lips.'

'I thought the red lipstick would look really good on you. Dead sophisticated,' Kerry ventured, holding up a tube of gloss that would make Hadley look like a teenage hooker. Not that she'd ever seen one in real-life, but she'd watched enough *Law & Order* reruns to get a general idea.

'No, definitely neutral,' Hadley said firmly. 'A dark beige, but not too dark, with, like, a warm tone to it.'

No wonder that by the time she was in front of the camera, wearing her own Juicy Couture camisole and Sass And Bide jeans, Hadley was feeling a little ragged. Actually, a lot ragged.

As Vince snapped away, she changed her pose by inestimable degrees; tilting her head, varying the width of her smile, adjusting her shoulders.

Click.

Click.

Click.

She'd missed that sound. Missed looking into the camera lens and doing what she did best: being Hadley Harlow. She pretended to laugh and she pretended to look surprised and she pretended that she was the multi-purpose, one-size-fits-all girl next door. But a slightly older version than the one that the general public were used to.

They finished shooting the black and white rolls and Hadley was just changing into a pink vest for some more upbeat pictures when Vince shuffled nervously into view.

'I want to do another roll of black and white and try something a bit different, OK?'

That was enough to make Hadley instantly suspicious. She didn't like different, unless she'd approved it in triplicate first.

'What do you mean by different? We didn't talk about different.'

Vince rubbed his chin anxiously. 'I just want to do some head shots, really simple, eyes nice and big and no smiling.'

'But I can't *not* smile,' Hadley insisted shrilly, following him on to the set. 'My smile is, like, my USP. That's my Unique. Selling. Point, fyi.'

'You have lots of unique selling points, Hadley,' Derek said from behind the camera. 'You're very pretty, and you said that you wanted to be taken seriously as a creative artiste. So if we got some more serious pictures, it would really capture people's attention.'

Derek had a point, but he was forgetting one important thing. 'I'm a girl next door type as well as a serious creative artiste,' Hadley reminded him. 'I need to look friendly.'

'Oh, you will. Kerry, can you flatten her hair down?'

Hadley put two protective hands over her hair, which had been carefully teased and back-combed to optimum levels of fluffiness. 'But I have big hair. That's another of my USPs,' she yelped.

'Big hair doesn't do so well in Britain,' Kerry piped up, brandishing some hair straighteners and a big round brush. 'And I could clip your fringe back. Look, sparkly slides!' She showed Hadley the glittery barrettes nestling in the palm of her hand, like that was going to seal the deal.

She winced as Kerry started spritzing her hair. 'We'll just do some Polaroids so I can see what the shots looks like,' she insisted, fighting to get some semblance of control back into her voice.

'Of course,' Vince promised, but Hadley didn't miss the conspiratorial look that he shot Derek, like they'd been planning this tag-team for days.

And when she didn't have time to even look at her *flat* hair in the mirror but was hustled in front of the camera, Hadley knew she'd been totally played. She sure as heck didn't feel like smiling, so that worked out super well.

'I want you to smile with your eyes, but keep your face still. Can you do that?' Vince asked doubtfully.

Well, duh. It wasn't rocket science. Hadley took a second to go to her one bullet proof happy place, the day she got Mr Chow Chow, her pet Mexican Hairless. She remembered him jumping up to lick her face, not at all put off by the spots and braces. Bless his little hairless paws.

'Lovely, lovely, nice wide eyes, look at me straight on,' Vince crooned. 'And just turn a fraction to the right.'

Hadley was so lost in her Mr C-C reverie (the first time they'd gone to the beach together: the time she'd had his nails painted pink to match hers) that at first she didn't realize that Vince was taking pictures. Taking proper pictures with a camera that wasn't spitting out Polaroids between takes.

'Hold it right there!' she snapped. 'We were meant to be taking a couple of shots so I could decide whether they were working for me.' Smiling with her eyes or any other body part was not an option as she pointed at the camera. 'Bring it here.'

Her Jedi mind-tricks were really way better than Hadley gave them credit for because Vince was creeping towards her. 'They look fantastic,' he insisted. 'I hardly recognize you.'

'That's not a good thing!' Hadley squinted at the tiny screen in horror. 'I look old. And sad. And my hair's horrible. I want you to delete them now. Come on, step to it!'

'But-but-but . . .' Was Vince going to get that sentence out anytime before the end of the week?

'Hadley, you look beautiful and understated.' Now Derek was getting in on the act too. Hadley felt under

53

attack from all sides. It was like being back home with her parents again.

'I don't want to look beautiful or understated. I want to look like me! I want to look like Hadley! Which part of that is a problem for you?' The heartfelt plea in her voice was pitch perfect. She'd always used it to great effect on *Hadley's House* when her screen parents wouldn't let her go off and have adventures.

It didn't get the same reaction from Vince. 'Screw this!' he snapped, snatching back the camera. 'I don't get paid enough to deal with divas like you.'

'I am *not* a diva,' Hadley gasped, but Vince was already stomping off with the camera containing those fugly pictures. She turned her anguished gaze to Derek who was staring after the photographer in disbelief.

'The artistic temperament,' he sighed knowingly. 'You know how it is.'

Hadley nodded her head. 'Kind of. And I also know that if you don't get those pictures destroyed then I'm not paying him a single cent for this shoot. I'm not being mean, I'm just saying it like it is, OK?'

It took hours, well thirty minutes, to get her hair back to its usual buoyancy before she dared to leave the studio and find a cab.

Chapter Six

The weeks drifted past so slowly that Hadley was convinced something wiggy was going on with the calendar.

She'd never been so deadly bored in all her life. There was nothing to do but go to the gym or the sweet little spa she'd found and pester Derek with phone calls about his complete failure to line up any ad work or TV spots for her.

So far she'd had one interview and photoshoot with a teen mag, as part of a round-up of new talent. She hadn't even had her own page but had to share it with someone who'd come third in a TV talent show.

Just how long did Derek intend to fob her off with any more lame offers for Australian ad campaigns or guest presenter spots on shows that aired after midnight that even Laura hadn't heard of?

At least Laura was equally mopey. Not that Hadley wanted anyone to be mopey, but if she had to be unemployable then at least she had company. She'd tried to tell Laura that they should use this time constructively, but Laura thought that meant eating her bodyweight in chocolate, not fitting in an extra spinning class or having an oxygen facial.

Irina and Candy were never home because they were both working. Which was good because Irina laughed every time Hadley so much as opened her mouth, while Candy was still being all kinds of frosty. And it was also bad because Irina had taught Hadley how to use the microwave and the DVD remote control but she was still having problems with the washing machine and sending out her underwear to be dry-cleaned was kinda expensive. Also, she did miss Candy a little bit, because they shared a common language where a tomato was a tomay-to and a pancake was not a crêpe.

Hadley sighed as she moisturized between her toes and heard Laura make yet *another* trip to the kitchen. Someone was going to have to do an intervention soon because last time Hadley checked, successful models didn't have love handles.

Back in her bedroom, she lovingly stroked her pink Viktor & Rolf dress before tugging it on. It had little puff sleeves edged in black lace and gave her an actual waist and hips. Normally she went straight up and down, like a fishing rod, as Amber frequently pointed out before the conversation veered towards butt implants and other things that Hadley really never wanted to think about.

Mervyn had organized a photo op at the opening of a Tiki Bar in somewhere called Kennington. To get into the Hawaiian headspace, Hadley pinned a flower barrette in her hair and was just spraying on some body glitter when there was a tentative tap on the door and Candy's head appeared.

'Are you going to this Tiki thing?' she asked, though the Hibiscus flower clip sort of gave it away. 'The organizers are sending a limo for me, do you want a ride?'

How Hadley wished she could regally inform Candy that she preferred to take a black cab, but boy, did she miss riding in limos. Great big stretch limos with tinted windows and fully-stocked fridges that blocked the entire street when they took a corner. It wasn't fair that Candy had limos sent for her or flew out to Miami to model shoes or got paid to go to Germany and wave at people. But it was Candy's fifteen minutes, so Hadley pretended to consider the offer while she waited for the glitter to dry.

'I guess,' she sighed, as if she was the one doing Candy the favour. 'As long as you don't think I'm flirting with the driver or anything.'

'Oh, whatever,' Candy snarled. 'I called you out about perving on Reed weeks ago. Get over it!'

She slammed the door, which was very inconsiderate, as Hadley was manoeuvering into a pair of five-inch high mules. But seconds later she was back. 'I'm leaving in ten, ready or not.'

The atmosphere in the back of the limo was so thick with seething that Hadley wished she'd made her own travel arrangements. The car seated at least twelve so thankfully there was plenty of seat between her and Candy, who was wearing a bizarre dress, possibly made out of old newspapers.

'When are you going to get over your snit?' Candy suddenly burst out. 'It's beyond immature.'

Candy was *so* confrontational. Sometimes she forgot that there weren't cameras on her 24/7 any more and life didn't need to be one drama after another. 'I'm not in a snit,' Hadley insisted. 'You were mean to me and you totally invaded my privacy. I was in the bath!'

'You're always in the fricking bath, and so? I was mean to you? Like, big deal.'

'It is a big deal when you disrespect people,' Hadley said simply, because it was.

'Well, you were disrespecting me and Reed by flashing your legs and your tits and—'

Hadley had never been so pleased to hear her Sidekick blare out the theme from *Hadley's House*. She eagerly rooted for it.

'Hadley speaking,' she chirped, ignoring Candy's snort of derision.

'Sweetie, it's Amber.' Hadley's heart sank. Amber only ever used that affectionate coo when she wanted something.

'Hey Amber, what's up?'

'I can't simply call my only child for a little chat?'

In Hadley's experience, no; but she played willing. 'So, is everything OK with you and the, er, foetuses?'

'Well, I've got them an agent and he's shopping around

for new shows to get them a series regular spot, so fingers crossed.'

'That's really great, Mom.' Hadley tried to inject her voice with huge amounts of enthusiasm. She wasn't convinced that she succeeded.

'When you were born you had jaundice for the first week.' Hadley could actually *feel* Amber shuddering down the phone. 'You were all yellow. It was so gross, but I've already organized the vitamin K shots and we can get Z-cards made right away. So, are you working?'

Hadley didn't even have to pause. 'I've got a couple of really exciting projects in development.'

'That means jackshit, baby! What do I always tell you? C'mon, what do I always say?'

'Things ain't fine until the contract gets signed,' Hadley gritted out, aware that Candy was totally listening in. 'I know that, but London isn't LA, and I'm having to build up some grass roots PR first.' Even to her own ears it sounded lame.

'Hadley, I'm going to cut straight to the chase,' Amber said quickly, because now they were done with the social niceties she could get to the real reason why she was calling for the first time in over a month. 'I need money. I've got medical bills, agents' fees and I need to put down a deposit on a bigger apartment . . .'

'I don't have any money, Mom, I told you.' Hadley had her fingers crossed, but she still felt a twinge of guilt tugging at her. 'When I get some work . . .'

'I can't wait that long,' Amber snapped. 'Face it, you're probably never going to work again. You're no Lindsay Lohan. But your old agent phoned to say that one of the cable channels are reshowing *Hadley's House* and we know what that means.'

Hadley knew exactly what it meant but she wanted to hear Amber say it. 'You know I'm not good with the business stuff,' Hadley said. Candy snorted from somewhere to her left, though Hadley couldn't imagine why.

'Repeat fees, sweetie.' The sugary endearments were back and Hadley didn't have to be a genius to know what was coming next. 'Could you sign them over to me, baby girl? Just this once. I'll get my lawyer to fax over—'

'How much?' she asked baldly.

'Well, they're stingy sons of bitches . . .'

'How much and how many seasons are they showing?'

'All the seasons, back to back,' Amber admitted after a pause. 'I don't have the exact figures to hand right now, but . . .'

'Well, when you do, have them sent over to Fierce and we'll sort something out. Like you can have half and off-set the repayments against the twins' earnings,' she said in a rush. 'Unless the accountants manage to find that off-shore account of Dad's that, like, vanished without a trace.'

'You know I had nothing to do with that.' Right on cue Amber burst into loud, noisy sobs. 'I'm not meant to get upset! Do you have any idea how high my blood pressure was last week? Jesus, Hadley, I went without food so you'd have pretty clothes for auditions. I gave up my career for you and you won't part with a few lousy bucks.'

Amber was shouting now, every word audible, so even Candy was shrinking back on the luxurious leather seat. 'Get me the figures and we'll come to an arrangement, Mom,' Hadley repeated. 'I promise I'll give you some of the residuals.'

'And I don't have to pay them back?' Amber clarified quickly. 'Because we're family and we have to stick together, right?'

'Right,' Hadley agreed weakly. 'I'll make sure that you get enough to cover all you need.'

'And I'd really like to put down a deposit on a condo.' Amber never, ever knew when to quit while she was ahead.

Hadley could feel every individual hair on her body standing up and waving as she bit down on the rising fury. 'Don't push it,' she advised softly and hung up.

The only good thing about the phone call was that Candy had been shocked into silence for the first time in recorded memory.

Sadly, it didn't last long. 'Did you just *growl*?' Candy breathed, her eyes cartoon wide. 'I didn't think you even knew how to growl.'

'Hey, she forgets that I divorced her when I was eleven,'

Hadley said lightly. Candy's mouth dropped open a little further so her bottom lip just grazed the plush carpeting. 'It's this whole child labour thing in California. If I was a legally emancipated adult then I could work longer without having to have rest and study breaks. Everyone did it.'

'I wish I could divorce my mom,' Candy said feelingly. 'She's such a bitch.'

Bette Careless didn't seem like a bitch on TV – flaky, self-obsessed, melodramatic; but not a bitch. Unlike Candy, who'd flinch every time Bette tried to kiss her. 'You shouldn't diss your parents, especially in front of other people,' Hadley said. 'It's way undignified.'

And for the second time in the space of five minutes, Candy was shocked into speechlessness.

Chapter Seven

Hadley didn't believe in what-might-have-beens. It was better to regret something you had done, than something you hadn't. That's what her yogi used to tell her. But then her yogi hadn't witnessed the moment that George and Candy first laid eyes on each other. If he had, he'd have given up on Buddhism and started stock-piling canned goods for the inevitable apocalypse.

'Oh my God, girlfriend!' George squealed, when he caught sight of Candy emerging from behind the velvet rope. 'I fricking worship you, you foul-mouthed little bitch!'

'I love you too!' Candy threw her arms around George as the cameras started flashing. 'You're the funniest thing in that lame-ass sitcom.'

Hadley impatiently tapped her foot and waited for Candy to back away from *her* pretend boyfriend.

In the end, she had no choice but to trail after them, like the original third wheel, as they made their way up to the VIP area. To add insult to injury, Candy and George sailed past the door whore without a backward glance while she was forced to insist sweetly that, yes, she was on the guest list, thank you very much.

'. . . nightmare, Candy,' she heard George say, as she

caught up with them. 'Used to step on all my cues and then Momzilla – that's what we called Amber on set – banned all baked goods because Hadley might get super-fat.'

'I'm wheat intolerant,' Hadley said icily, sliding into the booth. 'And I never stepped on your cues.'

'Take the stick out of your butt, Hadders,' Candy advised, flagging down a waitress who deposited a tray full of garishly coloured drinks on the table. 'It worked out OK in the end, didn't it?'

'How did it work out OK?' Hadley took a dubious sniff at one of the drinks and nearly got impaled on a stray cocktail umbrella. After her foray into champagne and the monster headache she'd had the next day, she was living alcohol-free again.

'Well, you and George are love's young dream,' Candy said archly, nudging George, who giggled. 'I mean, get a room, you two!'

That was obviously meant to be a joke, as they were sitting miles apart, but Hadley forced herself to turn her frown upside down and smile lovingly at George, who pulled a face.

'Hadley's all right,' he said grudgingly. 'But, hey, don't you think she's really bossy under that fluffy exterior? She's all, like, hug me there's a photographer, or, don't act so gay when people are around.' George clapped his hand over his mouth as he realized his monumental gaffe.

Candy's smile glittered. 'But you're not gay,' she pointed

out. 'Because you wouldn't be going out with Hadley if you were.'

'Everyone in London acts gay,' George hastily assured her. 'It's the cool, new thing.'

'Oh, *really* . . .' Trust Candy to be all suspicious-y.

'See, George acts all camp and stuff because he thinks it's funny,' Hadley bit out, which was quite an achievement given the way her jaw was so tightly clenched. 'Even though I've told him a million times that it's not.'

George slid across the banquette so he could sling a careless arm around Hadley's shoulder. 'You know I love to get a rise out of you, sweetness,' he cooed, planting a sloppy kiss on her cheek. She should have got an Oscar right then for resisting the urge to squinch up her face and rub her hand over the spot that George's lips – lips of George! – had touched.

'You're so funny, darling,' Hadley simpered, patting his hand. And if she dug her nails in just a teensy weensy bit, then even God himself would forgive her.

'Have a drink,' George whispered in her ear as Candy waved at someone on the other side of the room. 'Loosen up a little bit before she begins to realize that I can't actually stand the sight of you.'

'The feeling is beyond mutual,' Hadley whispered back and grabbed the nearest drink, a fluoro pink concoction with a stray piece of pineapple floating forlornly in its depths. Hadley took a cautious sip.

'This has pomegranate in it,' she announced, ignoring the acidic after-taste, which was more liquor-y than fruity. 'That's like a superfood.'

'See? It's practically a health drink,' George soothed.

Candy agreed with him. 'For God's sake, Hadders, stop sniffing it and just chug.' She took a long, enthusiastic gulp from her own glass.

It definitely tasted nicer than the champagne. And the second drink, a blackberry Martini, was almost approaching yummy, though the pips kept getting stuck in her teeth.

When Candy and George went off to dance, she even managed to wave them off with a carefree smile. Ooh, maybe she could get Mervyn to leak some bitter love triangle story to the gossip rags – as long as she emerged the eventual winner.

Hadley beckoned a tray-wielding waiter so she could have another blackberry Martini – they really were all kinds of moreish. She was starting to feel fuzzy round the edges. Fuzzy was good. For the first time since she sat in her lawyer's office all those months ago, the sharp, nagging anxiety had floated away.

She was just a girl with a pink flower in her hair slurping down a Martini in a club in London. She didn't have to tell anyone off or do their job for them, or remember to keep her left profile away from the cameras. If this was what drinking did for you, then she was a fan.

It was all going fine until Hadley tried to stand up and her legs registered their disapproval. She could do things in five-inch heels that most girls had never even dreamed about, but suddenly balancing on them was a problem.

Her knees knocked painfully together as she cannoned off the side of the booth and into the back of someone.

'Sorry!' And that was also weird. Her teeth had gone numb. Hadley ran her tongue over them experimentally and they all seemed to be present and correct, but actually her tongue felt odd too. Like it was made of rubber.

She needed to pee and she needed to find George and she might possibly need another drink too. It took a few seconds to get her priorities in the right order and then she was stumbling down the stairs, her hand clutched tight to the rail.

Pit-stop done, (two of the girls in the bathroom had broken into a tuneless rendition of *Feelin' Kinda Hadley* – the theme tune from *Hadley's House* – which Hadley had found hysterically funny) Hadley's next mission was to find her fake beau.

The problem was that George didn't really have any distinguishing features – apart from his spectacularly smug smile. And it was too dark in the club to be able to hone in on that. Every second boy had over-gelled blond hair and a white shirt.

'George's shirt is Comme des Garçons,' Hadley muttered

to herself, scanning the crowd of blond, white-shirted boys to see if she could spot the ruffle detailing that made George totally not stand out in a crowd.

In desperation, Hadley clambered on to a chair – almost putting her heel through a girl's leg, who took it with really bad grace – and peered over people's heads.

It was no use; she still couldn't see. Hadley carefully held aloft her Martini glass and climbed up on the table. This was so much better. Now she could see George and Candy, whirling around like they were on *So You Think You Can Dance?*

'George!' Her ear-piercing shriek didn't carry over the surf guitars bursting forth from the DJ booth, but the people sitting around the table she was currently standing on still started bitching. 'I'm sorry,' she hissed. 'But I have to find my boyfriend.'

'You spill my drink, you pay for it,' snarled one really surly girl, who got even surlier when Hadley told her that there was a free bar if you were a celebrity.

'Are you from one of those sad-sack reality shows?' the girl said belligerently. 'God, where do they find people like you?'

Standing on top of a table was not the best place to recite the highlights from your résumé, but Hadley gave it her best shot.

Her audience was less than impressed. 'Go fuck yourself.'

'Well, there's no need to get snippy,' she started to say,

when she felt two hands around her waist and she was lifted from the table and set on her own two, very unsteady feet. 'How dare you, you . . .'

'Do you stand on tables at home? I'm sure Candy would have mentioned that before.'

It was Reed. The man who'd manhandled her with his hands. At least her blackberry Martini was still intact. Hadley took a long, slow sip, because table-hopping was thirsty work. 'I've lost my boyfriend,' she informed Reed gravely. 'Your sister's run off with him. But he's my boyfriend. *Mine*.' She poked Reed in the chest with her finger so he'd get the seriousness of the situation.

Instead he looked down to where her finger was prodding what felt like rock-hard abs with a frown. 'How much have you had to drink anyway?'

Hadley finished off the rest of her blackberry Martini in one defiant gulp. 'You're not the boss of me. *I'm* the boss of me. And that whole stubble thing is so over. Would it kill you to shave?'

Reed rubbed the chin in question. 'Yeah, it might.'

Hadley squinted at him. In a sea of white shirts and blond hair, he stood out like some black-clad interloper, determined not to get into the Tiki swing of things. 'Are you allergic to shaving cream?' she breathed, because, hello, freaky.

'You really can't hold your drink,' Reed pronounced, deftly taking the glass out of her hand. 'I thought all you

LA kids were in rehab by the time you were fourteen. You're a real lightweight.'

Hadley liked to think that she was dignified in her alleged drunkenness. 'I never touched alcohol when I was younger. It would have totally stunted my physical development.'

And déjà ewwww! Because the mention of physical development made Reed remember he had a hard-earned reputation as a player to maintain, and he ran his thickly-lashed eyes all over her. She was obviously lacking – mostly in the breast department – because he turned away as someone touched him lightly on the shoulder.

Someone with straggly hair, gangly limbs and jutting cheekbones – obviously she was a successful model.

'Reed,' the girl said in heavily-accented English. 'This place sucks. I want to go now.'

He stroked the backs of his fingers down the girl's cheek but she pouted furiously and took a step back. 'Now. We go now,' she repeated emphatically.

'Will you be all right on your own?' Reed asked Hadley doubtfully. 'Should I go and find someone?'

'Who would you find?' she asked, but he'd already turned away.

'Later,' he called over his shoulder. She was left to go and fling her arms round George and nudge Candy out of the way with her hip, just in time for a stray photographer to take their picture.

Chapter Eight

Hadley stared at the front page of *The Daily World* in stunned satisfaction. There she was, standing on the table in the Tiki Club, with the headline *Good Girl Gone Bad*. OK, she could do without the comparisons to Paris Hilton in the actual article, but her legs looked smoking and everyone knew that there was almost no such thing as bad publicity.

It even made up for the fact that she'd been sick twice that morning already and had a thumping headache, even though she'd rubbed lavender essential oil on her temples.

'Laura, look, I've made the front page,' Hadley exclaimed excitedly, but Laura just flopped on the sofa and grunted disinterestedly.

'I can't believe that Irina's in fricking Milan,' she muttered vengefully. 'She's such a dog. I'm going to the shop, do you want some Paracetamol?'

Hadley shook her head. 'I don't believe in taking drugs,' she said primly. 'I'm willing my headache away through the power of positive thought.'

'You'd be better off with a Diet Coke and a really greasy fry-up,' Laura advised, getting up and flicking her fringe out of her eyes. 'Hmm, I could murder a bacon sarnie myself. Your chundering kept me up for hours.'

'Yeah, if you're gonna puke, do it quietly,' Candy said from the doorway. 'You were wasted last night and you practically threw me across the dance floor. I'm covered in bruises.'

Candy pointed to a minute red mark on her shin as evidence and Hadley tried to look suitably contrite. 'Sorry, Candy, I was just missing George and I was overcome with, like, emotion . . .'

'. . . and all those disgusting cocktails you drank,' Candy finished drily. 'Reed said you were yapping on about his stubble and allergies and a whole bunch of other stuff that he couldn't follow.'

Remembering Reed's presence cast a dark shadow over Hadley. But only for a second, until she looked down at the newspaper again. 'I'm on the front page,' she whimpered happily. 'I'm going to phone George and find out where we're going tonight. Gotta maximize my column inches while I can.'

But alas, when she phoned George he wasn't down with maximizing Hadley's column inches, even when she pointed out that his own inches could do with some work.

Then he said, 'We're pals aren't we, Hadders? Like, sort of.'

'Do you need to borrow money?' she asked him, suspicion writ large in every word.

'What? No!' George was really cranky first thing in the

morning. 'I just think it would be good to hang out at each other's houses. And watch movies together and eat fat-free, low-carb popcorn. Like we were proper friends.'

'But why would we want to do that?' Hadley was genuinely perplexed. 'Not being proper friends is like the cornerstone of our whole interaction.'

'I know that.' George seemed to be in some kind of emotional distress. 'But it's like we have a shared history or something and no one else in this godforsaken country spent their childhood on a studio set. When I tell them that my voice broke halfway through a recording of *Hadley's House*, they look at me like I'm crazy.'

'I remember that.' Hadley giggled. 'It was so funny. "But Hadley, the sheriff will never believe us if we tell him that the principal is actually a former Nazi war criminal." You started the sentence as a soprano and ended it as a baritone. God, my mom was pissed at you.'

'I'm glad that reliving my adolescent trauma is so amusing for you,' George said flatly. His unease seemed almost profound, and Hadley felt that she had no option but to give in to his unreasonable demands.

'Of course we can hang out properly. It'll be tons of fun. Come round on Sunday afternoon.'

Sunday had not got off to a good start. Laura had gone home to where she used to live. And though Hadley's newfound life-skill of being able to microwave stuff was coming along a treat, she still needed supervision when she was making oatmeal. Irina was MIA after a night out with her Russian friends, who were all called things like Nadja and Katja and had one facial expression – an intimidating blank stare, that they all shared.

Candy had refused to help. 'You're eighteen and as far as I know you're not completely mentally deficient,' she'd grumbled when Hadley had woken her up. 'Make your own fucking oatmeal.'

That was easy enough for her to say, especially as, half an hour later, Hadley had caught her on the phone to Conceptua, the Careless' housekeeper, getting step-by-step instructions on how to make coffee in the cafetière. What was the point of that when there was a Starbucks just round the corner?

Even having a long soak in the bath wasn't the same without Laura banging on the door and threatening to do unspeakable things to Hadley with a loofah if she didn't 'get the hell out of there in the next five minutes'.

But the worst thing was George ringing the doorbell. Ten whole minutes early, which was just rude, even if he did bring the previously mentioned fat-free, low-carb popcorn (Hadley checked the back of the box just to make sure) and the DVD boxed set of the first season of his sitcom (like, she wanted to see *that*). It was a real stretch for Hadley to act as if she was pleased to welcome him into her home.

Like, he'd actually been to the Malibu mansion for a carefully staged cast party that doubled up as an *At Home With the Stars*. He'd seen the specially imported Italian marble staircase, and the heart-shaped swimming pool. She'd even caught him snooping in her bedroom, so he'd also seen her princess bed. Like, *literally* a princess bed – it had come straight from a French palace.

Now he was carefully assessing the cheap cream sofa with the splodges on it from where her fake tan hadn't properly dried. The rickety coffee table groaning under the weight of teetering piles of fashion magazines, and the tiny rooms and the windows that didn't open with their charming views of sooty rooftops and anaemic, leafless trees. It was a million miles away from Malibu.

George opened his mouth and Hadley waited for the biting remark that he had all good to go, but he just nodded his head. 'Cool. It looks like the apartment in *Friends*.'

'Well, yeah – if it was half the size and the living room was painted purple,' Hadley said incredulously, then something very important occurred to her. 'Y'know, I always thought that the woman who played Phoebe was cast way too young for her actual age.'

'I know!' George clasped his hand to his heart and they had this connection, this special bonding moment, which lasted the whole time that it took to put on some deep cleansing facial masks and curl up on the couch to watch back-to-back episodes of the *Notting Hillbillies*. It was a really confusing show about a bunch of trust-fund kids ('They call them Trustafarians over here, Hadders, you need to know this stuff') who had lots of premarital sex and smoked lots of illegal drugs, as far as she could tell.

'Who is he again? Is he going out with the older woman, or is she his mom?' she asked George, as she tried to discreetly edge a stray piece of popcorn kernel out of her back molars. It might claim to be fat-free and low-carb, but it left an unpleasant after-taste that all the chai tea in the world couldn't wash away.

'I already told you. She's his step-aunt but they've been having an affair and now he's found out that she's actually his half-sister,' George explained, which just left Hadley even more confused. 'Never mind that. I'm about to come in. There I am. I'm in the kitchen, I'm looking around, cue shocked expression and "Yo, I need to borrow a tenner." What do you think of my delivery, Hadders? I think I didn't quite come in on the beat but my Brit accent rocks, doesn't it?'

Hadley stifled a yawn. 'You sound just like the Queen.'

There was the sound of a key in the lock and she looked up eagerly. She was saved. At last.

Candy burst in through the front door, followed by a gang of people. She'd been doing a guest spot on MTV UK and it looked as if she'd brought back half the audience.

'Oh, Hadders, you're in.' Candy didn't sound too thrilled, but then she shrugged and smiled. 'I'm having a party and everyone's invited. Even you!'

Hadley decided to let that little dig sail past her. At least she'd taken off her face-mask and applied her staying-in-make-up. Plus, her cashmere-blend lounging pants and matching hoodie were in a completely different league to the nasty nylon tracksuits that Irina favoured.

George waved gaily at Candy and, thank the Lord, switched off the DVD player. 'Hey there, gorgeous. What's new and different?'

'It's my absolute favourite person in the world!' Candy exclaimed, rushing over to give him an enthusiastic bear hug. 'Everyone – this is George, my new best friend, and Hadley – she lives here.'

'Everyone' consisted of four boys in tight black jeans, tight black leather jackets and black Converses. They were crying out for a splash of primary colour. There were also two tiny Japanese girls dressed in matching polka-dot outfits, and bringing up the rear was Reed, his arm around a straggly-haired, long-limbed girl who was a completely different straggly-haired, long-limbed girl from the other night.

'Who is that?' George hissed urgently in her ear. 'Because I think I've just fallen in love.'

Hadley definitely preferred George when he was being her fake boyfriend and not her new best friend.

'He's Reed,' she muttered. 'Candy's half-brother and a total modelizer.'

'He can modelize me any time he wants,' George breathed. Hadley couldn't stand it for another second.

'I need to talk to Candy,' she said, making sure that she banged her knee into his shoulder as she climbed off the sofa.

Candy was in the kitchen with two of the tousle-haired, kitten-hipped boys, who gazed adoringly at her while she mixed drinks in the blender that Laura usually used for chocolate milkshakes. Hadley hoped for Candy's sake that the generous helping of tequila she was splashing about didn't rust the blade.

Candy looked up and smiled vaguely as if she could barely remember who Hadley was. 'Oh, hey, do you want a margarita? And do you know how to use the blender?'

Candy could insult her. And she could criticize her on an hourly basis, but this was just too much. 'Do I *look* like I know how to work a blender?'

Even Candy's entourage were shaking their heads and murmuring no. 'OK, don't get your panties in a bunch, I'll call Laura.'

Laura wasn't there so Candy was forced to call Conceptua for the second time that day and conduct a very high-volume conversation in pidgin Portuguese.

Hadley flounced back into the living room, where George was eagerly chatting away to Reed as if they'd been best buds since kindergarten, while the straggly-haired, long-limbed girl perched on Reed's lap and played with his shirt collar.

'To be honest I found Araki's earlier movies too dark but I did love *Mysterious Skin*. It was so powerful,' George enthused. 'But since I came to London, I've really been into Mike Leigh and Ken Loach. Like, really raw film-makers.'

Reed couldn't be buying this BS. Hadley studied him from under her lashes, but he was leaning forward and looking more animated than she'd ever seen him. But considering that he only did snotty when she was around, that wasn't saying much.

'I think there's a real need for a new *cinema vérité*.' Reed suddenly flashed her a wicked grin, which made Hadley feel uncomfortable. Was there popcorn debris in her hair? 'Don't you agree, Hadley?'

Hadley blinked. The three of them, even straggly girl, were staring at her expectantly. They waited and waited. She wouldn't have been surprised if some tumbleweed blew across the room. 'Is *cinema vérité* a new chain of movie theatres or whatever?'

'Woo! Woo!' George pulled an imaginary lever. 'That was the clue train leaving the station. Hadley's strictly a Disney kinda girl, aren't you?'

Hadley wasn't going to have a hissy fit. Not in front of Reed, who already thought that she was an over-ambitious, alcohol-abusing, leg-flashing prom queen. Besides, Candy already had the monopoly on melodramatic snits. Best to play dumb and wreak her revenge on George at a later date.

'Gotta love a film that's fun for all the family,' she said sweetly, keeping the smile on her face as bland as a green salad without any dressing.

And she must have suddenly become invisible because George leaned across her and started up his conversation with Reed again, like they were doing their own special on *The Actor's Studio*.

'Hadders, are you having a margarita or not?' Candy called from the kitchen, and although Hadley had decided that drinking in clubs was OK if it furthered her career, drinking at home seemed wrong. Like, it was the first step on the slippery freeway that led to a check-in at the rehab motel.

'. . . but don't you love the way that he frames his shots so each one looks like a piece of art . . .'

On the other hand . . . 'Yes, please,' she replied. 'Make it a large one.'

And it wasn't that bad. Because the tequila worked much better than champagne at smoothing out all the rough edges and the niggling niggles that prodded at Hadley's brain. After two margaritas, she was happily ensconced between the two Japanese girls who couldn't speak a word of American but were big fans. *Feelin' Kinda Hadley* sounded majorly weird sung in Japanese, but it was the thought that counted.

Laura stormed in during the middle of the second verse, grunted something and disappeared into her bedroom, slamming the door behind her so hard that the walls shook, but by then Hadley was feeling no pain.

Maybe it was because Candy was sucking face with two of the boys, like, concurrently, which she was so going to regret in the morning if the curdled milk look on Reed's face was anything to go by. Or maybe it was because one of their bandmates had muscled in on the karaoke action so he could hold Hadley's hand and tell her that she was the standard by which he measured all other girls. 'I had my first crush on you when I was five,' he slurred in her ear. 'You were just so cute with that little gap in your teeth and freckles. Where have your freckles gone, Hadley?'

OK, maybe that bit wasn't so much fun. 'I never had freckles,' she declared, with her hand on her heart. 'They were drawn in by my make-up artist.'

His head got closer as he peered intently at her face, searching for supposed freckles, though Hadley was more worried that he'd spot the slight reshaping of her nose.

'I can't see any,' he announced mournfully and Hadley smiled, secure in the knowledge that her cosmetic secrets were safe. 'But maybe I should be extra, extra, extra certain.'

One moment he was moving closer to see what lay beneath the fake tan – so close that Hadley could see several open pores just crying out for a good exfoliation – the next his lips were on hers.

They rested there for a few seconds and Hadley waited for someone to give her direction. 'Just tilt your head slightly to the right and move the hair off your face,' but there was no one standing behind the camera. There was no camera. Just a few muted giggles and a sharp, 'Oh God, how much has she had to drink anyway?' from Candy.

And just as Hadley was about to pull away because she still had an almost-full glass of margarita with her name on it, a hand was cupping the back of her neck and his mouth was hard on hers.

Kissing was seriously overrated. It might look good in the movies but that was all lighting and skilful editing. In reality, it was someone trying to eat your mouth off your face while you get a crick in your neck. Then the boy added his tongue to the mix and batted it against Hadley's tightly closed lips.

She wrenched away from him and wiped the back of her hand across her mouth. 'Ewww!' she spat. 'Unhygienic much!'

Hadley took an long gulp of margarita to get rid of the greasy coating on her lips. What had he been eating? 'I just kissed Hadley Harlow!' the boy announced to the room at large and then punched the air as if he'd scored a winning touchdown.

George was red-faced with mirth, wheezy giggles leaking out from his mouth. 'You're the only person I've ever seen who kisses and looks like they're being covered in maggots at the same time,' he told Hadley as she inched back cautiously. There was a very real possibility that he might start snorting liquid out of his nostrils.

'George, don't you mind someone macking on your girlfriend?' Reed idly enquired, lounging back in the armchair with that stupid girl on his lap.

'Yeah, dude, Hadley just cheated on you. *In front of you!*' Candy gestured wildly with her glass and sloshed margarita mix on to the carpet.

George sobered up in record quick time. 'You . . . you floozy.' He wagged a reproachful finger at Hadley who was already regretting the last five minutes.

Her kissee was more interested in getting pats on the back from his bandmates than protecting her honour. Plus, Reed could stop smirking knowingly any time soon.

'You're a way better kisser than him, George,' she soothed, chugging back the last of her drink. 'You know you're the only boy for me.' Really, there was no justice in the world, because she couldn't get a paid acting gig and certainly wasn't going to be trotting up to collect any awards in the near future – but she still managed to get a collective 'ah' from the cheap seats as Hadley snuggled under George's arm and planted a kiss on his cheek.

Chapter Nine

Despite being tucked up in bed by George, who'd even helped her take her make-up off and left a glass of water and a couple of aspirin next to her, Hadley woke up at some ungodly hour in the morning to find the glass half empty (and not just metaphorically) and her mouth doing a good impersonation of the Mojave Desert.

Luckily, it was too soon for the inevitable headache to squat in her skull. Yay for her, Hadley thought as she stumbled out of bed, almost breaking every toe as she blundered into her vanity case.

Putting the hall light on would have been a step too far for her motor-visual functions so she groped her way towards the kitchen, only to get side-tracked by the sound of sobs coming from the lounge. But her need to rehydrate couldn't be ignored. Hadley had no choice but to give in to its siren song, even though that meant grabbing a mug from the draining board and filling it with *unfiltered* water from the tap. The sobs died down to a muted hiccup and there was Laura, hunched on the sofa. As Hadley emerged she straightened up and brushed a hand quickly over her face.

Laura looked beautiful when she cried. It really wasn't

fair. Hadley couldn't cry prettily; all her features scrunched up and a very unattractive line appeared between her eyebrows. But Laura's pouty lips quivered and her big, spiky lashes looked even bigger and spikier as a couple of stray teardrops clung to them.

Of course, she denied the weepfest but Hadley had seen enough teen movies to know that if she backed off, Laura would blurt out whatever was ailing her.

So Hadley 'ah' ed and tilted her head, just like her therapist, Dr Finklestein, used to, and before she could say 'tell me about your childhood', it all came spilling out like a particularly upsetting episode of *Ugly Betty*. Not only was Laura on the verge of getting pink-slipped by Fierce but her boyfriend with the muscular legs had cheated on her. Possibly with one of her friends. Or with the blessing of her friends. Hadley wasn't too sure about the small print as her hangover was starting to make its presence known.

'If I had a boyfriend and he did that to me, I'd leak a story to *E! News* that he had substance abuse issues.' Hadley shook her head in shared indignation until she realized that technically speaking, she was one half of a couple. 'But I *do* have a boyfriend,' she clarified for Laura's benefit. 'George is my boyfriend and I know for a fact he'd never screw around with another girl behind my back.' Which really wasn't a lie.

Laura was still going on about Tom; these perfect, photogenic tears slowly trickling down her cheeks, which were annoyingly flawless, considering she had no make-up on. Hadley felt a roiling wave of nausea buffeting her internal organs. 'Yeah, that sucks,' she mumbled, turning the first heave into a yawn. 'Going back to bed.'

When she was buzzed from whatever alcoholic beverage she'd been quaffing, Hadley felt good. Like 'the-world-is-mine-for-the-taking-and-there-ain't-no-one-or-nothing-can-harsh-my-mellow' good. But the morning after was not of the good. She always forgot that.

On her knees, the bathroom tiles hard underneath her, arms curled around the toilet bowl, was so undignified. It was even worse when she started throwing up; retching her throat red raw as mouthful after mouthful of acidic bile and undigested popcorn came up for their encore performance. At least she'd had the presence of mind to tie her hair back.

Hadley hauled herself to her feet and stared at herself in the mirror. A glob of spittle clung to her chapped lips. 'I look gross,' she wailed softly. The skin around her eyes was red-veined and bruised where she'd burst blood vessels from all the heaving, and the rest of her was ashen. Yesterday's pampering session had, quite literally, gone down the drain.

The front door slammed and Hadley gladly wrenched herself away from her reflection. At least she wasn't all puffy-eyed from a prolonged crying jag like Laura . . .

Laura, who might actually fill the vacancy to be Hadley's

very first best friend. Ignoring the searing pain in her head and yet another wave of nausea, Hadley skidded out of the bathroom, made a quick detour to the fridge and raced down the stairs after the other girl.

'Hey, Laura, wait up!' Hadley braced herself and then wrapped her arms round Laura for a count of three.

'I forgot to wish you good luck,' she gasped. 'I'm so "it's all about me" sometimes.'

Laura looked a little perturbed. She even yelped slightly, which wasn't quite the reaction that Hadley had been aiming for. 'You're freezing,' Laura pointed out. 'Go back inside.'

Best friends looked out for each other. It was in the best friend contract. Like Summer and Marissa. Buffy and Willow. Betty and Veronica. Hadley and Laura. Hadley pulled two cans of Diet Coke out from behind her. 'They're super cold,' she added helpfully.

'Right, OK.' Laura really wasn't getting down with the whole friend thing. She stared at Hadley's token of friendship with bemusement. It wasn't Hadley's fault that there'd been no time to order a fruit basket or arrange a spa day. 'Um, thanks, I'll drink them when I get back.'

'Don't be silly. They're not to drink. You put them on your eyes and they'll reduce the puffiness.' Hadley giggled. She kept forgetting that Laura hadn't been in the business that long. 'My make-up artist on *Hadley's House* used to swear by it.'

'That's so sweet, Hadders.' Laura was hugging her back. Proper hugging, that squeezed on Hadley's midsection in an alarming way. All she could do was clap her hand over her mouth and pat Laura's back with the other. 'Thanks. Well, I'll see you later.'

Finally Hadley was released from her enforced bondage and could rush back up the stairs for another appointment with what Candy called 'the great white telephone'. Which still didn't make any sense.

Hadley washed, got dressed and then promptly changed back into her Juicy Couture PJs so she could snuggle down underneath her comforter and pray for an early death. Anything to relieve her from what had become the worst of all five of her hangovers.

And that was when Candy walked in, without knocking, and sat down on the bed with no thought for Hadley's feet or personal space issues.

'What's up?' she asked casually. 'Bet you're glad you've stopped tossing your cookies?'

Hadley stared at Candy through eyes that were still the little piggy slits that she'd woken up with. 'What do you want?' she asked wearily, curling herself up into a tight ball so Candy couldn't sit on her feet any more.

Candy studied her chipped black nail polish. 'Reed says that I should apologize to you. He seems to think that I've been a shit-stirring little bitch.' She reflected on that for a moment, her lips pursed. 'Maybe I have, just a little bit, but you're so annoying.'

'You don't have to apologize,' Hadley assured her, tugging the pillow over her head. 'You can just pretend that you did and I'll pretend that you did and can you shut the door on your way out?'

Her voice might have been a little muffled but the meaning came through loud and clear – unless you were Candy and had skin as thick as a herd of rhinoceroses . . . rhinoceri . . . *elephants*.

'Get off me!' Hadley gritted out because all of a sudden she had 109 pounds of mouthy New Yorker lying on top of her.

'Oh, don't be mad at me, Hadders,' Candy drawled. 'C'mon, where's the Little Miss Sunshine we all know and sometimes love? She has to be hiding underneath that quilt.'

'She has a migraine . . .'

'You haven't got *another* hangover, have you? I could make you a fried egg – that's meant to work.'

Even when she was trying to be friendly, Candy was relentless. Hadley shucked off her pillow and sat up. 'The grease will clog up my pores.'

Candy gave a long, low whistle that pierced through Hadley's cranium. 'Jeez, you look like shit.' Then she laughed. 'That's probably not the best way to say sorry, is it?'

'You haven't actually said you're sorry,' Hadley pointed out, with the heel of her hand pressed against her forehead because talking hurt. Actually, everything hurt, including her ribcage, her hair and her little toes. 'You've just said a whole bunch of mean things to me. I don't need you to act like you're my friend.'

If you squinted just a little bit, it was possible that Candy looked ever so slightly hurt, which must have been a trick of the light. 'I'm not *acting* like I'm your friend. I am your friend – and so I say mean things. I only do that to people I like – you should be psyched.'

'Well I'm not,' Hadley said bluntly. 'And anyway, Laura's my friend now.'

'You can have more than one friend at a time . . .'

'We bonded this morning. It was really beautiful. She was traumatized because her boyfriend's been cheating on her and . . .' Hadley clapped her hand over her mouth. She was no expert but she was pretty sure that friends didn't blurt out other friends' secrets to really, really interested, begging-for-more, third parties.

'Anyway, I have to go and have a bath now,' Hadley said, getting out of bed and standing up with all the assurance of a newborn foal.

'Hold it right there,' Candy squeaked, barring the way to the door. And she had the chutzpah to accuse Hadley of being annoying? Not fair. 'Tell me everything and don't skip bits.'

Candy was like this vicious Pomeranian that Amber used to have, who would savage Hadley's Barbies in her snapping jaws of death. Candy was *exactly* like that.

She poked and prodded and pimped for details, until Hadley found herself shouting out all the sordid facts about Laura's relationship malfunction through the bathroom door, which made it circumstantial evidence that would never stand up in a court of law. Not that Laura would see it like that.

'But you mustn't say anything, Candy,' Hadley pleaded when she was finally out of the bathroom and nibbling tentatively on a dry piece of soya and linseed toast. 'She's very fragile right now and I think she might be getting sacked by Fierce today.'

'*Might* be?' Candy prompted, scrolling through the address book of her Blackberry. 'Might be isn't good enough.'

'Well, I'd tuned out by then,' Hadley admitted. 'Her accent is very monotone.'

'It explains why she's been so pissy. Like she always has something lodged up her ass,' Candy mused. 'OK, stop yapping now, I have calls to make. I'm taking the three of us for a night out on the town, to prove what a fantastic friend I am.'

Five hours later, an unsacked but still dumped Laura had been dragged to the limo Candy had booked. She was really going all-out on this friend thing. She'd even invited

Irina, who'd arrived back from somewhere abroad that afternoon, and George, who'd scurried round with indecent haste. He was such a slut sometimes.

Hadley was a rose between two thorns; wedged between George and Laura, who was unwrapping the foil from a champagne bottle with a grimly determined expression on her face. 'I'm going to get absolutely rat-arsed tonight,' she announced. 'I'm not coming home until I've committed at least five arrestable offences.'

'You go, sweetcakes,' George enthused, holding out his glass. 'We'll all get drunk so you don't feel left out.'

'Not a drop of alcohol is going to touch my lips,' Hadley said sanctimoniously, painfully aware of her sore throat and the five coats of foundation covering up the excesses of the night before. 'I'm going to try and get high on life.'

'You *have* to get drunk,' Candy insisted, brandishing another bottle of champagne like an offensive weapon. 'It's no fun unless we all do it.'

'You don't have to get drunk,' Laura assured her. 'Look, have one glass to toast my new life as a nun because I am never going near another boy as long as I live, and then you can switch to water.'

'Okaaay, I guess . . .'

Candy clicked her teeth in annoyance. 'Don't be such a pussy. I'm the offspring of two rock 'n' roll iconoclasts. I know about hangovers, and the best remedy is the hair of the dog that bit you.'

'I don't even understand what—'

'Just drink the damn champagne,' Candy growled threateningly. 'And stop pissing on Laura's parade.'

And either Candy was right (please God, no) or else she was what Laura called a lightweight, because tonight it only took one glass of champagne to have Hadley loose-limbed and giggly, clinging to George on the dance floor of the most grimy club she'd ever been to, and trying not to fall over.

'Oh, Hadders, you're such a cheap date,' George shouted over the deafening thud of the bass amp and some guy screeching about how chicks always abandoned him.

'I totally have this chemical imbalance that makes me get drunk too easily,' Hadley told him gravely. 'And I need to pee.'

The club was full of grungy hipsters in grey, skinny jeans who all looked as if they never got intimate with soap and water. Hadley's white Armani trousers and draped silver top were like a lightning rod for catty looks and snide remarks as she tried to find the others.

When Hadley felt a hand tap her on her shoulder she whirled round, ready to smile brightly in the face of sneering indifference, only to find a bored-looking Irina standing behind her. Being Irina she made no effort to introduce Hadley to the olive-skinned boy with the serious cheekbones who was holding her hand. 'We go, this club blows.'

'It sure does, sister,' Hadley said feelingly. 'Why are you holding hands with a boy? I didn't think you did that kind of thing.'

'I not your sister.' Irina gave her a gentle shove in the direction of the exit. 'I not holding hands with anyone, you're imagining it. You're drunk.'

Chapter Ten

Hadley jolted out of sleep and tried to sit up, until she realized she was already sitting up. Or rather, she was propped in the armchair, a blanket wrapped round her.

The clock on the DVD player told her it was 4 : 17 am, but she had no recollection of actually getting home or why she wasn't tucked up in her own bed. All she could remember was dancing on a podium with two girls who told her that they'd been in the last series of *Big Brother*.

'You're awake? How do you feel?'

The voice sounded vaguely familiar. Hadley could just make out a lumpen shape on the sofa, which suddenly elongated and stretched out to snap on one of the side lamps so she could see Reed lounging on the couch.

'You were pretty wasted,' he remarked as she ran tentative fingers through her hair, which was doing a good impersonation of wire wool.

Hadley had a dim memory flickering at the edges of her mind of someone force-feeding her a huge bottle of Evian. 'Well, I'm kinda sober. Actually, still kinda drunk. Maybe a bit muggy,' she finally decided. 'Why aren't I in bed?'

Reed sat up and rubbed his eyes. One benefit of the all-black ensembles and the stubble was that he looked the same as he always did. Standard issue hipster. 'Your friend George crashed out in there and anyway, I thought it would probably be best to keep you in the chair. Choking on your own vomit is so Eighties, y'know?'

'George is in my bed? Ewwww!'

Reed looked mildly confused. 'But he's your boyfriend.'

Which was still no reason why he should be in her bed. 'I'm saving myself for my wedding night,' Hadley gasped indignantly, because she *was* ... though hopefully her wedding night wouldn't feature George in any way, shape or form. Reed didn't seem to be buying it but there was a new crisis looming. 'Oh God, have I still got my make-up on?' Hadley threw off the blanket and was momentarily distracted by the black streaks of disco dirt striping her once white trousers. Grimy marks that not even the best dry cleaner in London could rectify. But there was an even bigger catastrophe that needed to be averted. 'I need the bathroom. I can actually *feel* my pores clogging up.'

The fact that she couldn't bear another second of Reed's most sardonic smile had nothing to do with it.

There was someone asleep in the bath under a pile of towels, but they barely stirred, only grunted, as Hadley switched on the light and began smearing Eve Lom cleanser on her face.

She'd toned and uber moisturized and still hadn't heard the front door shut behind Reed, when Hadley was forced to admit that she couldn't skulk in the bathroom staring at her blotchy reflection and wondering why her hair had had a fight with a tail comb at some unspecified point in the evening. Besides, she paid rent; she had every right to be in the lounge.

It sounded like a plan. And she was all ready to set it in motion, but as she slid the lock back on the door, Reed was standing right there, holding a mug of something that smelled of ambrosial nectar.

'I made you some hot chocolate,' he said loftily, as if he'd hunted it down, clubbed it over the head and dragged it five miles across frozen wastelands. 'Come back into the living room before you wake everyone up.'

'But I never have choc—'

'Shut up,' Reed suggested pleasantly. She definitely wasn't sticking around to be spoken to like that, no sir, but Reed already had his fingers looped about her wrist and her feet simply followed him down the hall.

The hot chocolate was yummy, even if Hadley could feel it going straight to her belly and turning into unsightly rolls of fat. She took baby sips and sneaked a look at Reed from under her lashes.

He was staring right at her, unblinking, until her gaze skittered away. It was way too late for these kinds of mind-games. 'Is there something you want to say to me or shall we just carry on doing the uncomfortable silence thing?' she asked dryly. Reed dipped his head as if to say kudos to her or whatever for not being a toe-dipper.

'You're quite the party girl, aren't you?' he said, steepling his hands under his chin. 'I think this is the first time I've ever seen you halfway to sober.'

That was unfair. She was all the way sober, like ninety-seven per cent of the time. 'You've seen me maybe four times in my entire life so I think your data might be a little skewy,' she told him tartly. 'I only had my first alcoholic drink a month ago.'

'And boy, are you making up for lost time.' Reed gave her another one of those smiles that didn't reach his eyes. 'Candy doesn't need to be around your addictive personality.'

Hadley nearly spat out a mouthful of hot chocolate at the total harshness of that statement. 'I don't *have* an addictive personality, and I wouldn't have drunk at all tonight if Candy hadn't force-fed me champagne. She's very domineering in a social situation, you know. Actually, in all situations.'

'She's a complete brat,' Reed corrected her. He looked so pretty when he smiled properly that Hadley wanted to take a mental picture to look at later. 'But she's *my* complete brat and I take my duties as an older brother really seriously. She's gone through stuff back in New York and she doesn't need to get dragged into your toxic lifestyle.'

Where to start? Had Candy been in rehab? Who cared about Candy – he'd just dissed *her*?! 'I do not have a toxic lifestyle!' Hadley hissed furiously. 'Yes, I go out a lot and maybe sometimes I have a little bit too much to drink, but it's, like, a carefully thought out career strategy.'

Reed snorted, which made the pretty melt away like it had never existed. Which was good, because Hadley was seriously starting to hate him. Not *hate*, because that was a negative, ugly emotion; but she was definitely feeling a serious dislike towards him and his collection of sneers and form-fitting black shirts and trousers. Could you say poser?

'Oh, like, getting your picture in the papers as you stumble out of a nightclub with your dress half falling off is going to have casting agents begging you to audition for them?'

'I don't do auditions . . .' Reed's face darkened just to let Hadley know that she was getting off-message. She was meant to be busy defending her very right to exist on the same planet as Reed and his sister. 'OK, I know you think I'm shallow because I actually brush my hair and stuff, but I care really deeply about things. And yeah, one of them is being famous again and how I go about achieving that has absolutely nothing to do with you. So butt out, mister!'

'Brush your hair?' Reed repeated. 'What has that got to do with anything?'

'All those girls you mack on with their limp, straggly hair because they think they're too good to use serum,' Hadley explained in one angry rush of breath. 'And before you start getting glowery with me, you're a total modelizer so don't be all preachy and judgmental because it won't wash. Have you ever been out with someone who works in Burger King?'

'Forget the booze, you obviously have to be on drugs,' Reed drawled, settling back on the sofa as if he were about to watch a movie.

'It was Cristal. And no I don't take drugs, thank you very much. Just answer the question! Have you ever dated someone from a service industry? Have you?'

Reed sighed because he was totally had and he knew it. 'No.'

'Aha!' Hadley crowed triumphantly. 'That's my point.'

'*What's* your point? Because I'm fairly sure I fell down the rabbit hole about ten minutes ago.'

'That you only going out with models is way more shallow and superficial than me doing whatever I can to relaunch my career.'

'I go out with models. Big deal.' Reed shrugged. 'They're beautiful and I like to look at beautiful things. Besides, they know how it works.'

'How what works?' Hadley echoed, trying to ignore the tiny, twisty feeling in her gut at Reed's dreamy expression when he thought about beautiful girls.

'The whole commitment thing,' Reed said vaguely, gesturing with his hand like that made it any clearer. Then his voice got crisper. 'But we're not talking about me. We're talking about you and your self-destructive search for fame and fortune. You're really living the cliché, aren't you?'

Oh, Hadley hadn't seen the lip curl for at least a week. And, surprise? She really hadn't missed it. 'So I want to be famous again? There's nothing wrong with that.' Hadley put down her empty mug with unwarranted force and folded her arms. Urgh! Not even Amber with her gloves off could ever make her feel this ornery.

'Why do you want to be famous again?' Reed asked, like she'd just given him two hundred and fifty pounds and signed up for some instant career therapy. 'Why don't you go to school or travel or work with orphans in Rwanda? What's the big deal with being famous? There's nothing wrong with obscurity.'

Which was all fine and dandy, and maybe Reed should try out that theory on the fame-hungry actors and actresses who came by for parts in his stupid, dumb movie. 'Look, I've been famous and I've been obscure and, believe me, famous wins every time.' Hadley tucked her legs under her and leaned forward because this wasn't shallow, this was her life. Maybe she hadn't had a say in the whole global celebrity thing first time around but now she was ready to pledge her allegiance loud and clear to anyone who happened to be listening. And right now, it was Reed. 'It's like, if you're famous and everyone knows your name, then you're real. You exist. You mean something to people.' Her voice was throbbing with the ache that was deep inside her chest. Hadley put her head in her hands so she wouldn't have to see the scathing expression that Reed had probably pulled out for this particular occasion. 'I want to feel that again, without having to be twelve.'

There was this deathly nothing. Hadley could hear Reed shifting on the sofa and she wished that he'd bite out one of his sneery one-liners so she wouldn't have to listen to her little campaign speech echoing around and around in her head.

'I think you have a very idealized picture of celebrity,' Reed said at last. 'Yeah, you're not twelve any more, but this whole wild-child routine is going to bite you on the ass. Global superstardom doesn't happen overnight. It takes time.'

'I don't have time,' Hadley said dully. 'I'm eighteen. I hit my twenties and then I'm just another model/actress/ whatever. LA is full of them. I have to make the transition from child star to young Hollywood elite in the next year or it's never going to happen.'

'So what the hell are you doing in London? Ah. Big fish; small pond, right?' Reed didn't sound like he was teasing her any more. But it was late and the lamp was casting shadows over both their faces and it was intimate. That kind of time in the morning when you share your secrets with someone that you hardly know and hope that when it gets light they wouldn't remember.

'I just need one lucky break,' Hadley said to herself. 'It can't be that difficult.'

'It really is,' Reed countered, sprawling full length on the sofa. He looked rumpled now, not so Mr Dark and Foreboding. 'Like, trying to get movie funding is turning into my own ninth circle, y'know?'

Circles? Hadley was all ready to be encouraging when she thought better of it. 'I'd ask you about it but you'd think I was angling for a role.'

'Yeah, I probably would,' Reed admitted with a choked laugh. 'Another time maybe. God, I hate these early mornings when you feel like you're the only person in the world who's awake.'

'People are probably awake in Japan and Australia and maybe Africa,' Hadley pointed out, snuggling deeper under the blanket because the chill was getting chillier. It was hard to keep her eyes open and her mind focused. 'I like being drunk. My brain just shuts up and I stop worrying about stuff just for a couple of hours.'

'You need to cut back – *way* back. And you need to refine your career plan 'cause what you're doing now? It's not doing you any favours, trust me.' And the strange thing was that in that moment, she did. Like, underneath the attitude and the modelizing, Reed was a sort of OK guy.

He stood up and wriggled his shoulders. 'I should get going.' He looked at his watch. 'I have a breakfast meeting in three hours.'

'Then I bag the sofa,' Hadley decided. 'Though by rights I should totally kick George out of my bed and make him sleep in here.'

That seemed like far too much effort when the couch was just in reach, so she crawled over the arm of the chair and collapsed into the warm imprint that Reed had left on the sofa cushions.

Reed was just a shadowy outline, scooping up wallet and phone from the coffee table and shoving them into his pockets. Hadley was almost asleep when she felt the warm press of lips brush fleetingly against her forehead. For a second she thought she was dreaming, until she heard Reed murmur in her ear: 'You're actually an all-right human being. Who knew?'

But she was dreaming, because when she opened her eyes, she was alone with nothing but the echo of the closing street door to keep her company.

Chapter Eleven

Hadley didn't stop drinking just because of her pre-dawn tête-à-tête with Reed. Even though she really, really hated it when he got so judgy. It was more because she didn't want to be just a footnote on the pages of *Celebrity Who's Who* as the child star who turned into a drunk. Besides, the hangovers were making her skin super-dry.

It helped that the other girls were, like, role models for the benefits of hard work. Candy and Irina were racking up frequent-flyer miles with modelling jobs in far-flung locations, which also meant that neither of them were around to foist alcoholic beverages on her. And Laura had this new work ethic, which mostly meant that she ate lots of oatmeal and yogacized her puppy fat away, and worked *for free*. It was cute and all, how she got all excited about working her newly svelte butt off for nila dinero, but as career plans went it was a salient exercise in how not to do things.

George was not happy when she switched to drinking lime juice and sparking water. 'You were more fun when you were wasted,' he complained bitterly, just because Hadley was sitting in a London nightclub stone cold sober.

There had to be more nightclubs in London than anywhere else on the planet. 'You were less obsessed with your plans for world domination.'

Hadley simply smiled in what she hoped was an enigmatic fashion and told him to kiss her and act like he meant it because she'd just spotted a photographer lingering behind some bizarro light installation.

But it was obviously really getting to him. 'If I leave your side for a minute, you get this pissy look.'

'What pissy look?' Hadley pouted and George pointed his finger at her face, which was benefiting from her new teetotal habits. Well that, and a recent oxygen facial.

'That look! I was just shooting the breeze with my friend Benji, and you come storming over to tell me to get back to the table.'

Benji was the little Asian boybander that George had to go and say hello to because he was at every single party they went to. 'He's always lurking,' Hadley said, twirling a strand of newly-lightened hair around her finger. 'Do you think he's a stalker?'

There'd been an assistant director on *Hadley's House* who'd been so frightened of Amber that he'd started breaking out in hives every time she cornered him to make script changes or rework Hadley's scenes. She didn't even know why she suddenly remembered him, except that George was scratching at his chest in exactly the same way. 'You talk such crap sometimes,' he said dismissively, but the pinched look around his mouth was the faintest trace of blood in the water. Which made Hadley the shark.

'Is he your boyfriend?' she asked calmly, looking over her shoulder at Benji who was talking animatedly to a girl wearing a last season's Chloe skirt. If he were five inches taller, he'd be an absolute heartbreaker. Benji glanced over in their direction, caught Hadley's eye and promptly spilled his drink. She turned back to George who was now clawing at his collar. 'So, is he? Like, you never talk about being gay or anything.'

'Oh God, shut the fuck up!' he whispered venomously. 'I'm not . . . why are you bringing this up? You might have been an enormo pain in the ass but you were never a bitch, Hads.'

'I'm down with the whole gay issue. My colourist and Derek and my part-time stylist are all gay, but I need to know that you're not going to do anything to jeopardize our arrangement.' George looked entirely unconvinced. 'And fyi, I'm not and have never been a b.i.t.c.h,' Hadley added. 'It's one of the reasons why I turned down a role in *Mean Girls*. Well, that and they wanted me to play second lead to Lindsay Lohan and I was all, like—'

'Hadley, I'm not gay and Benji's not gay either. We're not gay together. I mean, we're not together . . .'

It was ages since she'd had George squirming on the ropes and it was revenge for every single nasty comment he'd casually flicked her way over the last two months. As long as no one found out, Hadley didn't care if he was getting kissy with every cute gay boy in London. But what fun would it be to tell him that?

'Riigght,' she said sceptically. 'Whatever you say.'

'I mean it, Hadley, you can't say stuff like that. If Benji's manager found out . . . they're not even allowed to have girlfriends.' His eyes narrowed as, hallelujah! light finally dawned. 'Oh, I get it, this is a charming attempt to blackmail me. Go on then, spit it out.'

Blackmail was such an ugly word. And so untrue. But then again, desperate times and all that. 'A guest spot on your show would be a great way of helping out your loving, faithful *girl*friend,' she said slowly, because sometimes George needed extra help with long words.

'No way,' he breathed, his face flicking from horrified to panicked and back to horrified. '*Anything* but that. Hey, we could even say we're getting engaged! You'd like that, wouldn't you? Could probably get eight pages in *OK*.'

Eight pages in *OK* were the smallest potatoes compared to a primetime TV slot. 'Maybe I should ask Benji to come over, get to know him better,' Hadley mused, already raising her hand to wave.

She didn't know George could move so quickly as he yanked her hand down, hard enough for potential bone crushage. 'I could try and get you a walk on,' he capitulated grudgingly.

'Nuh-huh, Georgy.' Hadley gently peeled back his

fingers from her wrist. 'I want a walking, talking part, at least ten minutes of screen time and a special guest star credit in the titles.'

'It's not my decision – but I could get you in to see the casting director,' George backtracked furiously, clutching her hands again and giving them a frantic shake.

Being sober rocked. 'I offer to help you out in return for one tiny favour.' Hadley let her voice crack on the last word and threw in a lip wobble for good measure. Now was not the time for overkill. 'It's funny, 'cause I thought we were becoming friends.'

'We *are* friends, Hadders.'

Hadley shrugged diffidently. 'Yeah, whatever. I'm just going to powder my nose.'

She got up and looked around helplessly. 'Now which way is the bathroom? Maybe I should ask someone to help me. What did you say your friend's name was again?'

'You are a fucking piece of work, Hadley,' George gasped. He still went for melodrama when quiet restraint was so much more effective. 'OK, I'll get you on the show. Hopefully they can make sure that you're facially disfigured in some horrible, freak accident.'

'Thanks, baby,' Hadley cooed, patting George on the cheek. He flinched away from her as if she'd dipped her mitts in hydrochloric acid first. 'You're such a good friend.'

★　★　★

Despite George's recriminations and even tears at one point, the producers of the *Notting Hillbillies* were delighted to have Hadley on the show.

That's the word they used, *delighted*, as in 'We'd be delighted to have a star of Hadley's calibre, and we've got some really exciting ideas that will showcase her acting skills. We can't wait to start working with her.'

Hadley read the email print-out that Derek pushed in front of her with a serene smile. 'Do you know what I don't understand?' she asked.

Derek shook his head, a relaxed grin on his face because she wasn't riding his ass for once. He was very handsome – if George wasn't officially not gay, then she'd totally have set them up. 'No idea.'

'What I don't understand is that I've scored myself a role in a critically acclaimed TV show in the space of one five-minute conversation, and you've been working for me for two months and have managed to get precisely nothing. It's a complete mystery to me.'

That wiped the grin off his face pretty damn quick. 'I have come to you countless times with projects and you've turned each one down. It's got to the stage now, Hadley, where if it doesn't have an Oscar-nominated director attached, I don't even bother to mention it.'

'Like what? A few crummy presenter gigs; a one-spot ad for a fast-food chain that only has branches in the Midlands. I don't even know what the Midlands is!' Hadley tapped the email with her finger. 'Even this is a step down but you've set my relaunch back with your failure to do your job.'

If it came down to it, she would fire Derek. Ideally before she filmed *Notting Hillbillies* so she didn't have to pay Fierce any commission for doing absolute bupkis. But she couldn't go to another agency without something on her résumé for the last couple of months. It was a dilemma.

'We're just going round in circles,' Derek sighed. 'To be honest, Hadley, people aren't that interested in you as a more mature talent. Everyone loved you when you were an innocent little girl, but now it's a different story. They see the newspaper headlines, they've read all the stories about the business with your father and it makes them wary. Unless you can prove that there's more to you than what they already know, then you're screwed.'

Hadley gave a groan of pure, unadulterated frustration. 'How can I prove that when I can't get any work? Do you see my predicament, Derek? Do you have even the barest understanding of where I'm coming from?' Hadley groped for her bottle of Evian with a trembling hand. She was in serious need of rehydration – all this kvetching really took it out of her.

Derek seemed to share her pain. He slumped in his seat, his whole demeanour screaming dejection. 'I've had a big offer come in but I'm not even going to show it to you because your screams of protest will perforate my eardrums.'

Hadley narrowed her eyes. Her voice was at all times soothing and exceedingly well modulated, thanks to her speech coach. No way was she that demanding. 'Try me,' she challenged.

'It's for Australia's leading brand of loo roll,' he began carefully, before catching sight of Hadley's confusion. 'Er, toilet tissue?' He soldiered on before she could throw her hands up in horror and shriek out a refusal at a pitch audible only to bats. 'They've got wads of cash. Their opening offer was one hundred thousand pounds they'll fly you out to Sydney first class, put you up in a really lovely hotel.'

'That's almost two hundred thousand dollars,' Hadley noted. Derek obviously took her prowess with the exchange rate as genuine interest because he twitched another piece of paper in front of her.

'Here's the script.'

'My career isn't the only thing that's going down the dumper,' Hadley read with disbelief. 'But with Quilty-Lux loo roll at least some of my problems can be wiped away . . .'

'Obviously it's just a first draft, Hadley,' Derek interjected hastily. 'I'm sure we could suggest some changes . . .'

'Oh, no. A world of no. There's not enough money in the world that would make me . . . *prostitute* myself by schilling for toilet tissue. I can't believe that you even considered this a viable option.'

'Why don't you think about it?' But Derek was already breathing a sigh of relief as Hadley pushed her chair back and grabbed her Louis Vuitton bag.

'There's nothing to think about,' Hadley snapped. 'Like, I want the whole world to know that I have bodily functions? I don't think so!'

Chapter Twelve

Walking on to a studio set with rooms made out of plywood, cables coiled up like sleeping snakes on every available surface and lights hot enough to melt off your make-up made it seem like the last five years had never happened.

Hadley hadn't realized how much she'd missed it. Seeing her costume changes neatly labelled; hanging out at the Craft Services table; even the really tiresome script read-through, where every single member of the cast angled for more lines.

By the time Hadley was being cued for her first scene, she'd commiserated with Wendy in make-up about her gran's hip replacement and complimented Mike, the runner, on his bitching choice of new sneakers. Because if there was one thing that she'd learned from her years in the biz that she prized above all other lessons, was that you had to be nice to the little people. It was the little people that would rat you out to the tabloids, screw up your lighting and put white sugar in your decaff latte.

'Quiet on set,' the director bellowed. 'Act one, scene four, action!'

Hadley carefully opened the door, remembering that

Mike had told her that it stuck a little, and walked into what looked like the front room of a mansion but was meant to be a one-bedroom flat on Westbourne Grove.

'Tiffany, what the hell are you doing here?' asked the actor who was playing Tai, her step-cousin.

Hadley paused, looked round the room as if she was seeing it for the first time and hung her head. 'I've been expelled,' she exclaimed sorrowfully. 'There was this teensy incident with the headmaster's son, but I swear I was framed.' She paused again, to let one tiny tear trickle slowly down her cheek. 'He said he was going to help me revise, but I certainly don't remember *that* being on the curriculum.'

Shakespeare it so wasn't, but compared to the last two seasons of *Hadley's House*, when the show was seriously jumping the shark, it was practically Emmy-winning material.

Hadley didn't know where the *Notting Hillbillies* powers-that-be had found their cast (possibly in a dumpster) but the fact that she turned up on time, remembered her lines and hit all her marks seemed to impress the heck out of everyone. Except George, but Hadley got to smash a prop lamp over his head on her last day so, hey, added bonus. Honestly, the week just flew by.

She was just wrapping her final scene, fake baggage packed and waiting by the door, when she saw the series director walk on to set with Derek in tow. There was a whispered confab as she had the shine on her forehead dusted away and then the director, Brendan, said, 'Can we take five everyone? Hadley, my love – a word, please?'

Hadley carefully picked her way across the set through the missing fourth wall and over some camera leads. 'I'm sorry I fluffed that last line. I keep forgetting that you pronounce *route* to rhyme with boot and not, um, like, shout.'

Brendan, a big burly Irishman with ruddy cheeks, put an arm round her shoulder. 'Not a problem. You've been a total pro all week. Most of my cast can't even pronounce their own names properly. You've met Anjali, haven't you?'

Hadley bestowed a friendly smile on the series director, before dialling it down a few megawatts for Derek because he was still on her to-do list under the words 'Fire Derek'.

'We love what you've done with the part,' Anjali gushed. 'To be honest, Tiffany was meant to be a typical, airhead Valley Girl, but you gave her depth.'

'It was nothing, just doing my job. I've had such a great time.' Hadley adjusted the yellow boob-tube she'd been not too happy about wearing. It really clashed with her, well, everything.

'We were wondering how you were fixed for the next few weeks as we'd like to extend your contract through to the end of the season,' Anjali said. 'But we need a decision now because we'd have to rescript this final scene and we only have an hour of shoot time left.'

Derek was nodding his head eagerly, his mouth open wide to start agreeing, but Hadley slipped her arm round his waist just in time to give him a vicious, warning pinch to shut the hell up.

'My schedule's kinda busy,' she said regretfully. 'I'm due in Sydney at the end of next week. For a very lucrative ad campaign,' she added conspiratorially.

'If it's a question of money, I'm sure we can come to some arrangement,' Anjali butted in. Really, the woman had no idea how to play hardball.

Hadley tilted her head as if she was deep in thought. 'Why don't Derek and I find a quiet corner to look at my itinerary and see if we can make the numbers work?' she suggested. 'And I'd really need a special guest-star credit higher up in the titles.'

Chapter Thirteen

It was majorly odd to think how much Hadley's life had changed in a few short weeks. There were still miles to go before she clawed her way right up to the top again. But she'd successfully negotiated those pesky bottom rungs and now the world was her oyster.

Not her *oyster*, perhaps, because they tasted icky. But the world was definitely her salmon nigri again.

Operation Stardust had gone storming ahead in the most unexpected way. Because now there was a buzz about Hadley; a buzz that was quickly becoming a deafening roar.

At first, she'd been jazzed just to have a call sheet again and a reason to get up in the morning that had nothing to do with her goal to get up to eleven on the elliptical trainer. But now she didn't just have a call sheet but, like, a packed itinerary.

It started off with a couple of shoots for proper fashion magazines and not weekly gossip rags. After that, an interview with the style supplement of a Sunday paper and a guest spot on a primetime Friday night chat show. And then Derek was getting flooded with calls from every casting agent in London who wanted to know how her schedule was looking once *Notting Hillbillies* wrapped.

But it wasn't until BBC America started showing the current series and *E! Tonight* filmed an interview with her for a last-minute segment on Hollywood stars living in London that the LA casting agents wanted to know when Hadley was going to be back in town. Her triumphant homecoming was pencilled in for the week after they finished shooting the last episode.

'I'm lining up meetings with CAA, PMK, NBC, CBS and the CW. So many initials,' she giggled to Manda, her screen next-door neighbour, as they sat having their make-up done for the final day's filming. 'And of course my mom's going to be induced while I'm over so I'll have two cute little babies to visit while I'm there. I'm already on the wait list for two Hermés baby slings.'

'It sounds so glamorous,' Manda mumbled, keeping her lips motionless as a coat of lip-gloss was applied. 'I've got a week in Ibiza with my little sister and maybe a guest appearance on some rubbish quiz show, but that's it.'

'Oh, you should so come to LA. They'd eat up your accent with a spoon.' Hadley obligingly lifted one leg so Wendy could apply another coat of body shine to her calves. 'You've just got to keep on keeping on and eventually people take notice.'

Manda leaned in closer. 'I s'pose. So have you heard George's news?'

From her relaxed posture, no one would have guessed that the mere mention of George's name made Hadley's tummy muscles clench. The official word was that they were still going out but keeping things casual while they were working together. He was like her own personal storm cloud, his sulky face promising a cold-weather front every time he even deigned to look in her direction, which wasn't that often. 'Oh, we haven't had a chance to hook up for a couple of days,' Hadley said blithely. If he'd got a new pretend girlfriend she was going to sue his ass off for breach of contract.

'Word is that he's been in to see Spielberg about his new movie,' Manda hissed. 'But that's strictly hush hush.'

'Yeah, like every guy under twenty-five with an Equity card has been in to see Spielberg about his new movie,' Hadley bit out before she could stop herself. 'But I'm really pleased for him. I'm sure we'll have a chance to catch up at the wrap party.'

She had no intention of catching up with George at the wrap party, or anywhere else, for that matter. Because the other big change on the good ship *Hadley* was that she had actual real friends now. Friends who *liked* her for her – not because they were contractually obligated to. When Hadley could actually find a window in her schedule, she hung out with the cast of *Notting Hillbillies*, who thrilled to Hadley's every word as they lounged in their favourite Soho club, which was so exclusive that you needed a secret pin number to tap into the front door's keypad.

Of course, she totally wasn't drinking anything other

than virgin caphinairas and having her car come at ten so she had a chance to go memorize her lines for the next day – but work came before everything else.

Now she just had to get rid of the one less-than-bright spot on her new sunny horizon that was George. 'We can still be friends,' Hadley told him as they sat in their limo on the way to the *Notting Hillbillies* wrap party. 'I can get into cool clubs and have my picture taken on my own merits now, but we had fun hanging out, didn't we? Kinda.'

George petulantly pursed his lips so his fringe lifted in the slipstream. 'I was just following orders,' he snapped out. 'And I guess I'm not needed now to guarantee your part for next season.'

There was no time to sugar-coat it. 'Oh, but, hey, I'm not doing another season. I'll be back in LA by then – I'm up for a new pilot from the team who did *Santa Monica Boulevard* . . .'

And instead of being pleased for her, like a proper friend would, George actually shuddered as if his body had been plunged into piranha-infested waters. 'Say what?' he hissed. 'I've been on the show for three fucking years and all I've been offered is a spot on *Dancing With Stars.*'

Hadley paused from reading a message from Manda on her Sidekick, pleading with her to get to the party soon. 'Well, I can't help having star quality, George. It's not like I can turn it on and off.' OK, not the most tactful thing to point out. 'Look, we can carry on the arrangement for a bit and if you did ever manage to get work in Hollywood *again*, I could get you in to see some people. Not even as a favour but because I really want to help you.'

Revenge was so sweet and it had, like, zero calories.

'Fuck you, Hadley,' George spat, scrambling out of the limo and almost ripping the sleeve of his Helmut Lang jacket in his haste to get away. It reminded Hadley of why she'd never liked him in the first place. She didn't actually owe George anything and it was time he realized that.

But first she had to brave a phalanx of photographers as she glided up the red carpet in a silver twist of a dress that an up and coming designer had made just for her. As soon as she entered the party, at an old fire station transformed for the night, a glass of champagne was thrust into her hand by her press agent.

'Hey, Merv, is that shirt actually ironed?' Hadley asked him playfully.

Mervyn peered down at his snowy white front. 'New, actually.' He looked at the glass in her hand. 'Didn't know if you were on the wagon or not?'

Hadley held the glass up and considered the contents gravely before taking a tiny sip. 'Well, I don't have to get up early tomorrow and it *is* a celebration. I'll just have one glass though.'

'So, what do you want to do about gorgeous George then?' Mervyn asked. Hadley was totally down with the way he got straight to the point. If only Derek could be that direct. 'Is it worth keeping him around in case this Spielberg rumour turns out to be true?'

'D'you think?' Hadley rolled her eyes. 'He's not exactly *Actors Studio* material.'

Mervyn didn't seem to care either way. 'Your choice, princess.'

'He's jealous of my charisma,' Hadley confided out of the corner of her mouth. 'People love me; it's just who I am. Always has been.'

'We do love you,' said a voice in her ear and then Lorne, who played Tai on the show, was wrapping his arms round her, which she didn't mind because he always smelled really nice and worked out a lot. Hadley patted one rippling bicep.

'So what do you want me to do?' Mervyn asked again. 'Or do *you* want to do it?'

Dump George? In person? Hadley shuddered at the thought. 'As if ! That's what I pay you to do. And make sure that I get last month's bonus from his publicist for the five front pages.'

Mervyn touched his forehead in what Hadley guessed was like an ironic salute or something but Lorne was already whisking her away to the VIP booth and even if it *were* a new shirt, they'd still never let Mervyn past the velvet rope.

★ ★ ★

One glass of champagne turned into three bottles, ordered on Hadley's credit card, for toasts that got more preposterous as the evening wore on.

'To Vi in the canteen for making the best tea,' someone shouted, and Hadley dutifully held her glass aloft.

'To Fiona in the press office for blagging us all MP3 players,' Kiran added. Hadley pouted. She'd never got a free MP3 player.

'Why aren't you joining in the toast?' the boy sitting next to her asked, and Hadley began to launch into an indignant explanation when she realized her glass was empty.

'I have no more champagne,' she announced mournfully, upending her glass and catching the solitary drop that slowly trickled out on to the end of her tongue.

'We can't have that,' he said, snapping his fingers at a passing waiter. 'More champagne for my beautiful friend here, please.'

Two bottles of Cristal appeared on the table in the time it took for introductions to be made.

'I'm Hadley.'

'I know. I'm a big fan and I'm Alain,' he said, handing her the brimming glass that the waiter had just poured. 'I've been trying to pluck up the courage to talk to you for the last hour.'

Alain was gorgeous. Heart-breaking, drop-dead, make your heart skip a beat gorgeous. His close-cropped hair showed off a pair of cheekbones so pointy, they could double as a coat-rack; Bambi-big eyes the exact colour of a Starbucks triple espresso with just a smidge of half and half. And then there was the mole, nestling just under his elegant nose, which existed just to signpost the way to a mouth that was so kissable he could have made a fortune advertising lip-balm.

The urge to drool was almost too powerful to resist. Hadley contented herself with a teensy tremor that skittered down her spine. 'Am I that frightening?'

'Beautiful women are *always* frightening,' Alain stated emphatically. Amber had warned her about boys like this.

'They might be smooth-talking and pretty, honey,' she used to say. 'But scratch each one and you'll find a cold-hearted bastard underneath.'

But then again, Amber wasn't nestled so close to Alain that their thighs rubbed against each other. Hadley was feeling things that she didn't think her body knew how to feel. Squishy, girly feelings that made her skin itch.

Somehow, she managed to summon up a cool smile. Interested, sure, but not *that* interested. 'So what do you do when you're not practising your chat-up lines?' she teased.

Alain's lashes swooped down and really, it was a crime for a boy to have the kind of lashes that took her three coats of Diva Mascara to achieve. 'Oh, I'm a producer. I'm working on this hip, indie movie.'

Ker-ching! It was like she'd put her money in a slot machine, pulled the lever, and watched the dials align themselves so each one showed a cute little pot of gold. Cue the crashing cacophony of coins. Hadley had hit paydirt.

Never mind TV pilots. She could be hip! And indie! And in a hip, indie movie! Without the help of a certain Reed, who'd gone AWOL since that weird early-morning confessional.

'Tell me more,' she husked invitingly and Alain was incredibly obedient; telling her about this film that would be absolutely perfect for an eighteen-year-old ingénue with an American accent and 'legs all the way up to her armpits'.

It was kinda hard to pay attention. The champagne was making her feel sleepy and when more people piled into the VIP room and congregated around their table, Alain pulled Hadley on to his lap, which was even more distracting, what with concentrating on making herself seem as light as thistledown (whatever the heck that was) and leaning back against the tightly muscled wall of his chest. It was, like, the best night ever.

'Are you falling asleep on me?' Alain wanted to know as the house lights came up and Hadley whimpered in protest.

'Champagne usually enervates me,' she mumbled, pressing her face against his shoulder, awake enough to hope that she wasn't getting Mac tinted moisturizer over his T-shirt. 'Guess I've been working too hard.'

'Well, let me get you home before you turn into a

pumpkin.' Alain gently slid her off his lap and then hauled her to her feet.

'Hey, Hadders, we're going to an after-hours club if you're interested,' Manda called out, but Hadley waved a feeble hand.

'I'm beat,' she whined. 'I need to go to sleep.'

A general chorus of 'Where's George?' sounded, while Hadley slumped against Alain. Those arms of his weren't just aesthetically pleasing; they were doing a really good job of keeping her upright.

George duly appeared, like the most bad-tempered genie to ever pop out of a lamp. 'I thought you weren't drinking,' he demanded belligerently, when Hadley stumbled her way through the introductions of 'Alain, George. George, Alain. He has nicer hair than you.'

'I'm going to take Hadley home.' Alain sounded as if he was daring George to argue the point. 'Is that OK, mate?'

'Saves me having to hold her hair back while she pukes,' George said indifferently. 'By the way, Hadley, you're so very dumped.'

There were shocked gasps but Hadley merely wagged her finger at George as Alain very kindly led her towards the exit. 'Like, whatever,' she slurred. 'I asked Merv to dump you hours ago, so you're the dumpee, not the dumper. Are we clear on that, George?'

'What did you ever see in that loser?' Alain asked, as he half carried her down the stairs. Her legs were being way uncooperative. Hadley almost toppled over as the double whammy of the cold night air and the pop pop pop of the camera flashes registered simultaneously.

'I didn't see anything in him,' Hadley hissed, reliving that last venomous look on George's face. 'He has no loyalty and he's, like, two hundred and fifty per cent gay.'

Chapter Fourteen

Waking up was not one of Hadley's best ideas. Opening her eyes came a close second. The ceiling didn't look like her ceiling. Her ceiling didn't have a patch of mould on it the exact same shape as the logo for The Coffee Bean and Tea Leaf.

The last thing she could remember was having a collision with the sidewalk as she'd tried to get in a cab. She'd definitely skinned her knees because she could remember looking down and seeing rivulets of blood streaking her tan. Her knees gave a warning throb just then to remind her and when Hadley pulled back the grubby sheet (like, ewwww!), she made the worst discovery yet.

She was naked! Bare-ass naked in someone else's bed!

'Oh, crap!' she groaned out loud and then clapped her hand over her mouth. If she was *nude* in someone else's bed, then where was the someone else whose bed she was in? It was like one of the tongue twisters her speech coach had drilled into her to get her to stop lisping.

Alain. What had she done? More to the point, what had he done to her? Because there was no way she'd have done anything. She was saving herself for the man she married. Or Orlando Bloom. Preferably she was saving herself for her wedding night with Orlando Bloom. Not blacking out because she'd drunk too much and giving it up to some passably cute boy because he had a six pack.

But despite her knees, they were no other twinges or aches in places that Hadley really didn't want to think about. Just a deep, hollowed out feeling in her head that wasn't like her usual hangover.

Hadley gingerly wrapped the quilt around her and hauled herself out of bed. Her slinky silver dress and underwear were strewn over the scarred wooden floorboards. She was just about to dive for them when the door opened and Alain walked in.

It was a relief that he still looked handsome this morning. Handsome and sheepish, as he rubbed his chin and looked resolutely at the floor. 'About last night . . .' he began but Hadley held up her hand imploringly.

'Don't say anything else,' she begged. 'I've never—'

'You didn't,' he interrupted. 'We didn't do anything. I slipped something in your drink to get you back here.'

'You did what?' Hadley was stunned. 'Huh? Did you date-rape me?'

His look of outrage was pretty ironic considering he'd just admitted to drugging her, abducting her and stripping her. 'I said, nothing happened. It wasn't personal. I just need the money.'

Keeping a death-grip on the quilt, Hadley tugged at her hair with the other hand. 'What did you do to me?'

134

'Look, I'll say really nice things about you. I'm not going to make out like you were a slut or anything. Just that we hooked up and you rocked my world.' The words poured out of his beautiful mouth in this giddy rush like he couldn't wait to be done with them. 'I'm sorry but, hey, you've been in the biz long enough that you know the score.'

Hadley stared at him in disbelief. None of it made any sense. Not the kind of sense that she wanted it to make anyway.

She must have stood there for a while, opening and shutting her mouth and not able to make anything resembling a word come out.

'Say something,' Alain said at last, when he couldn't take the silence any more. 'You can call me a bastard if you like. I deserve it.'

'Did George put you up to this?' Hadley hardly recognized her own voice.

'Got a friend who's got a friend on the *Daily News*; he tipped me off as to where you'd be.'

'So you're not a movie director?' Hadley asked tremulously, though really that was the least of her problems.

Alain shook his head. ' 'Fraid not. You'd probably better go now, but I think there's a few snappers outside.'

Hadley padded over to the window and poked her fingers through the slats on the grubby Venetian blinds. There were a couple of photographers milling about in the street and also a couple of really trampy looking tramps.

'Where am I?'

'Oh, I live above a betting shop in Hackney,' Alain explained. And somehow, though it didn't seem possible, everything had just got worse.

Engage your brain and start thinking, Hadley. She turned round so she could fix Alain with her scariest look. The one that made Derek twitch and even Amber mind her manners.

'I have money. I can give you money,' she said decisively. 'Whatever they'll pay you, I'll double it – but you'll have to sign a sworn affidavit that you'll leave me alone and if you break it, I will sue you. I will sue your friend. I will sue—'

The long list of people that she would sue, including Alain's grandparents, landlord and the vicar who baptized him – and obviously did a crappy job because he was severely lacking in Christian values – was cut short. 'Aw, man,' Alain moaned. 'That would have been sweet but I've already given, my mate the photos. I took them on my digital camera, then emailed them to him.'

'THERE ARE PHOTOS?! You took photos of me?' Hadley shut her eyes and wondered if her frantically racing heart was going to bust out from her ribcage. 'Was I naked?'

'I really want you to go now,' Alain insisted weakly. 'Just get your clothes and get out.'

'Was I naked?' Why couldn't she get angry, instead of talking in her stupid, babyish voice that didn't seem to be instilling the fear of God into Alain?

'It was tasteful,' Alain admitted. 'It's a family paper, so there was, like, um, your tits but they might put black blobs over your nipples.'

'Turn your back so I can get dressed,' Hadley demanded furiously. No way was he getting another look. She sent icy daggers of loathing right between Alain's shoulder blades as she dragged on her clothes. 'What's the address here?'

'Why do you want to know?'

'Just tell me the address and I won't tell the police that you slipped me an illegal substance,' Hadley clarified.

Alain reeled off the address but she had to make him repeat it twice because her brain still wasn't properly engaged. Luckily, Mervyn's number was on her speed dial. 'Now give me some privacy,' she snapped as she pulled her Sidekick out of her clutch bag.

There had been times, many times, that Hadley wondered exactly why she was paying Mervyn a three grand a month retainer – especially as he wasn't using any of the money on a good laundry service.

But she didn't have to wonder any more. He listened to her garbled explanation and said tersely, 'Get the hell away from the windows, sit tight and I'll be there in thirty minutes.'

He was there in twenty-three, hammering at the door and shouldering past Alain with a contemptuous sniff. 'Not a bloody word out of you, pal,' he'd grunted. 'Give me your camera now.'

Alain gave up his Sony gizmo without a protest. Hadley had never noticed it before but Mervyn made up for his lack of height with bulky shoulders, meaty fists and a nose that looked like it had been broken at least three times.

Merv fiddled with the camera, then dropped it on the floor with a satisfying thwunk. 'Right, me and my client need some privacy so go somewhere else. Do not phone anyone, do not speak to anyone, do not pass go or we're going to have a problem.'

'Look, you've got the . . .' Alain began, then immediately regretted it as Mervyn backed him into the wall and, like, totally invaded his personal space.

'What part of "do not speak" is giving you trouble, mate?'

Alain sidled out of the door back first, as if he wanted to keep an eye on Mervyn and his fists. Hadley finally shifted from the bed where she'd been kneeling.

'This is bad,' she stated for the record. 'It's really bad, isn't it? Badder than bad.'

'Just tell me what happened,' Mervyn advised, grabbing a rickety chair, turning it around and straddling it.

It was hard remembering what had happened and in the right order, especially as there were parts that she couldn't

138

recall and only had Alain's side of the story to go on.

'Did he say what he'd given you? GHB? Rohypnol?'

'Are you sure that nothing happened; you didn't have sex?'

'Who's seen the photos? Have you seen them? I wiped everything that was on the camera but I'll sort out his computer before we go.'

Hadley sat on the edge of the bed with her head in her hands as, mercifully, Mervyn's inquisition came to an end. 'I'm such an idiot,' she wailed pitifully. 'I should have known that he was too good to be true. I shouldn't have had any champagne . . .'

'Shoulda woulda coulda,' Mervyn replied, leaning over to pat her perfunctorily on the shoulder. 'Buck up, Had. It's a mess, yeah, but I'm one of the best clean-up guys around.'

Hadley allowed herself one small trembling flicker of hope. 'Can you get them not to publish the pictures and, well, not to publish anything? 'Cause we could call the police and tell them that he drugged me! And that he took off my clothes. That's assault, right?'

Mervyn shook his head. 'There's at least ten photographers outside. We get the police involved then it's going to be all over the front pages.'

'There really is such a thing as bad publicity,' Hadley agreed. 'I don't want my boobs in the paper. I know that sex tape worked out for Paris Hilton but she wasn't a successful child star. This will kill my career!'

Her voice was creeping up the hysterical setting again. Even Mervyn winced. 'We'll see if we can cut a deal. You tell your side of the story. You'd been arguing with George, he made you feel undesirable so you ended up doing something you really regret. I'll see if we can dig up some dirt on your little friend, Alan . . .'

'His name is Alain and he's no friend of mine,' Hadley insisted vociferously but Mervyn was already pulling out his phone.

'*Daily News*, right? One of the girls on the entertainment desk owes me a favour.'

It was hard to follow what was going on from Mervyn's end of the conversation, which mostly consisted of a series of grunts. The ten minutes that he was on the phone seemed to last for an eternity as Hadley scrutinized his inscrutable face for any clues.

Finally, Mervyn hung up the phone. 'Right, get your stuff and let's get out of here.'

'But what—'

'Some time in the next five seconds would be good.'

Running a gauntlet of photographers was not fun. Not when there was a complete absence of red carpet or friendly cries of 'Hadley, show us a bit of leg, love.'

Hadley emerged from Alain's flat with Mervyn's coat – which smelled distinctly of armpit – over her head and his arm firmly round her waist so he could guide her through a wall of flashes, people shoving, pawing and shouting at her. 'So, Hadley, we heard that you and George have split up? Is the new guy just a rebound thing? Can we just have a quick quote for tomorrow's edition?'

Nothing could be as bad as the press scrum outside the Malibu mansion the day that it was repossessed. The only time that they'd stopped thrusting their cameras into her face was when her princess canopy bed was hoisted on to the bailiff's flatbed truck. But this – this came a close second.

Mervyn had phoned ahead after putting his foot through Alain's computer, and there was a car waiting at the kerb with its engine running. Hadley was forced to curl up on the floor between the seats with the coat still over her head as Mervyn slammed the door and swore at the press pack.

It was another five minutes of high speed excitement before he said, 'I think we lost them. You can come out now.'

Hadley threw off the smelly raincoat and took deep, shuddering breaths. 'Where are we going?'

'I'm going to drop you off at a hotel and then you're going to give me your door keys so I can pack a bag for you.'

'I'm staying at a hotel? Oooh, can it be The Sanderson?'

'We're meeting someone at a hotel and then you're going to get the hell out of Dodge for a week or two. That

Ozzie bog roll ad you were bitching about? Might be worth giving Derek a call and seeing if it's still a goer,' Mervyn advised. It was just the thing to take her mind off her current woes.

'You're kidding me? I'm not that desperate.' Hadley climbed on to the back seat and removed a piece of grit that was embedded in her shin. She also needed some antiseptic for her skinned knees, though all the stress had made her forget the pain.

'Do I sound like I'm kidding?' Mervyn didn't sound like he was kidding at all. In fact, when faced with a crisis situation, he sounded all take-charge and don't-mess-with-me. 'When you get to the hotel call Derek so he can get you on a plane tonight.'

Hadley folded her arms and gave the back of Mervyn's head a baleful glare. 'Anyway, who are we meeting at this hotel?'

Mervyn turned around so he could give her a grin that was meant to be reassuring but actually not so much. 'The chief showbiz reporter of the *Daily News*. We've come to an arrangement. You give them what they want and they'll kill the story.'

Chapter Fifteen

Hadley couldn't stop shivering, even though the limo driver who'd picked her up at Sydney Airport had already whacked the heating right up. What had happened in that London hotel room was going to ensure that she was in industrial strength therapy until she was eighty. At least.

She'd sold her soul for fifty thousand pounds and forgotten about all those important things like morals and ethics and maintaining a sunny disposition at all times. As the steely-hearted woman from the *Daily News* kept pointing out each time Hadley had tried to backtrack, anyone would have done exactly the same thing in her precarious position. Anyone. Candy, definitely Irina, and absolutely, positively, George.

It was a whole world of heinous but, as Hadley stepped into her suite at the Inter-Continental and saw the smooth, ghostly curve of Sydney Opera House and the twinkling harbour lights from the floor to ceiling windows, her spirits soared just a little. Then she thought about Mervyn waving her off at Heathrow and they plummeted back to the ground.

'With a bit of luck one of the Royals will die or some

premier league footballer will have screwed around behind his wife's back,' he'd said in a not very comforting way. 'Bet the story won't even make the Sunday papers. And at least you made some cash out of it, right?'

Derek phoned as she was slipping between four-hundred-thread-count sheets. He'd stung the toilet tissue peeps for double the money and had lined up a meeting with the director of a new show who didn't even want her to audition.

'It's like *The OC* meets *24*,' Derek explained, as Hadley arranged the pillows behind her for maximum lumbar support. 'Seems like your star is firmly back in the ascendant.'

' 'Bout time too,' Hadley murmured feelingly. There was a brief pause and then something occurred to her. 'So, I guess if everything works out in LA next week, I won't be coming back to London. I just wanted to say thank you for all your hard work.'

Derek sounded as if he was choking on something. 'Oh, that's OK. Just doing my job. I take it you'll need your stuff forwarded?'

'Yeah, and I guess I should call the girls or send them some flowers or something.' She'd been so busy with the *Notting Hillbillies* and her new friends that she'd barely seen or even thought about her erstwhile roomies for aeons.

'Can I just ask why you rushed off to Sydney so quickly?' There was a faint note of suspicion in Derek's voice that Hadley could have done without.

'Me and George split up,' she said in a rush. 'I just needed to put, like, half a world between us. It got really messy, y'know?'

Derek was put off the scent. Well, he was making sympathetic noises at least. 'That explains why there's a picture of you in the papers this morning—'

'Say what?!'

'Oh, you're leaving a club – well, actually you're sprawled on the pavement while some little hottie tries to pick you up. Nice pants though.'

Pants was English for underpants. That much Hadley knew. 'You can see my underwear? I so won't miss British tabloids. They're, like, *evil.*'

She just wanted Derek to ring off any time in the next three seconds, because it was late, and they were done. He hadn't been a huge help in Operation Stardust but at least he'd got Tegan to pick up her dry-cleaning.

'. . . didn't always see eye to eye.' Derek was still not shutting up. 'But I have to give you credit, you're more driven than any other celebrity I've ever met.' He'd got that right. 'And actually I've learned a lot from you. You'd make one terrifying agent.'

Way to dish out the backhanded compliments. 'When you've been doing it for as long as I have, you pick up some tricks along the way,' Hadley said wearily. 'Derek, I've got to get some sleep. I have a really early call-time. And did you get them to agree to the script changes?'

The minute Hadley's head hit the Pratesi bed-linen, her eyes snapped shut. Huge waves of tiredness were licking at the edges of her mind but just before she gave in to the pull, she remembered something her father had always said, 'You lay down with dogs, then you wake up with fleas.'

It took all week to shoot the toilet tissue ad. Or rather it took them five days to come up with a script that didn't mention, in any way, shape or form, what the toilet tissue was going to be used for or the blip in her career trajectory. The actual ad only took one day's work.

Hadley spent most of it perched on a pink, glittery toilet in front of a blue screen. Animated toilet brushes doing a soft-shoe shuffle would be added at a later date.

'Sometimes it's hard to be a star,' she chirruped gaily, swinging her legs from side to side. 'Turning up at a premiere in the same designer dress as the director's mom, living on a diet of lettuce leaves and hot water, getting sore wrists from signing so many autographs. But at least there are some things in life that never let you down.'

Then she tossed a roll of Quilty-Lux high in the air and caught it (though that took more than one take) before winking at the camera as it moved in for her contractually obligated close-up. 'Quilty-Lux, because everyone deserves a little star treatment.'

What*ever*!

She had one day to do a shoot for an Australian fashion

magazine and buy several new pairs of Uggs when the call she'd been dreading came.

'It's going in this Sunday,' Mervyn said, without preamble. 'Unless Posh leaves Becks for Brad Pitt.'

Hadley stared out at the intense blue stretch of Sydney Harbour where sea met sky. A little white sailboat bobbed on the water as she clutched at a straw and gave it an almighty tug. 'Do you think there's any chance that might happen?'

Mervyn gave a short, sharp laugh. 'In a word, no. You're not planning on coming back any time soon, are you?'

She was done with London. Grubby London, with its scuzzy boys, grimy reporters and sub-standard sushi. 'I never want to set foot in the UK again. Like, ever. I can't wait to get back to LA. It's sunny there all the time, Merv.'

'Can't get a decent cup of tea though,' Mervyn grumbled. 'But home's home, right?'

Chapter Sixteen

The industrial grey arrivals lounge of Los Angeles airport was the most welcome sight Hadley had ever seen. Apart from the time when she'd found the most perfect pair of black boots in the Prada store on Rodeo Drive.

She was back. And this time there was a driver, provided by Fierce's LA office, holding up a sign with her name on it.

Even the two photographers waiting listlessly outside customs for any stray celebrity to saunter past were pleased to see her. 'Good to have you home, Hadley,' one of them called out.

It was good to be home too. Good to be having meetings on studio lots again, with executives who turned up on time. And took her to lunch at the Polo Lounge. That was a big deal because it meant that they wanted to be seen with her. It was so different from the months before she left, when she couldn't even snatch ten minutes with some assistant's assistant.

'You're so hot, Hadley, that I can hear the sizzle as you walk into the room.'

'We're thinking primetime, we're thinking star vehicle, we're thinking movie spin-off.'

'I had the VIP manager from Hyde on the phone, practically begging me to bring you along tonight.'

Hadley had heard it all before and talk was cheap. But the offers starting to line up would have her back in a Malibu mansion faster than you could say, 'I want three million and five per cent of the box office receipts.'

Even Amber was pleased to see her as she lay in state in a private room at the Cedars Sinai with her humungous bump obscured by a La Perla peignoir. It might have had something to do with the one hundred thousand dollars that Hadley had put in a Tiffany's box tied with pink and blue ribbons. Despite all her pleas, Hermés had been unable to fast-track her up the wait-list for their baby sling.

'I knew it would all come good,' Amber said as she sipped an organic mango smoothie. 'Thank God I sent you to London.' That wasn't exactly how Hadley remembered it, but Amber was pleased to see her and she wanted it to stay that way.

'You're so big,' she breathed, wide-eyed. 'Like, are you a size ten now?'

Amber waved a dismissive hand. 'They're going to whip out the spawn and give me a tummy tuck right there and then. And I'm doing this lemon water and honey fast so I'll be back in my Gucci bikini before the end of the month.'

That made sense. Hadley nodded and tried not to stare at the obscenely huge bulge where Amber's flat stomach used to be. No wonder everyone adopted orphans from

Third World countries. She gave a start as Amber reached over and squeezed her hand affectionately.

'Well, get your skinny ass over here and give me a hug,' Amber ordered, holding out her arms. 'It's so good to have you here, sweetie, looking out for me. Why don't you talk me through some of the offers and we can decide which ones to throw out and which ones to put on the "give us some more money, right the hell now" pile.'

Yeah, it was *so* good to be home.

Amber went into labour late on Saturday night while Hadley was tucked into one of the booths at Hyde with Mischa, Nicole and some whey-faced skank who claimed to be an Internet 'it girl'. It took some time to register her vibrating Sidekick, then she was running through the kitchen and out the back door.

It was kinda inconsiderate of the twins to put in an early appearance when Hadley had scheduled an emotional reunion with Mr Chow Chow for the next day. He'd been languishing in a doggie hotel since Amber had been in hospital.

But that was all on hold now as Hadley paced the waiting room anxiously, with a publicist from a multinational baby toiletries brand who was all ready with endorsement contracts, 'as long as they don't have any weird birthmarks or harelips'.

It was sort of exciting to think that she wouldn't be an

only child any more. She'd be the cool older sister who'd swoop in to whisk off her sibs to Disneyland. Hadley could just see the 'at home' shoot in *Life & Style* with the twins gazing adoringly up at her, their blonde curls glinting in the sun as they frolicked around the pool. Maybe she could get her own hair lightened a couple of shades.

'Ms Harlow?' She looked up as the doctor suddenly emerged from the delivery suite.

'Is everything OK?' she asked, and for one moment she was frightened because he had a strained expression on his face and Amber wasn't exactly a spring chicken. Though she *was* eleven years younger than Madonna. What if she'd died in childbirth like they did in the olden days, and Hadley would have to assume legal guardianship? Would she have to stop going out? Were all the good nannies taken?

'Congratulations. You're the big sister to two healthy babies,' the doctor said. The baby prods publicist sighed in relief but the doctor took Hadley's arm and tugged her to one side. 'Your mother's fine, health-wise, but she got rather upset when she realized that both babies were boys. One of them had their legs crossed every time we did an ultrasound . . .'

Hadley gasped. No one had boy babies. Celebrities had girls – Shiloh Jolie Pitt, Suri Cruise; only Britney had boys and she was beyond yesterday. Amber must be pitching an absolute fit.

'We've had to sedate her,' the doctor murmured. 'I'm sure once she's calmed down she'll be delighted with her sons.'

Yeah, keep clinging to that illusion, doctor dude. Hadley smiled at the publicist, who was looking anxiously in their direction. 'Are you sure?' she asked. 'Do we need a second opinion?'

'I'm a hundred per cent positive that both babies are male,' the doctor said dryly. 'Do you want to come and say hello to your brothers?'

Hadley really didn't. Sure, they'd be cute and everything once they were crawling and smiling, but she'd seen newborn babies on the Home & Health Channel and they were red, wrinkly and screamed a lot. 'I need to have a word with their publicist first. I won't have to hold them, will I?'

Hadley turned and beckoned the publicist over. 'You know what I was thinking,' she said brightly. 'I'm so sick of seeing girl babies. Like, you can't move in this town for falling over a pink stroller. Did you know that sixty-three per cent of all babies born are boys?' (Statistics always sounded good even if she was making them up on the spot.) 'So sixty-three per cent of all parents who spend money on baby shampoo and diapers have sons . . .'

'Oh my God, are they boys?' the publicist shrieked in disbelief. 'I need to talk to head office stat.'

* * *

It took hours to convince the publicist and the company's CEO that boy babies were going to be the next big thing.

They'd gone to look at the twins, sleeping peacefully and unaware that their whole financial future rested on the fact that, thank the Lord, they were both fair-haired and blue-eyed. Eventually the contract was signed and Hadley had enough time to go back to her hotel and slip into something a little more 'sisterly' for the photo call that had been organized.

Hadley was just admiring what her new Calvin Klein trousers did for her butt, when the fax machine started beeping and spewing out paper.

If it was yet another version of the contract, she was going to seriously lose it.

If only. It was the front cover of the *Sunday News*. Mervyn had scrawled a little message on the top sheet. *Benji's new single went straight in at number one this week. Great timing! M x*

'BOY BANDER BENJI AND "GORGEOUS" GEORGE IN SORDID LOVE TRIANGLE', screamed the headline. ' "I'm devasted", sobs George's ex, Hadley Harlow.'

With shaking hands, Hadley scooped up the pages and began to read.

'George was the love of my life,' Hadley was quoted as saying. 'But our lovemaking was always unfulfilling and George was becoming more and more distant. That was when I realized that he was seeing someone else. I just never imagined that the someone else was a boy. George always seemed so manly. I can't believe that he'd do this to me.'

She hadn't said half of that stuff. Not even a quarter of it. In fact, she'd refused to answer any of the sex questions.

It ended with a terse statement from Benji's management: 'We make it a policy never to comment on our clients' personal relationships.' George's comment was less evasive. 'My private life is no one else's business and Hadley Harlow is full of s★★★.'

OK, that hurt a little bit, but it wasn't as if she'd had any choice. Hadley scrunched up the papers and stuffed them in the wastepaper basket, before picking up her quilted Chanel bag. That part of her life was done, now she had a whole 'nother chapter to look forward to.

Hadley was expecting photographers to be camped outside the hospital. But she hadn't been expecting quite so many of them as she gracefully climbed out of her town car and posed for pictures. After all, it wasn't every day that a soon-to be global superstar welcomed twin brothers into the world.

'Any comment on what the UK papers are saying about you?' asked an aggressive reporter, shoving a mic in her face.

Hadley arranged her features into a carefully distraught

expression. 'I guess I'm doing as well as can be expected.'

'Are you going back into rehab?' someone else demanded and Hadley's face dropped all the way to the floor.

'They're calling you the most hated woman in London. Is that why you came back to LA?'

Something was wrong. In fact, Hadley's wrong-radar was going into overdrive. She needed to call Mervyn ASAP and start screaming at him.

'No comment!' she hissed and with her head down, she fought her way through the crowd, elbows sharp and at the ready.

The *Sunday News* story had portrayed her as a wide-eyed girl in love who'd had all her hopes and dreams dashed because her boyfriend had been cheating on her. With another boy! People should be sorry for her – not hate her.

It was at times like this that a girl really needed her mom. Hadley ignored the signs for the elevator and raced up the stairs two at a time, which was really difficult when you were wearing four-inch heels.

The publicist was *still* waiting outside. Had she even gone home? Then she took one look at Hadley and turned away so she could start barking into her cellphone. Could you say rude?

Hadley strode through the double doors and followed the trail of blue balloons to Amber's suite. Hopefully the sedative would have worn off and she'd be thrilled about all Hadley's sterling work in securing the contract.

'You stupid little bitch!'

Or maybe not. Amber was sitting up in bed, fussed over by her hair and make-up stylists who scurried out of the room as Amber shooed them away.

'Hey Mom,' Hadley said, keeping a watchful distance. The postnatal depression had obviously kicked in. 'How are you feeling?'

'You've got a damn nerve showing up here,' Amber spat. 'Well, you can just turn around again and leave before you ruin everything.'

It was then that Hadley noticed the black and white pages scattered on the bed. Hard not to when two words screamed out at her in big, black type: 'Hadley Harlot!'

Hadley inched closer and snatched up the first page and there she was in all her bare-breasted glory. Alain was right; they had totally blacked out her nipples.

'What the hell have you been doing in London, you little slut?' Amber demanded belligerently, but Hadley barely heard her, she was too busy staring at George and Benji on the front page of the *Sunday World*. They were dressed in matching white T-shirts and beaming happily like they were doing a toothpaste commercial.

Turned out that they'd found love only after George had had his heart broken by Hadley's constant stream of infidelities, fuelled only by her alcoholism. 'Hadley was a complete trainwreck,' George was quoted as saying. 'She drove me into Benji's arms. It was so refreshing to be with someone who could love me for me.'

Just in case the British public were in any doubt about her suitability as a girlfriend, they'd published Alain's photos. On the inside pages, they'd even decided not to put black blobs over her breasts. There were also a series of pictures of her coming out of nightclubs looking a little the worse for wear and a shot of her sitting on the lap of some geriatric soap star, while George stood off to the side, biting his lip. 'Hadley constantly taunted me about being gay and would throw herself at other men. I realized that I'd rather be gay than stuck in a relationship with such a damaged person.'

The *Sunday World* had rounded up a whole queue of people to describe Hadley as 'a diva', 'a screeching drunk' and 'a sad character clinging desperately to the last vestiges of her celebrity'. They'd even dug up all the stuff about her dad and implied that her problems stemmed from having such a weak paternal role model. The eight page special ended with a picture of a door-stepped Candy who was shown giving the camera a one-fingered salute, under the quote, 'Hadley just lived here – we weren't friends.'

'Oh my God,' Hadley whispered weakly, collapsing into a chair. 'What am I going to do?'

Amber had been silent for all of ten minutes while Hadley's world crumbled, but now she came to life again.

She stabbed at the air with her finger. 'You can get on the first plane back to London and stay there.'

Hadley stared at her in disbelief. Despite the carefully applied make-up, Amber's face was red and twisted with anger. 'I can't go back there. I've got all these deals lined up,' Hadley said weakly.

'Yeah, and when the US press pick up on this, the only deal you're going to have is stacking shelves at Wal-mart,' Amber informed her venomously. 'You're finished and if you think I want your toxic influence anywhere near those goddamn babies, then think again.'

'But what about the photo call . . .'

'Really, Hadley, sometimes you have no dignity,' Amber snorted, clutching her heart. 'Don't just stand there bleating, get out!'

Other girls had moms who drove them to their piano recitals or watched chick-flicks with them. And sometimes they'd row about curfew but they'd always make up because they had like, this unbreakable mother/daughter bond that nothing could tear down. Hadley knew this because she'd been playing that daughter for the last eighteen years. Amber, though, didn't even have a copy of the script.

Hadley turned to watch two nurses wheel in the twins' little cribs. She'd just been cancelled, with no chance of her contract getting renewed.

Amber was already cooing over the twins like they were

birthday, Thanksgiving and Christmas all rolled into one photogenic package.

Amber lifted her head just long enough to snap: 'And you can take that little rat-dog back to Britain because I'm not looking after it any more,' as Hadley walked towards the door.

Chapter Seventeen

'What the hell have you come back for?' Candy screamed, when she saw Hadley standing on the doorstep. 'We've been trapped in here for days because there's paparazzi camped on the doorstep.' She stopped to draw breath and caught sight of Mr Chow Chow, still drugged out from the doggie sleeping pill Hadley had disguised in some smoked salmon before the flight. 'What is *that*?'

'He's a Mexican Hairless,' Hadley explained, peering through the wire mesh of her Louis Vuitton dog carrier. 'Can you lower your voice? He's really sensitive to loud noises.'

Candy didn't lower her voice or budge even one inch so Hadley could step over the threshold. 'Dude, just piss off. You get one whiff of success and dump all your friends and then you think you can stroll on back when it suits you and—'

Like, who'd died and made Candy the boss of the house? 'Is Laura here?' Hadley asked hopefully. Even though she was an almost successful model these days, Laura didn't usually get uppity, unlike certain New Yorkers with anger-management issues.

'She's in Miami, having the fat from her ass sucked out,' Irina said, coming up behind Candy, who turned and whacked the Russian girl in the side.

'No, she's not. She's shooting bikinis.'

'I like my version better,' Irina insisted. Hadley knew that Irina and Laura had had some big modelly dance-off over a perfume ad but she couldn't remember the details. Maybe Candy was just a teensy bit right about how she'd been neglecty. But friendship was hard to maintain when you had your own stuff going on. It wasn't as if there was a self-help guide on the subject.

'You're just jealous,' Candy taunted Irina. 'Because Laura's the Siren girl and you're not.'

Irina studied her nails and refused to crack a facial expression. 'Whatever,' she deadpanned. 'I say Hadley can stay and is much my flat as yours.' She gave Hadley a sly smile. 'She just got her underpants in a twist 'cause she using your room as an atelier.'

Hadley took advantage of Candy shifting forward so she could hit Irina again to step into the hall. 'Atela-what?' It had been like, the longest week ever. She was so tired that she didn't even know if she had the energy to do her skincare regime. She just wanted to go to bed.

'Atelier,' Candy panted, as she tried to free herself from Irina's vice-like grip on her wrists. 'It's a dressmaker's studio and no one told me you were coming back!'

Candy and Irina followed her down the hall into her

room. She'd forgotten how small it was – just as well that Mr Chow Chow was so tiny. And yup, Candy had totally turned it into an overspill dressmaking salon. Though why she had to make her own clothes, Hadley didn't know. Like, why couldn't she just go and buy new ones? She could so afford them.

'How could you have done that to George?' Candy suddenly piped up as Hadley surveyed the bolts of material piled on her bed. 'You destroyed him!'

'I've tried to make it up with George!' Hadley protested. And she had tried. God knows, how hard she'd tried. During her last three days in LA, not having any of her calls returned by studio execs, she'd sent him balloons, flowers, a basket of fat-free, low-carb muffins and countless texts saying she was sorry.

Then she'd received a fax from George's lawyers telling her to stop harassing their client or they'd be forced to obtain a restraining order.

'Can you blame him?' Candy was struggling under the weight of a sewing machine as Irina watched with undisguised amusement. 'It was bad enough that you dumped us when you got that part in *Notting Hillbillies*, but what you did to George? That was low, even for you.'

Mr Chow Chow was starting to show signs of extreme agitation from all of Candy's yowling. His funny little face puckered up before he crawled under the bed.

'Mr C-C, come out from under there,' Hadley pleaded.

'You know the dust will just aggravate your allergies.'

'You have nice tits,' Irina said abruptly and Hadley nearly banged her head on the bed-frame as she turned to stare at her in amazement. Was Irina gay too? 'Are they real?'

'Of course they're real!' Hadley exclaimed, peering down at her chest. They were small, but they were all kinds of perky. About the only part of her that was at the moment. It was weird to think of the British public getting a good look at her breasts when she'd never even undressed in front of anyone. Except Alain. And in that case she'd *been* undressed and that was too seriously traumatic to think about.

Irina shrugged. She could say a lot with one simple wriggle of her shoulders. This one said that whatever Hadley had or hadn't done, they were still cool.

'I go to Brazil tomorrow,' she informed Hadley casually. 'Then Prague, then Berlin. After that, I don't know but you can stay in my room for a bit.'

There had to be a catch. Irina wasn't given to random acts of kindness. Hadley studied her intently and waited for the punch line.

'One more day with that noisy bitch and I kill her in her bed,' Irina sneered with enough menace that Hadley totally believed her. 'I hate her worse than Laura and her fat ass!'

It was too darn much. She'd left one war-zone for another. 'Hate is a really strong word, Irina.'

'It's not strong enough!' declared Irina and swept out,

making sure to crunch over a couple of patterns that Candy had left lying on the floor.

Two weeks later and Hadley was over it. She'd moved on. In fact, she'd moved precisely the five hundred metres it took to walk to the supermarket and buy lean steak mince (Mr Chow Chow didn't eat anything else) and fresh soup. She had mad microwave skillz these days and that was a good thing. Like her therapist used to say, if you weren't moving forward then you were standing still.

Or actually lying down, because horizontal was her current position of choice. As soon as she got back to the flat, she'd ignore Candy who'd ignore her right back, and take refuge in Irina's room, despite the faint aroma of stinky Russian sausage lingering in the air. She'd curl up on the bed with Mr C-C and bury her head in his little hairless neck. He really was a girl's best friend. Or was that diamonds? She never could remember.

Finally the paparazzi had got bored of her twice-daily trips to walk Mr Chow Chow, though they never tired of taking shots of Hadley scooping his poop. And they always shot her mid-conversation with Mr C-C so they could print stories about how she was wondering the streets of London talking to herself: 'Has horrible Hadley officially gone bonkers?' But she wasn't horrible. She was still the same old Hadley.

Still, she didn't look like the same Hadley that had

glittered and shone on the red carpet in those same papers. Now the grainy black and white pictures showed a girl who looked kinda ordinary. Her roots were coming through, the platinum of her hair (heiress blonde as she'd used to call it) fading out to something softer because she was too embarrassed to see Guido, the best stylist/colourist in north London. Not because of her shocking root growth but because he was gay and would probably put hair remover in the hydrogen peroxide solution.

For the record, Hadley wasn't cloistered away because she was feeling sorry for herself. She was cloistered away because she had nothing to wear. Tegan had followed the instructions Hadley had sent her from Australia and packed up her luggage, which the airline had then lost, so she had to make do with one measly suitcase of clothes.

Even if she was feeling a tiny bit . . . *down*, that was also good because the only direction that was left was up.

'Well, I'm glad you're still managing to stay positive,' Derek had said doubtfully when he'd finally got it together to return her many, many phone calls. 'I've got nothing except a shoot in one of the lad's mags. Will you do topless?'

'Hasn't everyone in the UK already seen them?' Hadley asked. 'Like, seriously.'

'Are you sure you're all right? You're usually telling me how to do my job at this point.'

'Oh, I'm fine,' Hadley assured him. 'I'm just using this

downtime to regroup and take stock and figure out my next move. Everything will be fine. I'll be fine.'

'You've already said that,' Derek pointed out gently, pausing for a little cough. 'This is slightly delicate but as you can't guarantee your agency commission out of future earnings, you're going to have to pay our monthly retainer and the rent on the flat in advance.'

Hadley tickled Mr C–C under his chin as he snuffled his approval. 'Cool. I totally understand,' she agreed brightly. There was still a little bit of her Australian money left over – though she'd given most of it to Amber – and she could eke out her *Notting Hillbillies* cash for a while longer. She'd cut way back on her spa and salon appointments by not booking them any more. 'I have to go now, Derek, 'cause I'm, like, totally busy. But if anything comes in, anything, even stuff you think that I think is beneath me, you'll call me, right?'

'Right. Look, are you sure you're going to be OK?'

But Hadley was already switching off her phone because if Derek kept yapping, she'd totally use up her free talk time.

Chapter Eighteen

Laura came back the next day in a cloud of Siren perfume and expensive designer clothes. Hadley had been dozing but her sleepy fug was interrupted when Laura and Candy began cooing at each other right outside her door.

'What's up, bitch?' Candy cried.

'Same old, same old. How about you?'

Hadley had actually missed Laura's funny accent and her willingness to make a never-ending supply of tea. Now she had to work the kettle all by herself and try not to spill boiling hot water when Candy walked into the kitchen and knocked into her. Yes, Candy was mad at her because George was her new best friend (and in that case why weren't they hanging out 24/7?) but that was no reason to disrespect Hadley's personal space boundaries.

'. . . worried about her.' Hadley raised her head off the pillow, which took a superhuman effort, as she caught the tail-end of Laura's conversation. 'Her agent asked my booker to have a word because she refuses to go into the agency. She keeps telling him that she's fine but he says she sounds funny.'

'She always sounds funny. That stupid little-girl voice

stopped being cute when she was, like, five,' Candy snorted. And to think that Hadley had almost stood up for Candy when Irina got her hate on. 'She deserves to suffer after what she did.'

'But what did she do? She sold a story and George got outed. It hasn't done him any harm. Then there was that topless shot of her, which didn't make any sense because Hadley would never sleep with someone and let them take pictures. She's very prudish for a girl who wears such short skirts.'

'It makes sense if she was drunk at the time,' Candy supplied helpfully. 'And also, she's not that bright. The guy probably promised her a part in his next movie and down came her knickers.'

Oh, she *hated* Candy. And if Irina really did want to kill her then she'd totally help to hide the body and wash bloodstains out of her clothing.

'She's not stupid, Candy,' Laura said firmly. 'I know you have issues about the whole kiss and tell thing but Hadders needs someone to look out for her right now. Has anyone even heard her side of the story?'

Candy's reply was muffled but it contained at least one really offensive swear word. Hadley scooped up a magazine from the floor with Candy's face staring sulkily from the cover and began ripping it methodically to shreds.

'Hadders? You in there?' There was a polite knock on the door. 'Can I come in and see how you are?'

'I'm fine,' Hadley called out. 'I'm in the middle of something. I'll catch up with you later.'

'Are you sure?'

'Honestly, I'm peachy. Just waiting for a really important call from the States.'

It took another few seconds but finally Laura got the message and walked away.

Hadley managed to avoid Laura for most of the day by staying in her room even though she was dying for a pee.

Eventually, *finally*, Laura and Candy went out.

There was time to quickly walk Mr C-C, who got really moody when his routine was interrupted, make a quick mug of soup and head for the bathroom.

When she was really little, like, pre-*Starr Family* little, they'd lived in a tiny apartment in the Valley. She'd had to sleep on a camp bed that smelled of damp, but mostly Hadley remembered lying awake at night and listening to her parents row. Her dad had been out of work and Amber had been waitressing at a little diner off the Strip in the evenings so she was free to take Hadley to auditions during the day.

They argued and argued about money. But it was about her, really. How to afford new photographs to send to casting directors and the new outfits she needed and the speech coach to correct her lisp. It would go round and round in circles until her dad would storm out and Amber would run a bath and stay in the bathroom for hours.

Maybe it was the one useful thing that Amber had ever really taught her – the healing properties of a good, long soak. She stayed in the tub long enough to become prune-like, before hauling herself out of the bath and swiping a razor half-heartedly at her legs.

She also managed to squeeze most of Candy's very expensive body lotion down the sink, before she carefully pulled back the bolt and poked her head round the door.

Laura was there in a nanosecond. As Hadley tried to retreat, she clamped a hand round her wrist and dragged her down the hall. 'I made you a cup of tea,' she said cajolingly. 'Lapsang Souchong, your favourite – and I even remembered a slice of lemon. Let's have a nice chat.'

There was the murmur of voices from the lounge. Candy's laughter (probably about someone's downfall) and a deeper chuckle that could only belong to Reed. She really wasn't in the mood for a two-pronged Careless attack. And Reed's lips would get all tight and thin and . . . Hadley dug her heels into the carpet.

'Not in the living room,' she whispered urgently. 'Candy's been really disrespectful to me and I'm, like, not dressed for company. Look at me!'

Laura stopped trying not to spill tea everywhere and did an almost cartoon-like double-take. 'Christ on a bike – *what* are you wearing, Hadders?'

They both looked at Hadley's fetching ensemble of

bikini bottoms and a Quilty-Lux T-shirt. 'I don't know how to use the washing machine and Fierce packed up all my stuff but it got lost in transit. Like, they think it's been tracked down to Karachi. Or maybe Caracas,' Hadley added doubtfully.

'Oh my God, you've got freckles!' Laura yelped.

At the mention of her least favourite F-word, Hadley turned tail and scampered for the sanctuary of Irina's room, Laura hot on her heels.

'You have roots too. Are you naturally ginger?' she demanded, shutting the door behind her but not before her words leaked down the hall to Reed and Candy, who were probably crying tears of mirth.

'It's just the contrast between the bits that have been lightened a teensy, weensy amount and the bits that haven't,' Hadley insisted firmly, clamping a hand over her parting because Laura was standing over her and squinting. Damn her for being so tall.

Thankfully Laura's attention was diverted to Mr C-C, who chose that moment to scurry out from under the bed and growl at her.

'Oh, is this Mr Chow Chow?' Laura took a cautious step back – which was wise, because he loved to nip ankle bones – and placed the mug of tea on the bedside table before sitting down. 'So, anyway, how have you been?'

'Absolutely fine,' Hadley stated for the record. 'I don't know why everyone keeps asking me that. This is, like, a temporary glitch in Operation Stardust, but I've been through way worse than this.' There wasn't a tremor in her voice. She could even look Laura right in the eye as she said it.

But really? Nothing had ever been as bad as this. Not *Hadley's House* being cancelled. Or her dad stealing from her and telling her that she was dead to him when the police came to arrest him. Not Amber replacing her with two younger models. Nothing was as bad as being universally loathed instead of universally loved. Only this morning eighty-six per cent of callers had voted her the most hated person in Britain in a phone-in poll on the radio. Even Mervyn couldn't spin that, which was probably why he hadn't returned any of her calls.

'I just want you to know that I consider you a mate,' Laura said, holding out her hand to Mr Chow Chow and snatching it back when he snapped his teeth. 'I'm not around much but if you need anything or you just want to vent, you can always call me.'

Hadley nodded politely. Laura was nice, even if she did spend way too much time hanging with Candy. But there was no way she was going to over-share all the sordid details of what had happened in that completely gross apartment. She couldn't expect other people to clean up her mess; she had to do it for herself. The buck stopped with Hadley and really she was totally AOK with that.

'So how have *you* been?' she asked Laura brightly.

'You look like a proper model now, even when you're off-duty.'

It was true. Laura had that glossy patina that only really successful people had. Even though she was wearing a simple pair of jeans and a black sweater she looked great; it was the way she held herself and didn't slouch like she used to. Even her hair, which was gathered up in a messy ponytail, had that rich-girl sheen.

'I'm cool,' Laura answered with a sigh, like she wasn't fooled by Hadley's diversionary tactics. 'It's a bit mind-boggling how your life can get transformed in, like, five minutes. Do you know what I mean?' Hadley nodded carefully. Laura was about as subtle as acne. 'But it's all good,' Laura continued. 'I went to a Buddhist shrine when I was in Tokyo and Hello Kitty World. Never seen so much pink in my life. But anyway, I have the next couple of days off and we should have a spa date. I went to this great one with Candy . . .'

Her skin might be screaming out for a good buff and fake tan, but no way was Hadley accepting Laura's charity. Nope, it was pity. And there were three things that Hadley didn't do: white sugar, off-the-rack and other people's pity.

'Oh, I can't,' she demurred, biting her lip sorrowfully. 'I've got a really full schedule this week.'

'Doing what?' Laura persisted, giving Hadley one of her looks. Hadley had met Laura's mum precisely once but she'd given them all exactly the same look when she'd discovered that none of them had ever washed the kitchen floor.

It was a good question. She planned to stay indoors for as long as humanly possible while she hatched a dastardly masterplan which would clear her name, make the public love her again and result in several serious product endorsements and the lead role in a big box office movie franchise. Until then . . . 'Sorry, can't say,' Hadley cooed regretfully, making sure to lower her voice as she leaned in conspiratorially. 'I had to sign, like, a non-disclosure agreement. Strictly on the down-low.'

Laura's eyes widened. Bless her little cotton socks, or Fogal stockings or whatever, but she was so gullible. 'Wow. It sounds like you're going into the spy business or something,' she said, sounding suitably impressed. 'Well, I guess all publicity is good publicity, though Ted says otherwise.'

Any time Laura wanted to leave and take her suburban brand of naïveté with her was just fine with Hadley. 'So I've got a ton of stuff to do, sweetie,' she said pointedly. 'Scripts to read, motivation to find, y'know.'

'That's the spirit!' Laura slapped Hadley's back with enough enthusiasm to leave bruises. 'Take your mind off everything.'

Urgh, stop talking to me like I'm a normal person, Hadley wanted to scream, but she just shrugged in the exact same way that Irina did when she wanted to let someone know the conversation was over.

Laura got the message and slid off the bed. 'Do you wanna hang out in the lounge?' she asked hopefully. 'Give you and Candy a chance to make up. And Reed's been asking about you.'

Probably wanting to know why she hadn't been evicted yet because she was a poisonous influence on his potty-mouthed, evil little sister.

'Mr Chow Chow is still jet-lagged,' Hadley prevaricated. 'I can't socialize him too soon.'

'But Reed's telling us all about the actresses who've been auditioning for him,' Laura pouted. 'I never realized he was so funny – once you get past the sneer.'

Hadley neither knew nor cared. 'Those two,' she sniffed contemptuously. 'Take away the sneer and the attitude and you're not left with much of anything.'

She could hear their voices floating through the wall as she went through a very half-hearted Yogalates routine. It was hard to do a good Mermaid stretch when you kept banging your hand on the wardrobe door.

'Reed, I'm gonna pee my pants!' Candy yelped at one stage, her next sentence lost in a choky wheeze of giggles.

Hadley strained her ears so she could hear Laura exclaim, 'She so did not say that! You're making it up.'

'She did,' Reed insisted and he sounded much younger than he normally did. But then whenever Hadley had talked to him, there seemed to be a lot of growling and lip tightening going on. 'I asked her to read the part with a British accent and she said, "I don't know any other languages." Honestly, those LA girls share one collective brain cell.'

Hadley bristled with indignation on behalf of the girls of her native city. Her ears were pinned to hear the next slew of insults when her Sidekick started to ring. She glanced at the screen.

Weird. Why was Derek calling her at 10pm on a Thursday night? Then again, it was only two in the afternoon in LA. Maybe it was good news?

'Hey,' she said eagerly. 'Got anything for me?'

'Have you got any plans for tomorrow night?' Derek asked.

Ah, plans. Hadley could remember having plans. 'Nothing I couldn't cancel. Why?'

Hadley could totally read Derek's silences now and this one, punctuated by a slight clearing of his throat, meant that he was going to try and sell her a bridge. 'It's a one-off TV presenter gig for a late night show on Channel Four,' he said in a rush. '*Life Begins at 9.30*. Have you seen it?'

'I think so.' Hadley vaguely recalled a really skinny man who looked like Johnny Depp in *Pirates of the Caribbean* acting like he had ADD, while this girl did most of the work and tried not to get upset when he made fun of her. 'That guy needs a Ritalin prescription, stat.'

'It's just that Marika, the girl, she fell off a ladder while she was . . . long story short, they need guest presenters each week until the end of the run and they specially requested you.'

'They did?' Hadley couldn't hide the excitement bubbling up and threatening to spill over. Somebody wanted her. About time too. 'Me? I'll do it!'

Derek was now doing the snuffly silence that meant he wanted to talk her out of it. 'I only mentioned it because I said I'd let you know if any offers came in.'

'Yup and I said I'd do it.'

'They've already made it very clear that they're going to bring up the George thing and the drinking thing and the topless photos thing. They've already got a sketch scripted,' Derek told her dejectedly. 'I really don't think—'

'But I could go on there and clear my name,' Hadley exclaimed. 'Tell my side of the story.'

'Talking of which, what exactly *is* your side of the story because you still won't go into any details?'

'Oh, it's so boring, like hardly worth mentioning.' Hadley brushed him off. 'And so they want to do a sketch? How bad can it be?'

'They had that singer on who lip-synched through her performance at the MTV awards until her backing track broke down. She left the show halfway through in tears, Hadley. I really strongly advise you not to do this.'

Hadley thought about it for five seconds. She'd already suffered through weeks of public humiliation. Half an hour more wouldn't make much difference. And it would show that she could be a good sport. The British public loved good sports. She knew that for certain.

'I hear you, Derek, but this could be the way to get people back on side,' she said firmly.

'But they also want you to interview a rock band,' Derek said desperately, 'who spit on their audience. Actual *spitting*.'

'I can read the questions off an autocue,' Hadley replied implacably. 'I'm very good at doing that. What time do they want me?'

This silence was Derek's defeated silence, punctuated by a heartfelt sigh that all his efforts had been in vain. 'They need you at the studio by six-thirty. I'll get a car to pick you up, OK?'

'Oh Derek, this is fantastic,' Hadley trilled, pushing away a half-eaten bowl of pad Thai. Thanks to Laura, curves were back and Hadley, who'd lost seven pounds on her enforced soup diet, was in danger of becoming fashion backwards. 'It's going to be a real reversal of fortune, y'know?'

'I know. And it's your funeral,' Derek muttered, but Hadley was already switching off her phone because Derek's negativity might be contagious.

Chapter Nineteen

It was like riding a bicycle. Or getting back on a horse after it had bolted. Or some other dumb metaphor for hurling yourself back into the spotlight when it had already chewed you up and spat you out.

That had to be why she was nervous. Quivering with terror at the prospect of being beamed into the nation's homes so they could judge her all over again. Hadley sat in make-up, clutching Mr C-C to her chest and stroking him again and again, like a mantra that would calm her down.

'I can't do your lip-liner if you won't hold still,' the make-up girl said crossly. She already hated Hadley because she'd had to go out to buy some colour rinse to cover up her roots.

Hadley raised her hand. 'Just give me a minute, OK?' She grabbed her bottle of water and took several long swallows. But what if she needed to pee once the cameras started rolling?

Hadley shuddered all over again and the make-up girl flared her nostrils in annoyance.

'You have a rash all over your chest,' she said accusingly, slapping foundation over the offending area. 'Is it an allergic reaction?'

And she could check her attitude at the door too. 'I'm just a little stressed,' Hadley admitted.

'Oh, it'll be fine. They'll give you a hard time but it's nothing personal. You'll have a drink about it after and Ross will apologize.'

Hadley had already met Ross when they'd had a quick script run-through. He wasn't even a tenth as hyperactive off camera as he was on. In fact, he'd talked with a really posh accent, like Prince Charles, and kept saying, 'It's all just a bit of a laugh, nothing to worry about.' Which should have made her worried, especially as they never rehearsed the infamous sketch that Derek had been bugging about.

'Well, you're done,' the make-up girl announced flatly. 'I did the best I could.'

Hadley peered without interest at her reflection. Her skin was still so blotchy that it looked as if she had serious stubble rash and that frosted pink lipstick . . . 'Could I have slightly darker lips, please? Maybe something in the berry family? I'm more of an autumn than a summer these days.'

The make-up girl snatched up a tube with the air of a woman who'd like to ram it somewhere ouchy. 'What a diva,' she muttered under her breath.

But the moment she walked out on to the set and felt the burning hot glare of the lights, Hadley found her calm place. Then she looked up to see hundreds of pairs of eyes staring back at her.

'No one told me this was a live show,' she hissed into her mic. 'I thought you added in a laugh-track.'

'Thirty seconds,' came back a harassed voice. 'Ross, where the hell are you? Get your arse on stage now.'

Hadley gave a start as Ross bounded on stage and the audience burst into frenzied applause.

'Ten seconds and roll the autocue, seven, six, five, four, three, two and one! Hadley!'

Hadley faced the camera to her right and grinned, as if everything in her world was dandy. 'Hi, I'm Hadley Harlow, the most hated girl in Britain and this is . . .'

'I'm Ross Thomas, the sexiest man in the solar system, here to frolic with each and every one of you in a saucy manner guaranteed to bring mutual satisfaction,' Ross purred, eyebrows and fingers wagging. 'Let's introduce you to tonight's guests . . .'

Hadley moved across the set on autopilot, hosting a live studio discussion about why dog poop sometimes went white in summer. She introduced a live performance from the really hairy, ugly rock group that Derek had warned her about (though they'd seemed like absolute honeys when she'd met them in the green room before the show) and got through the sketch that tested every last ounce of her professionalism.

It was based around the newsflash that she was totally flat-chested. Apparently her lack of breasts made straight men turn gay. Ross Thomas had a pair of tiny, fake boobs strapped to his chest that looked like fried eggs while Hadley was wearing a huge 'I'm the only gayer in Hollywood' T-shirt, as she read off the autocue, 'Well, if there's no tits in it for me then I might just as well go gay.'

It went on like that for another painful three minutes but Hadley didn't care because she'd died of shame and was already in hell.

'Isn't she a good sport, people?' Ross declared when they got to the end of the sketch, lifting Hadley off her feet in a ferocious bear hug, which made her clutch frantically at his shoulder. 'She might be the most hated girl in Britain, but I love her. Now give her some noise or I'll kill each and every one of you.'

Hadley never knew that applause could sound so grudging or half-hearted. There were a few isolated claps and one solitary whoop before they cut to a commercial break.

'OK, you can put me down now,' she suggested and her feet hadn't even made contact with the floor before a studio flak was hurrying over.

'You're not going to leave, are you?' he asked, flapping his hands in an agitated manner. 'You were great. All the production team are loving it. So you're not going to walk out?'

Both Ross and the lackey were watching her anxiously like she was about to throw the hugest strop this side of Candy Careless. Which, not even. 'I have never walked out on a job in my life,' she informed them tetchily. Like, did they think she was a rank amateur?

'Good, good, let's get you into make-up to take the shine off your face,' the minion said hurriedly, hustling Hadley off set. He didn't leave her side until she was back in front of the camera, ready to host a game with contestants pulled from the audience who were all giddy with delight at the prospect of winning a mini-break to a gross holiday camp in the north of England.

The interview with the rock band, Raised By Wolves, was scheduled just before the second commercial break. As they lumbered over to the squashy sofa where Hadley perched, she was almost asphyxiated by the beer fumes oozing from their collective pores. And actually a little glass of champagne was just what she needed to take the edge off – but so not going there.

Instead, she shook each proffered sweaty paw as they sat down and glanced quickly at the autocue.

'You saw them perform their new single, "Jailbait Rock", earlier and they'll be playing us out at the end of the show but right now Raised By Wolves are going to answer a few questions texted in by viewers.'

The band were nudging each other and snickering but Hadley bravely soldiered on.

'OK, our first question is from Gary in Norwich. Who in the music biz do you think you could have in a fight?' Hadley felt the need to point something out to the audience. 'Not that violence is ever the answer. But guys, who makes you want to put on a pair of boxing gloves and go ten rounds?'

She looked expectantly at the lead singer, who hadn't shaved in for ever; his lips were completely obscured by his matted beard. Hadley peered curiously to see if there was a vaguely good-looking person underneath it all. It seemed extremely doubtful.

He matched her scrutiny to the power of a hundred. 'Sorry,' he smirked. 'It's kinda hard to listen to the questions when I've got a picture of your tits taped up on the tour bus.'

'Just ignore him,' a voice in her earpiece commanded.

Hadley snapped her fingers to get his attention. 'My face is up here.'

He reluctantly shifted focus from Hadley's chest. 'I'm a lover, not a fighter, sweetheart,' he leered.

'OK, good to know,' Hadley said brightly. 'Next question from someone called Death To Emo. Would you ever shave your beards if the fate of the world depended on it?'

The band were whispering and giggling like a bunch of toddlers dosed up on sugar and there were still five minutes before the ad break. Truly, this was the suckiest day in the history of suckiest days. And she'd had a few of them.

'C'mon, boys,' she cooed. 'Just what are you hiding beneath all that stubble? It can't be that bad?'

'I'll show you what I've been hiding,' announced the big

burly one sitting on the end, suddenly standing up. Hadley gazed blankly at him. No one had said there'd be this much ad-libbing.

It seemed to be happening in slow motion as he began to unzip an absolutely filthy pair of jeans. This was not going to end well. Hadley waited for the voice in her ear to cue her into the commercial break but all she heard was a panicked, 'Oh, shit!'

'What do you think about this then?' Mr Burly asked, pulling down his jeans and bending over so Hadley could get the full benefit of one of the flabbiest, hairiest, spottiest butts she'd ever seen.

She couldn't stop herself. 'Ewwwww!' she squealed. 'That's so icky. You must have a really unhealthy diet to have so many zits. Also, you need to see a dermatologist. I could give you some numbers.'

Someone was definitely saying something in her ear now but Hadley couldn't make it out over the roar of the audience. Besides, her attention was riveted on the most repulsive man she'd ever met, turning round so he could wave his *thing* in her face.

'Heard you liked real men,' he grunted. 'Well, what do you think about this?'

Hadley clapped a hand over her eyes before the miso soup she'd had at lunchtime could put in a repeat performance. 'Ewwwwwww!' she winced again, but with a lot more force. 'What is wrong with you? Why would you do this to me? And, like, your mother's probably watching this or, like, your grandma, and they'll be devastated. You should be ashamed of yourself.'

'You'd know about that,' piped up another member of the band. 'Bet your mum was real proud when you had your boobs splashed all over the paper.'

Hadley could feel herself starting to lose it. It was like being plunged headfirst from an airplane without a parachute but in a really, really bad way. 'If my mom had made some money from the picture rights, she'd have been cool with it,' she flung back at him. 'But it's OK. Why don't you make a few more lame jokes at my expense? It's not like I have feelings that get hurt. I totally get off on being the most hated girl in Britain. It's like the best fun ever!' Hadley's shoulder slumped as she suddenly realized that it was her mouth saying all this stuff. 'Believe me, I wrote the book on being ashamed,' she added quietly, before lifting her chin. 'Questions? Comments?'

There was a stunned silence from Raised By Wolves. Apart from the pig with the skin issues – who'd got his dick caught in his zip as he frantically tried to pull up his jeans.

'Go to commercial break! Hadley, commercial break! Now!' Her earpiece suddenly burst to life and her show-must-go-on gene kicked in.

'We'll be back in a little while,' Hadley gritted, smiling manically at the camera, as she listened to the series of

188

instructions being bellowed at her. 'And we'd just like to apologize if any of the contents of this interview caused offence. See you in a few!'

The split second that they went to the adverts, Hadley stood up and ripped out her earpiece as the producer and band's manager ran on to the set.

'What the hell do you think you were doing?' the producer screamed. 'We could get a huge fine from the ITC. You are finished!'

It was just too much. 'Don't you mess with me!' Hadley screamed right back until she realized that the producer wasn't screeching at her but the members of Raised By Wolves, who were getting it on the other side from their manager.

'You bloody idiots,' he shouted. 'You can wave goodbye to your Christmas special. We were going to have a kiddie's choir and everything – that's not going to happen now.'

'It was just a bit of fun,' the lead singer muttered. 'Like, we were being anarchic, wild, crazy.' He waved his hands in the air to show just how anarchic, wild and crazy he was.

'I'm finished,' Hadley said to no one in particular because no one was actually listening to her. Lots of people clutching clipboards were rushing about, but only the make-up girl came towards Hadley, brandishing a powder puff to take the shine off.

'My God, you're even blotchier than you were before,' she gasped. 'I'll go and get the airbrush foundation.'

Hadley followed her into the make-up room where she calmly gathered up her matching Louis Vuitton accessories and pulled on her jacket.

'Where are you going?' one of the dressers asked her. 'You're back on set in thirty seconds.'

'I'm done,' Hadley said, her voice as croaky as someone with a forty-a-day cigarette habit. 'I'm absolutely, completely and totally done.'

'But you can't . . .' The make-up girl was still holding the powder puff in the air. 'We've still got fifteen minutes of airtime and the big song and dance number at the end.'

'Not my problem,' Hadley decided, pushing open the door. 'If they want to sue me, then they should contact my lawyer in the States.'

Outside it was raining. Big fat droplets soaked her the minute she stepped out of the stage door and found herself in a little alley.

She didn't have a clue where she was. A car had brought her here and she'd assumed a car would take her back home.

Mr C-C gave a whinny of disapproval as he got splashed on the nose, and rocked his carrier as he dived away from the wire mesh. 'I don't know what *you're* in a bad mood for,' Hadley told him crossly. 'It's not like you've just quit the business called show and have no idea how to get home.'

She started trudging up the alley towards the road and decided that halfway there her boots were pinching. She couldn't even walk in measly three-inch heels any more.

Hadley sat down on a step, pulled off her boots and tucked them under her arm before heading for the lights. She searched in vain for the little orange glow of a vacant cab. There was always the bus. She'd caught a bus once with Laura when she'd been really drunk and it wasn't an experience that she was particularly keen to repeat.

Hadley impatiently shook back a sodden strand of hair as a car slowly came to a stop right where she was standing.

She'd seen a *Law & Order* episode once about street walkers, and her skirt *was* kinda short. Not that short though. The driver leaned over to open the passenger side door and Hadley was all ready to give him a piece of her mind. She was getting real good at that.

'Get in before you're washed away,' said a voice that she couldn't quite place over the steady drone of the rain. 'Come on, princess, you're soaked.'

Reed. Confused, Hadley peered into the car's interior. Reed stared back at her, his fingers drumming impatiently on the dashboard. 'Wow, it's a weird coincidence you passing like this. I don't even know where I am,' she said.

'Waterloo,' Reed supplied. 'And it's not a coincidence. We were watching the show. It was obvious something bad was going to happen so we decided to come down and blag our way in.'

Why would they do that? And just who was *they*, anyway? Hadley squinted furiously and there was Candy draped over the back seat, talking quietly on her cellphone. It was too dark to see her facial expression but Hadley would have bet all her worldly goods that it was smirk-shaped. 'Well, I could have spared you a trip because I walked out before the end of the show,' Hadley hissed, straightening up so she could start walking and really Reed shouldn't be driving along next to her with an open door because it was way dangerous.

'Hadley,' Reed called, his voice exasperated. 'It's cold; it's raining down in biblical proportions; you're acting even more crazily than you normally do; so get in the car before I put you in.'

'Quit bitching and get the hell in the car,' Candy yelled suddenly. 'We're getting rained on!'

He had a point, Hadley decided, and scrambled inelegantly on to the seat. It took a moment to untangle herself from her many bag straps and shut the door. But then she was leaning back with a grateful sigh, which quickly became a whimper when her wet denim jacket made contact with the leather seat. Just her luck; she'd catch a cold, which would turn into pneumonia and then she'd run up a huge hospital bill before she died.

'For the record,' Reed bit out as he started the car, 'we came down to see if you were all right and then shout at someone, probably Ross, if you weren't. Are you all right?'

'I'm fine,' Hadley replied automatically, digging into her bag to pull out her ringing, vibrating, flashing phone. Derek's number was blinking gaily. Hadley switched it off, opened the window and hurled it out on to the street.

'You could have just put it on divert,' Reed said mildly, turning left. 'Are you sure you're all right?'

'I already told you; I'm fine,' Hadley said, then burst into tears.

Chapter Twenty

Reed and Candy were super nice about it. Like, the whole crying thing. Even though Hadley sobbed all the way home.

'God, even Mom doesn't cry this much when she's drunk,' Reed hissed at Candy, as he scooped up Hadley's bags, Mr C-C barking furiously throughout the whole operation, and guided her up the stairs.

'No one cries as much as Mom,' Candy stated emphatically, unlocking the door and stepping aside so Hadley could run in and throw herself on the sofa. Hadley wasn't liking the tears any more than Reed and Candy.

Crying had never got her anything but a blank indifferent stare from her father and a sharp 'cease and desist' from Amber, followed by a smack for emphasis. 'Don't act like a big baby,' she'd snap. 'Nobody has time for your crap.'

But Reed and Candy had time for it as Hadley curled up on the couch with a cushion clutched to her chest. 'Everyone hates me,' she spluttered. 'I can't bear it!'

'You were fine,' Candy assured her breezily. 'You pretty much kept your cool but then we only watched to the first commercial break. What happened after that? Why did you storm out?'

Reed emerged from the hall and threw a towel at her. 'Your hair . . .' he murmured vaguely, gesturing with his hand. 'Um, it's leaking.'

Hadley rubbed her head and stared at her stained hand in confusion. The colour rinse was now making a bid for freedom and leaving dirty yellow streaks over everything it dripped on.

'I'm so gross,' Hadley announced woefully, looking around for a tissue as her nose had decided to start running too. How they could bear to look at her without wincing she didn't know. 'People shout at me in the street and everyone's seen my breasts and they all think I'm a skeevy, stupid b.i.t.c.h.'

'Oh, come on, Hadley,' Reed said, crouching down in front of her so he could take one of her frozen hands. 'Everything will seem better in the morning . . . Why is one of your bags ringing? I thought you'd violently disposed of your phone.'

Hadley lifted her head, then collapsed back on the sofa. 'It's my Sidekick,' she wailed. It was indeed. It stopped ringing for a scant three seconds, then started all over again. 'It will be Derek and I just can't talk to anyone. Reed, will you get rid of him?'

She closed her eyes as she heard Reed answer her phone. 'Hadley isn't available right now,' he said tersely. 'No, I'm just a friend. Sorry, she'll call you back,' Reed added, ignoring Hadley's frantic hand gestures. The moment that he terminated the call, it started ringing again.

'Switch it off,' Hadley begged. 'I'm never talking to anyone ever again!'

'So, what happened?' Candy prompted, sitting cross-legged on the floor, her huge blue eyes fixed unwaveringly on Hadley's face. 'Did they make you do another sketch? 'Cause that first one was kinda mean.'

'I don't want to talk about it.' Hadley closed her eyes because now Reed was sitting down in the chair opposite, casually crossing his long legs and staring at her like she was the evening's entertainment and he wasn't going to budge until he got his money's worth. 'Why don't people take me seriously?'

It was so meant to be a rhetorical question but Candy was already there with an answer. 'Because you're so funny, Hadders. And you don't even know how funny you are, which makes it even funnier. You're like a real-life cartoon character.'

Hadley blinked rapidly. 'I am not. I'm a human being and I have feelings and emotions and stuff.'

'There you go!' Candy crowed, pointing an accusatory finger. 'That's exactly what I'm talking about. You're like *Legally Blonde* meets *Clueless*. Seriously, who writes your lines because there is no way you could make this shit up all by yourself?'

Hadley narrowed her eyes. So she hadn't read the *Complete Works Of Shakespeare* or whatever. It didn't make

197

her stupid. And it didn't mean that she was going to stand there and let Candy trash-talk her. 'You are rude and nasty, Candy. Just because you've been on some stupid reality TV show with your punk parents and you dye your hair black it doesn't make you cool,' she ranted, jumping up so she could rap her knuckles against Candy's furiously scrunched-up forehead. 'It just makes you a walking hissy fit with a tiny girl attached to it.'

'I am not fucking tiny!' Candy screamed so loudly that all the dogs in the neighbourhood should have been howling in solidarity. Mr C-C certainly was, but before Hadley could point out that Candy was doing a good impersonation of a tiny person having a hissy fit, she felt a heavy hand on her shoulder and turned around to witness Reed's most disapproving look yet. If he glared any harder, then his eyebrows would fall off his face.

'I think you should apologize to my sister after she's taken time to make sure if you're all right,' he said in a tone which Hadley guessed made lesser girls wilt.

Hadley wrenched herself away from Reed's bone-crushing fingers so she could scoop up Mr C-C, who was attacking the coffee table. He really had lost all the socialization skills that the five hundred dollars-an-hour dog psychologist had taught him. 'Don't hold your breath,' Hadley suggested sweetly. 'Your sister's the biggest brat I've ever met and you need to stop sticking your nose in other people's business and, like, shave once in a while.'

The shocked silence was punctuated by a growl of pure rage from Candy, but Hadley wasn't waiting around for it to evolve into a stream of high volume F-words. She darted neatly out of the room, eyes downcast but still aware of Reed's skin-blistering gaze.

Storming into her bedroom wasn't great, as game-plans went, especially as she stubbed her toe as she stormed, but Hadley found slamming the door very hard immensely satisfying. Mr C-C cowered under the bed as Hadley stood there, fists clenched. She had a compulsive urge to throw her head back and scream or start hammering at any vertical surfaces with her bare fists. It was very unsettling. This is what everyone meant when they said that anger was a really negative emotion.

Instead she got into the lotus position on the bed and tried her deep-breathing exercises. Hadley even tried to visualize her third eye, though it was proving very elusive. Outside her door, she could hear Candy shouting, but it was more volume than actual words. Though what she could catch ('. . . that goddamn *bitch* . . . I'm tall enough to become a cop . . . I'm out of here . . .') was classic, hissy-fitting Candy. The front door suddenly opened and then slammed shut, which meant the apartment was empty and Hadley had other storming options.

She cautiously stuck her head out to make sure the coast was clear, just in time to see Reed beetling towards her, almost falling over a pair of Laura's shoes in his haste.

'We're going to have a talk,' he growled, bearing down on Hadley before she even had time to shut the door in his fuming face.

'Get out!' she yelled, but it sounded squeaky, rather than menacing. 'You don't live here and you're not the boss of me so just go away!'

Reed wasn't going anywhere. Hadley found herself backed up against the wall, Reed's hands on either side of her head, boxing her in with no exit strategy.

He bared his teeth in something that didn't even remotely resemble a smile and up close, yes, Reed was properly handsome with his chiselled jawline and pouty mouth but he was also properly terrifying because the jaw was clenched and the mouth was curled up in disdain. 'What is wrong with you?' he asked, like it was the most reasonable question in the world. 'What the hell is wrong with you?'

People never got this close to Hadley. It wasn't in her contract. Her eyes skittered to the left and if she could just duck out from under his arm . . . but as soon as she thought it, a hand clamped down on her shoulder again. Hadley looked at Reed's fingers as they flexed like he wished they were around her neck so he could squeeze the life from her.

'If you don't stop touching me then I'm going to sue you for physical harassment.' It would have been intimidating if her voice wasn't shaking like a hyperactive kid playing Dancemat Revolution.

'Jesus, Hadley, everything that comes out of your mouth is ridiculous,' Reed said softly. 'How do you even manage to get dressed on your own?'

'I'm not ridiculous. I'm serious.' But when she heard her words in her breathy little baby voice they lacked feeling. Hadley tried again. 'OK, I've done some ridiculous stuff since I got here but I'm a serious person. I'm, like, a serious artiste.'

It was hard when you had to make up your lines as you went along. And it really didn't seem like Reed was going to give her any rave reviews. 'You're a fake,' he told her in that same gentle voice, which was way worse than when he growled at her.

And all she could retaliate with was a very whiny: 'Didn't I already tell you that I was having a really bad day?'

Reed's hand tightened on her shoulder as he sniffed contemptuously. 'You're unbelievable. You sob your heart out because you got humiliated on some dumbass TV show, which no one forced you to appear on. So, big deal. If that's the worst thing that's ever happened to you then, princess, you have my congratulations. Go out and actually pay your dues, put in some real work and you might get a little sympathy from me.'

'You don't know anything about me,' Hadley said quietly, because one loud noise and she might just shatter. 'Not one thing.'

'I know plenty about you because it's there every time I pick up a paper,' Reed insisted, lowering his head so his lips were millimetres away from hers as he trashed all over her. 'I'm sure the biggest tragedy of your full and varied life was when you thought it would be a really good idea to whip your top off for some opportunist with a camera and it ended up biting you in the ass.'

All Hadley could do was stand there mesmerized, nails scored into her palms as she looked into Reed's cold eyes. 'The naïve waif routine isn't cutting it. Time to give the real world a whirl . . .' he continued.

The real world sucked, sucked, sucked and was full of people ready to sell her out for their own ends, if Hadley didn't do it to them first. 'I don't know how,' Hadley's voice was tight and throbbing with something dark that she didn't even recognize. 'I didn't graduate High School. Fyi, I didn't *go* to High School. I didn't go to the prom. I didn't date. I didn't do anything but show up every day at eight am to the studio and stayed there for fourteen hours straight . . .'

'I don't see how that's got anything to do with—'

'Yeah, because, dude, there's a lot you don't see about me,' Hadley told him in that terrible voice that she really didn't like the sound of. 'Every day I pretended to be this all-American, well-adjusted girl with a happy family, no matter what other crap was going on in my life. And believe me, there was plenty. So don't tell me that I'm a fake and don't tell me that I haven't paid my dues. I paid for them with my *fucking* childhood.'

Hadley was shaking so hard that Reed was the only thing holding her up, while he stood there looking like someone had hit him over the head with a two-by-four.

Hadley summoned up every last ounce of strength to push him away; fingers curling into the soft wool of his jumper for the briefest moment before she stalked towards the door. Halfway there, she whirled round so she could stab a finger in Reed's direction as he stared at her warily. 'I might not have lived in some crummy walk-up in New York or backpacked round Europe with a bunch of other trust-fund kids but I was too busy earning a living. And for the record, I was damn good at it. I entertained people. I made them fall in love with me and I've got nothing to show for it but a whole bunch of people trying to use me like that "opportunist" who dosed my drink until I passed out and then made a quick buck from it.'

Reed gasped, his arms hanging limply at his sides as he took a step back. His skin turned ashen in, like, a split second, which would have been interesting if Hadley had finished setting him right. But she hadn't. 'Stop riding my ass because you think you know everything about me. Well you don't, so you can chew on that while you're getting the hell out of here because if you're not gone in one minute, I'm calling the police for real.'

He walked past her, his sleeve catching agaisnt her arm,

but then Reed turned his head so she could get a ringside seat of his anguished expression. It needed some work. 'God, Hadley, I'm so sorry . . .' he began helplessly, groping for the words like English wasn't his first language. 'I didn't . . . I thought . . .'

'Why are you still here?' Hadley shut her eyes because really she couldn't look at him for another second.

Only when she heard the front door close quietly behind him did Hadley finally throw her head back and let out one long, painful scream.

Chapter Twenty-One

It still felt like she was screaming when Hadley woke up the next day. It was very strange to have this anger bubbling inside her like a nasty case of acid reflux.

Hadley wanted to throw and smash and rip every single one of her worldly possessions (apart from her Prada boots) until her bedroom matched the jagged landscape inside her head. But that would have involved actually getting out of bed. And she was never getting out of bed again. What was the point? There was no point. Her life was pointless, that was what Reed had said.

Just thinking his name in her head made Hadley grind down on her very expensively capped back molars. He was the first person she'd ever *hated*, though she also hated that this gave Reed a distinction which he didn't deserve.

She tossed from side to side for a bit, kicking out her legs because even the quilt was irritating her, and then settled back into a fitful snooze, which was interrupted by someone opening the door and plonking themselves down on her bed.

With a furious groan, Hadley sat up to see Candy sitting there looking like the evil gnome that she really and truly was.

Hadley folded her arms and leaned against her bashed-up pillows. 'Get off my bed and get out of my room,' she snapped in a voice so vicious that it surprised even her.

Candy shifted ever so slightly but tilted her chin to show that she was in her usual defiant mood and not planning to budge any time soon. 'Look, you said some things, OK, I definitely said some things and then Reed said—'

'Were you planning to get to the point, some time before, like, Christmas?' Hadley icily enquired, pushing back the covers so she could grab Candy's arm and haul her up. Just as well that Candy really was minuscule. 'I don't want to talk to you ever again. And I certainly don't want to talk about your *brother*.' Afterwards, she'd be pleased that she managed to sound the word out like 'brother' was a secret code-word for 'serial-killer' or 'badly dressed ugly person with body odour issues'.

'But, Hadders, you're being—' Candy protested, wriggling in her grasp.

'Not another word! In fact, I don't even want you looking at me or breathing near me.'

It was a bit melodramatic but then it wasn't as if Hadley lived in the real world to know any better. It was amazing how much that still stung.

Candy wrenched herself out of Hadley's hold. 'Well, if you're going to be like that, then screw you,' she snarled, reverting back to form. She was so predictable, like, all the time. 'I'm not even going to show you today's papers.'

As punishments went it was pretty random, so Hadley just shrugged. 'I don't care about today's papers. Or yesterday's papers,' she added thoughtfully. 'I'm through with it.'

And as soon as she said it, Hadley realized that she wasn't just saying it to get a rise out of Candy. It was really true.

'I quit,' she said for the seventh time. 'Derek, how many more ways do you want me to say it? I'm done, retired, giving up the business called show.'

'But have you seen the papers this morning?' Getting fired must have short-circuited Derek's brain because he wasn't listening to a single word that Hadley was saying.

'No, because I'm not interested. I'm, like, ridding myself of the burden of celebrity.'

'Yeah, whatever and I had the executive producer of *Life Begins at 9.30* on the phone first thing,' Derek happily chirped.

Hadley pulled a face at Mr C-C. 'Yeah, I'm sorry I walked out but hey! Wait a minute. Actually, I'm not. And I was going to send a muffin basket but now I'm all like, why should I? They set me up and they let that band of hairy jerks diss me. People might think I'm fake but I'm not. I have feelings and they got seriously hurt last night, Derek.'

'I know,' he cooed. 'I know and I'm not even going to say I told you so because water, bridge. But they loved you, sweetie. Even before the incident that we're not going to talk about again. They called you a comic genius . . .'

'But I wasn't being funny!'

'And the clip of the you-know-what is the most watched video on YouTube today,' Derek finished smugly. 'Now, do you still want to quit?'

'What's a YouTube?' Hadley asked, but Derek was so not finished.

'And they want you back for the rest of the season. They're *begging* me for some Hadley, and they're prepared to pay very well. I think I can get them to add another nought on.'

'I'm not doing it because I'm retired. I'm through with living my life in the glare of the media spotlight and with hateration from people who don't even know me. It's all totally shallow and meaningless,' Hadley bit out. Every time she said it, her resolve strengthened.

'There's no hateration any more,' Derek insisted. 'Only love. Everything's about to change. I can feel it. One of the Sunday supplements is going to run a piece, a nice, in-depth profile and I said I'd get you on the phone today for some quotes and—'

'No, Derek, no!' Hadley rasped, smacking her hand against her forehead. 'You know when we used to do that thing? That thing where I'd turn stuff down because I wanted you to go back to people and get me more money? That thing?'

'Ah yeah, happy days,' Derek sighed with a side order of sarcasm that was badly timed and totally unnecessary.

'This isn't that thing,' Hadley said. 'It's a new thing, when I say that I don't want to do something because I don't want to do it. Derek, please, I need you to respect me.'

'I do,' Derek said smoothly. Way too smoothly. 'Why don't we do lunch on Monday, my treat. I'll take you to Nobu and we can talk about drafting out your retirement statement. And before then, I want you to make a list of what you plan to do with the rest of your life.'

'What do you mean?' Hadley asked.

'Well, if you don't want to be a superstar then you must have other career options in mind. We'll talk about on Monday. Later darling!'

Derek had a point. Sort of. Hadley had been so busy quitting that she hadn't given a thought to how she was going to spend the rest of her life. She was in excellent health so there was no reason why she shouldn't live to a hundred.

Hadley sprawled out on the sofa, Mr C-C on her lap, to work on her list. Candy had tried to come in and watch something on TV, but abandoned that idea when Mr C-C went into attack mode. He really was the most thoughtful little critter sometimes.

When Irina breezed in, laden down with a really expensive Balenciaga bag and several taped-up carriers festooned with airport baggage stickers, it was a welcome relief. Writing a list of her future career plans had turned out to be much harder work than Hadley had realized.

'You really need to invest in some proper luggage,' she told Irina kindly as the other girl collapsed on the floor. 'Those carrier bags are not giving the right impression.'

'I wait until someone gives me suitcase for free,' Irina yawned, stretching out her long limbs like some exotic creature from the depths of the ocean. 'I shagged out and hungry. We get pizza, ja?'

Irina and Hadley had this whole arrangement. In exchange for microwave tuition, Hadley made phone calls for quattro formaggio pizza and a side of buffalo wings because Irina got blind-sided by the pizza guy's Italian accent.

'You all over the papers again,' Irina said later, through a mouthful of cheesy dough. She'd offered Hadley a slice but it was swimming in grease so she'd politely refused. One day Irina was going to wake up and find herself the size of a house with her modelling career in tatters. 'If some guy waved his dick at me, I do serious damage.' She snapped her teeth to illustrate her point and Hadley was just on the verge of asking Irina what *exactly* she meant by serious damage, when the front door opened and they both heard Laura yapping at someone on her cell.

'Well, if he wants me to do it then he's going to have to rethink his sample size,' she was saying crossly. 'I'm not a six,

I'll never be a six and I'm not doing a shoot in one of his dresses which will leave my boobs hanging out.'

Irina rolled her eyes so hard that her pupils completely disappeared. 'She's so fat,' she noted savagely, stuffing another slice of pizza into her mouth as Laura stuck her head round the door.

'I heard that,' she gritted. 'And you know when you were being a bitch on that shoe shoot? They booked me for their winter campaign, so thanks for that.'

One of Irina's fingers slowly moved into the upright position as she spat out a stream of clipped Russian that had to contain language that even non-Russian people would find offensive.

Laura didn't even flinch, but stood there with her hands on her hips, pretty smudge of a nose wrinkling in distaste. 'And don't leave your empty pizza box lying on the carpet. Put. It. In. The. Bin. You're a disgusting slob, Irina.'

'I thought I heard your voice, bitch!' Candy came careering into the lounge, and with all these people arriving and standing about, it was beginning to feel like a bad am-dram staging of *Our Town*.

'I just got back,' Laura said distractedly, staring at the wadded tissues with Irina's discarded chicken bones resting on them as if they were causing her immense inner pain. 'You all right?'

'No, I'm pretty fucking far from all right,' Candy hissed, shooting Hadley a pointed look, which she returned with interest. Hating someone was actually a lot of fun. Who knew? 'We need to talk,' Candy said in a low voice and dragged Laura bodily from the room.

Irina watched them go, then turned back to Hadley with her most exaggerated sneer. 'I hate those bitches,' she stated for the record. 'You phone up and get me another pizza now?'

Candy claimed first dibs on the living room the next morning. She must have got up as the cock crowed (not that there seemed to be that many cocks crowing in Camden) to stake her claim. She even covered all available seatage by spreading out the Sunday papers so that when Hadley emerged all ready to watch *Popworld*, she could give her a smug smile.

'I would make room for you,' she said, her sweetness as fake as a tub of aspartame, 'but there was that whole "don't look at me, don't breathe near me" speech.'

'But you have the biggest room,' Hadley burst out, vibrating with the unfairness of it. She was still finding it very hard to hold back the cranky. 'I don't even have a closet, so I should get to hang out in here whenever I want.'

'What*ever*,' Candy drawled, stretching out on the sofa luxuriously. 'Go away, *Sad*ley, your squeaky voice is giving me a headache.'

Candy was completely lucky that Hadley was a nice

person who wouldn't give in to her baser urges to storm into the other girl's room and rip up every single piece of fabric and dress pattern in there. Instead, Hadley had to make do with drawing zits and a monobrow on the publicity shot of Candy that was pinned to the kitchen notice board. It was a real pity that there wasn't a company who made voodoo dolls and did Sunday delivery.

There was nothing for it but to skulk in her room and work on her list until the smell of coffee (proper coffee made from beans rather than a glass jar) wafting under her door and Laura's gentle knock coaxed her out.

'House meeting in the lounge in two minutes,' Laura said casually, like a house meeting was no big deal. 'There's some brunch stuff in the kitchen.'

The kitchen counter looked like the breakfast buffet at the Four Seasons. There were mounds of bagels, glistening slices of smoked salmon dotted with lemon wedges and tubs of thick, fattening cream cheese, as well as a basket of flaky croissants and pain au chocolats. Hadley could feel herself ballooning two dress sizes just from inhaling the smell of warm pastry. She loaded up a bowl with fruit salad and went into the lounge, where Irina and Candy were sitting at each end of the sofa with matching mutinous expressions and laden plates.

'I only here for the food,' Irina said, picking up her bagel. 'Then I out of here.'

Candy assumed an air of martyrdom that looked as fake

as her hair. 'I was trying to watch TV,' she moaned to no one in particular before she crammed a pain au chocolat into her mouth sideways.

Eventually Laura appeared with a smoked salmon bagel. She'd have to run an extra fifteen minutes just to work off the cream cheese, Hadley thought to herself sagely. Also potential supermodels had no business having their big toe poking out of a hole in their sock, but Laura simply sank down gracefully on one of the floor cushions and declared the inaugural house meeting open.

'Right, guys,' she announced firmly. 'All of us work really hard and have to travel a lot and when we get home, the place looks like a bomb's gone off. So I think the first thing we should do is just have a civil discussion about what's going wrong.'

The floodgates opened on a stream of accusations and counter-accusations. Yes, Candy could do what she wanted in her own room but every single one of them had had pins embedded in their feet from her dressmaking experiments. Plus, it was selfish of Laura to leave her washing in the machine and then disappear off to another continent for days at a time. And Irina left greasy plates with discarded stinky sausage on them, but if she refused point blank to own the problem then Hadley was damned if she was going to be strung up for spending too much time in the bathroom.

'I have the smallest room,' she pointed out for what

seemed like the gazillionth time. 'And I can't afford to go to a spa so you're all being, like, unreasonable. And I have NEVER left soapscum on the bath. I don't even know what that is.'

'Well, my room's the size of a potting shed,' Laura exclaimed angrily. 'But I don't feel the need to spend three hours moisturizing or whatever the hell it is that you do in there.'

'I can't believe that you want to rob me of my sanctuary and I don't see why I should have to clean the bath,' Hadley all but whimpered. 'I'm not like other people.'

There was a definite and unmistakable snicker from Candy but she tried to turn it into a cough. 'I can't do a thing about Hadley's bathroom vigils but there is a really simple solution to everything else.'

Three pairs of eyes looked at her expectantly.

Candy nibbled the edge of a croissant as the tension slowly mounted. Nobody should be able to look that smug while eating that many calories, Hadley thought crossly.

'Go on, spit it out,' Laura snapped. 'Your solution, not the croissant.'

'Well, duh, Irina and Sadley move out and we can cover the extra rent.' Candy licked her fingers daintily. 'I'll call the agency tomorrow and get them to sort it out.'

'Do not call me Sadley.' Hadley banged her elbow into Candy's arm and watched with satisfaction as a glob of jam slowly but surely dripped on to her T-shirt. It was already smeared from a disastrous home-bleaching experiment so there was reason for Candy to start shrieking like her first-born was being murdered. 'I think your hostility stems from being so short. You should talk to your therapist about it.' Hadley realized she'd gone off-message. 'And I'm not moving out. I can't afford to. London's the most expensive city in the world after Zurich. You move out.'

'I was here first,' Candy pointed out smugly. 'I'm not budging.'

'You were here five seconds before me. You move out and take your fugly clothes with you,' Irina deadpanned. 'I not move out. This flat convenient for West End and airport and cheap rent.'

'I can't move out,' Candy protested, dabbing ineffectually at the jam stain while glaring at Hadley. 'Conceptua and my mom tag-teamed and I only get to stay in London if I live in the agency-approved apartment.'

Hadley recognized her cue. 'Go back to NYC then,' she suggested brightly. 'I'd help you pack except I can't because I don't like you.'

'I would never let my mother tell me what to do,' Irina added darkly. 'Is so immature.'

Candy was making a noise that no human being should ever be able to make. It sounded a bit like someone trying to start an ATV that was stuck in a gravel pit. Hadley watched curiously as Candy opened her mouth and tried to make actual words.

'Jesus wept!' Laura suddenly shouted, throwing a cushion across the room in her distress. 'All right, we'll get a bloody cleaner but first we need to work through all this shit because the tension in this flat is seriously ugly.'

Hadley wanted to hug herself in glee. She'd really missed having domestic staff who'd rearrange her closets for her, put her shoes in order of genre, make sure all her bottles of nail polish were facing the right way—

'. . . that horrible little rat dog . . .'

Hadley returned from her little fantasy of a neatly-ordered vanity case to the reality of Candy pointing an accusatory finger at Mr C-C, who was trying to kill a stray doughnut by seizing it in his teeth and violently shaking his head. 'Don't do that, sweetie,' Hadley cooed. 'You know you're not allowed to have sugar.'

She reached down and scooped him up so she could kiss his darling little mouth. 'Hadders, that is so unhygienic,' Laura frowned.

'Actually, dog saliva is much cleaner than human's,' Hadley informed her. 'And Mr C-C is a Mexican hairless, so he doesn't shed. Really, he's the most perfect little doggy in the world, aren't you precious?'

'He drools everywhere,' Candy said in a low, dark voice. 'He's vicious and yappy and I caught him trying to pee up the kitchen bin yesterday.'

Hadley clapped her hands over Mr C-C's ears so he wouldn't have to hear Candy's outrageous character assassination. 'He does his business outside and he has the sunniest temperament, unless he's provoked.'

'I like the dog,' Irina butted in. 'He never attack me, maybe he just has good taste.'

'You're saying that because Hadley is your only ally in the house,' Candy hissed. 'I want that dog gone. I bet if I got my lawyer to look at our tenancy agreement, he'd find a "no pets" clause.'

Hadley couldn't believe what she was hearing. All she could do was gasp so indignantly that it made her light-headed. 'You lay one of your stubby fingers on Mr C-C and I'll sue you,' she threatened, because Candy was just a jumped-up reality TV celebrity and didn't have the power to start issuing decrees. Besides, if ever there was anybody who needed to not be in the apartment . . .

'I'm sick of your brother constantly hanging around and taking up sofa space and using our hot water and, like, oxygen,' she choked out.

At least it shut Candy up. Hard to talk when her jaw was hurtling towards the floor.

'And he's totally rude and disrespectful and he's here all the time and he doesn't pay any rent,' Hadley continued, warming to her theme. 'Mr C-C has way more right to be here and he smells much nicer.'

When Reed had been looming over her and getting all judge, jury and executioner on her ass, he'd actually smelled rather yummy – citrussy and spicy. Not that she'd paid much attention at the time. And in no way was Hadley going to let the truth get in the way of managing to royally piss Candy off.

'Look, this isn't getting us anywhere,' Laura sighed. 'We need to stop hurling the hate about and find a way to live together.'

'I've still got plenty to get off my chest,' Candy growled, still visibly fuming over the criticisms of her overbearing jerk of a brother. 'Irina is heinously rude and if I have to hear Hadley squeaking in that baby voice one more time, I'm going to rip my ears off.'

'The problem is you,' Irina declared serenely. 'You a very noisy little girl. All the time, you make the fuss and the tantrums.'

'Are you going to let them talk to me like this?' Candy demanded of Laura, who'd had the totally bad idea of calling a house meeting. 'You're meant to be my friend!'

'I'm trying to be neutral, like Switzerland,' Laura insisted weakly. 'I don't hate anyone.' She thought about it for a second. 'Except I intensely dislike Irina.'

'What*ever*,' Irina scoffed, like being intensely disliked wasn't a problem. 'You stole my Lanvin dress though you too fat to get in it.'

'Well, you drowned my iPod in a cup of coffee,' Laura shouted, her face red with anger.

Irina shrugged and didn't even attempt to deny it. 'That was outside the flat, it doesn't count.'

Hadley cuddled Mr C-C closer, her head whipping back and forth as Irina, Laura and Candy bickered in a never-ending stream of 'but then you said, so I said . . .'

It all ended in a trifecta of flouncing and 'fine'. 'OK, fine.' And one last, 'Fine, whatever!' Hadley found herself all alone in the lounge, the sound of doors being slammed still ringing in her ears. It was going to be really unpleasant living with three other girls who all hated each other, she mused. But on the plus side, at least she had the TV all to herself now.

Chapter Twenty-Two

Hadley made an effort for her lunch with Derek. She'd even managed to find a hairdresser at short notice to do her roots, although she'd abandoned her usual platinum blonde for a softer, honey-tinged shade that didn't need touching up so often.

Her Marc Jacobs court outfit said loudly and clearly that she wasn't to be messed with as she kissed the air above Derek's cheek and slid into her chair in the private dining room. He was obviously anticipating tears and tantrums.

Derek eyed her carefully. 'You've lost weight,' he said at last. 'Your face is looking a little gaunt, but I love the hair.'

Hadley nodded her head in tacit agreement. She'd always believed Amber when she'd said that you could never be too rich or thin but if she stuck with her soup-only regime, she'd end up looking like Nicole Richie. Besides, Derek was paying.

'I'll have the blackened cod and a salad with Ranch dressing, please,' she said to the waiter, without even bothering to open her menu. 'And a Diet Coke with shirred ice, not cubes.'

'So, let's talk about the piece in yesterday's *Sunday Style*,' Derek began, not taking his eyes off her face. 'Must have come as a bit of a shock but I think that ultimately it will do a lot of good. Go some way to redressing—'

Hadley held up her hand. 'I'm not reading the papers, Derek. I'm sure I told you that on the phone. Now, do you want to see my list that I've been working on?'

Derek nodded, his sleek, shaven head catching the light. 'Go on then,' he said as if he was simply humouring the crazy girl sitting opposite him.

'Just ignore the hearts and flowers,' Hadley advised, pulling the piece of paper out of her bag. 'I always doodle when I'm thinking.'

She watched Derek scanning the list, his eyebrows quirking and then meeting in a furrowed line. She couldn't imagine why. It was a good list.

POSSIBLE NEW CAREERS
1. Personal shopper.
2. Dog trainer.
3. Motivational speaker.
4. One of those people who runs seminars for businessmen on how to use acting to make their presentations less boring.
5. Diet coach.
6. Real estate agent – check if High School diploma needed.

What she'd realized was that there were tons of things she

could do with her important life skills. There was no way she'd end up in an overall made from icky man-made fibres, stacking shelves.

'I wanted to ask you what the starting salary was for an interior designer, because I'm very visually aware,' she told Derek eagerly. 'Not a lot of people know that about me.'

Derek took a sip of his San Pellegrino and folded his arms. 'How much money do you have left?' he asked baldly, smiling faintly as Hadley made a silent 'oooh' of disapproval. Everyone knew it was vulgar to talk about money. 'I'm your agent, for the time being, so you're telling me on a strictly need-to-know basis,' he explained smoothly. 'And I bet you can tell me right down to the last cent.'

'Twenty-five thousand, three hundred dollars and forty-seven cents,' Hadley blurted out. 'I checked my balance this morning. But I'm still waiting for my *Notting Hillbillies* money – you should get on to that – and there'll be syndication fees and residuals and stuff,' she tailed off weakly.

'That's about sixteen thousand pounds. You shouldn't have given all that money to your mother,' Derek scolded as Hadley's Diet Coke arrived. 'Are you going back to LA?'

At the mention of Amber, Hadley had visibly flinched, but now she put her hands in her lap so Derek couldn't see them twisting nervously. 'That's not an option right now,' she said vaguely. 'I think London is a good place to . . . y'know?'

'No, I don't, I really don't,' Derek said softly, urgently. 'Listen to me, Hadley. You're eighteen and I know that makes you an adult in the eyes of the law but I have a personal responsibility to you.'

Hadley blinked slowly. Derek's words seemed to be having an effect on that place where the tears came from, though possibly she had something in her eye. No one had ever had a personal responsibility towards her. It was always the other way round. 'That's really sweet of you,' she started to say but now it was Derek's turn to hold up his hand in the universal sign language for 'do not interrupt me'.

'I understand you wanting to give up the fame thing, you've had a rough ride – but we're in a position to make a lot of money.' He paused to let this sink in. 'Kid, you need all the money you can get your hands on right now. You're still Hadley Harlow and that's your most bankable asset.'

'Derek, I am so tired of being Hadley Harlow,' she breathed. 'It's like everyone thinks that they know me because they've seen one of my movies or a picture in a paper. But the thing is even I don't know who the real me is. I just got given scripts and told who I was playing that week. I don't feel like a real girl. I just pretend to be one and I'm not doing a very good job of it.'

You're a fake. The memory of Reed's scathing comment was so loud that Hadley gave a nervous start.

'I think that you don't give yourself enough credit,' Derek said gently. 'Despite your childhood, you're actually a pretty nice human being. Tegan says thank you for the dress by the way.'

Hadley looked at him blankly. How did he know anything about her childhood? And who was Tegan? 'Oh! Assistant Tegan!' Hadley cast her mind back. 'I have everyone's birthdays in my Sidekick.' She paused as the waiter reverently placed her blackened cod in front of her. 'I didn't do it to be nice, Derek, I did it because Tegan has a crappy little job with lots of things to do but she'll do my stuff first because I bought her a pretty dress. See? Not a nice human being – I just played one on TV.'

'Eat your lunch before it gets cold,' Derek said mildly, picking up his knife and fork and turning the conversation on to the less dangerous topics of where he should go for his winter vacation and whether Laura and Irina hated each other as much as everyone at Fierce thought they did.

It wasn't until they were waiting for coffee that Derek launched into Round Two. He slipped a large manila envelope across the table like it was a ticking bomb. 'That's the *Sunday Style* piece. I want you to read it,' he ordered her implacably. 'You're not going to like it. You're going to be furious with me about the cover image and the piece itself will make you very angry. And the fact that it's already been syndicated worldwide will just about make you go ballistic. But I hope you'll understand why it's going to have people beating a path to your door. Go on, open it.'

Hadley had a feeling that if she didn't, Derek might put a gun to her head. He had this resolute expression that she really didn't like. Gingerly, she extricated the magazine with her finger and thumb and yup, he was right.

'That is not an approved shot,' she hissed, staring at her black and white face, almost scrubbed free of make-up and with *flat* hair. 'I didn't even pay the photographer.'

'I paid the photographer,' Derek said calmly. 'And I don't want you to look at the picture, I want you to read the words.'

Reading the words took her over an hour. Not just because some of them were really long and she was just a dumb girl from the Valley who'd never graduated High School. No, it was kinda hard to read when the tears kept blurring your vision.

Hadley got to the end of the piece and closed the magazine with trembling hands, before taking the snowy white linen handkerchief that Derek proffered.

She scrubbed at her eyes as the waiters cleared the lunch settings and started preparing for the evening service. Derek poured her a glass of water and reached over so he could stroke her wrist.

'It seems like the end of the world now, I know, but pieces like this completely redefine a person. You have to trust me.'

'I can't believe the things people said,' Hadley

whispered, shoving the magazine aside. 'Like, I'm some . . .' Something she didn't even want to think about.

'Hadley, darling, you're going to give me six months, a year tops, to make you a ton of money, none of which you are going to give to your mother, no matter how many more children she has and then, if you still want to, you can retire, OK?' Derek's grip on her wrist tightened. 'You deserve the right to at least get rich.'

'I don't know,' she said weakly. 'I can't even think straight right now.'

'Fine. I'm going to do the thinking for you,' Derek purred, leaning forward so he could wipe a stray smear of mascara from her cheek. 'I'll draw up a strategy and we'll talk tomorrow.'

Hadley sat there dumbly, all her concentration focused on forcing the magazine back into the envelope so she wouldn't have to look at it any more. 'I have to go home now,' she whispered finally.

Derek sighed in capitulation, before tucking the envelope into her bag and guiding her through a sea of tables and concerned-looking wait staff, as if she was made of the most fragile, spun glass.

Twenty-Three

When she got home, Hadley shoved the magazine right to the bottom of the kitchen bin, but ten minutes later she squinched up her face, took a deep breath and braved the congealed rice noodles to retrieve it.

It was like looking at those 'When bad clothes happen to good people' spreads in the gossip rags. Part of her wanted to turn the page and a much larger part of her with really poor impulse-control couldn't look away.

LITTLE GIRL LOST
The rise and fall of Hadley Harlow, Hollywood's most tragic child star

blared out from the cover in big black letters. Inside it was even worse.

Hadley took a fortifying gulp of water enriched with added calcium and began to read.

> *Once upon a time there was a little girl who lived in a beautiful house in Malibu, the playground of the rich and famous. The little girl had a heart-shaped swimming pool, a bed*

229

imported straight from a French château and closets full of designer dresses.

Every day a shiny black car would arrive at precisely 7.42am to take the little girl to a big TV studio, where she'd play another little girl who didn't have the big house, or the swimming pool or any of the other luxurious trappings of stardom. This other little girl had something better: a doting dad, a loving mum and a spaniel called Scamp who followed her everywhere she went.

Welcome to the strange world of Hadley Harlow, America's favourite gap-toothed, freckle-faced sweetheart ... until adolescence kicked in, the bubble burst and she was cast aside by the public who once loved her.

'Hadley grew up on a studio lot,' says Marlene Weisman, the casting agent who discovered her at the age of three when she was looking for a child to star in a cereal commercial. 'She learned to read from scripts, she cut her teeth between takes and was expected to behave like a seasoned pro by the time she was five. Somewhere along the way, her childhood got lost.'

Born in Encino, California to bartender, Mark Harlow, and Amber Spillane, who described her

*career as 'actress' on Hadley's birth certificate,
though her biggest role was a three-episode run
in the cult soap,* Passions, *Hadley Harlow signed
with her first agent at three days old.*

Hadley stared at the huge picture of her taken on the set of
The Starr Family. Her screen mom and dad were looking
proudly on as she blew out the five candles on a pink
frosted birthday cake. But inset was a tiny black and white
snap taken of her and Amber in a dressing room around the
same time. Hadley's hair was in curlers and she was holding
a script, while Amber was pointing at the page, her face
screwed up in irritation.

'I don't care if you can't read the goddamn thing,'
Hadley remembered her saying frequently. 'You are going
to stay here and learn these lines until they're stuck in that
pea-brain of yours.'

It was all there in black and white. A three-thousand
word story about a lonely little girl who spent all her
waking hours on a TV set designed to look like an
American dream home, with a screen mother who got the
sack after Hadley started calling her Mommy off set too. A
girl who 'was a forty-year-old woman in a seven-year-old's
body' according to a *Hadley's House* staffer who wished to
remain anonymous. Oh, yeah, there were a whole bunch of
no-name insiders who'd queued up to over-share about
defining moments in Hadley's life. From the time that she'd

had mono and Amber had paid a doctor to give her vitamin B shots so she could carry on shooting to Hadley being banned from mixing with the other children on set in case they slipped her a donut.

> *'We're talking about a little girl who knew the intricacies of television backwards but had no socialization skills,' remembers a* Hadley's House *staffer. 'Neither the Harlows nor the studio gave a rat's ass about Child Labour laws. That kid worked fourteen-hour days, would fall asleep on set and sometimes get brought back in the middle of the night for a last minute reshoot.'*

Hadley stopped reading for a moment so she could rush to the bathroom and throw up her lunch. Then she sat down on the closed lid of the toilet, magazine still clutched in her hand. It was weird because when this had all been going on, she hasn't thinking that much about it. It was just, like, how stuff was. But reading it; seeing it through other people's eyes, was majorly, majorly distressing. Like scenes from a really bad made-for-TV movie.

> *So, where did it go wrong? How did the biggest star in America simply disappear from view between the ages of fourteen and seventeen?*

And why didn't anyone care? 'Puberty was not kind to Hadley,' says her former make-up artist, Carol Kent. 'Everything that could go wrong did. She shot up seven inches in six months, got acne, lost the baby face but not the baby voice. It was a disaster. That picture of her on the Little Girl Lost *posters, where her eyes are open wide and she's screaming – it's an iconic image. It's like Marilyn Monroe in the white dress. There's no coming back from a picture like that.'*

So Hadley Harlow was confined to that fairytale mansion in Malibu, only visited by a steady stream of diet coaches, personal trainers and an eminent plastic surgeon. 'I think the worst day of Amber's life was when Hadley got her first period,' Maria Suarez, their old housekeeper confessed. 'She cried and cried and told Hadley it was all her fault that her career was ruined. She had Hadley working out for four hours a day and a therapist scheduled every afternoon because Hadley's hair started falling out due to all the stress. It was like living in the middle of a ticking time bomb.'

The bomb went off in Hadley's accountant's office on March 13th 2006, when staff noticed her bank accounts had been emptied overnight

233

by Mark Harlow. 'Mark handled the business side of things. He was never around and when he was, he had no interest in Hadley. I don't think I ever saw him speak to her, let alone give her a hug,' says Linda Chiarusco, who played Hadley's screen mother for the first three seasons of Hadley's House. *'Hadley was desperate for approval from him but Mark was too busy wheeling and dealing – though it was Amber who always had to step in to close the deal on the negotiations with the studio after Mark had screwed things up.'*

WHERE DID HADLEY'S MISSING MILLIONS GO?

It was something Hadley was also eager to know and her attention was directed to a handy graph at the side of the page, which made no more sense than when the lawyers had read out the evidence in the courtroom in LA.

For the London portion of her total humiliation, they'd dug up Mervyn from under the stone where he'd been hiding for the last few weeks. He was at great pains to point out how she'd plotted her own downfall. *'Underneath it all, there was a nice kid struggling to get out,'* he noted. *'But her own ambition just got in the way. Talking to her was like having a conversation with a publicity still. The lights were on, the doors were open but the real Hadley*

*wasn't at home. You wanted to shake her a lot of the time,
try to get her to see sense.'*

It ended with a short summing up from Lorena Carr, a
former Broadway star who'd been delaying her retirement
by appearing as Hadley's glamorous grandmother on the
show. *'I think the only time that Hadley felt free was in
front of the cameras. She just lit up. Everyone's so quick
to knock her but they forget how damn good she was.
Hadley has a wonderful sense of comic timing and she
brought a pathos and vulnerability to the shallow
characters that her parents insisted that she play.'*

Hadley lifted her head as she heard someone come in
and head for the kitchen. There was the sound of the
fridge opening and then closing, and muffled footsteps
before one of the bedroom doors shut. She forced her eyes
back to the page.

*'I think that Hadley could have a long and wonderful
career,'* Lorena Carr continued. *'Talent like hers comes
around once in a generation but her parents never
recognized that. They treated her more like an ATM
than a daughter. I find it ironic that Mark's in prison
for fraud when he should be there for child abuse. And
Amber should be in the cell next to his. You can quote me
on that.'*

She was crying again, hunched forward on the seat, arms
wrapped round her body to try and tamp down the
anguished sobs rising from her throat. It *hurt* so much. All

235

her life, laid out in six pages; all her dirty little secrets weren't secret any more but up for discussion over breakfast. She'd given them her brightest smile day after day and it hadn't been enough. They wanted to suck out her insides and pick over her bones too. There wouldn't be anything left; just a hollowed out girl where Hadley had used to be.

It took a while to realize that someone was stroking her hair. Hadley looked up through red-rimmed sticky eyes to see Irina standing over her.

'Hey, it's not worth crying about,' she said, her clipped vowels softened. 'Your parents, they shits, but you put that behind you.'

Hadley let Irina pull her up and half carry her to the bedroom, where she wrapped Hadley up in a quilt. Five minutes later, her sobs had quieted to an occasional hiccup and Irina was back with a cup of tea.

'Did you read it, Irina?'

The other girl sighed. 'It's in all the papers today. I just get back and there's photographers setting up outside. One of them ask me if you wear a wig.'

Hadley could feel herself getting ready to unleash a fresh volley of sobs. 'I had alopecia. It's a medical condition, and I'm better now.' She caught sight of the magazine clutched in her hand and shuddered. 'They made out like I'm some kind of victim and it wasn't like that. It was just, like . . . I don't even know what it was like.' Hadley struggled to get up, though she had no idea where she actually wanted to go. Her escape plans were blocked by Irina, who sat down and wrapped a bony arm around Hadley's shoulders.

'You'll get over this,' she said, like it was a statement of fact. 'You prove to everyone that they talk out of their asses. You better than this.' She waved a dismissive hand at the magazine that was still clutched in Hadley's clenched hand. 'Give it to me.'

'No, I want . . .' Hadley stirred herself from her funk so she could hold on to it for dear life but Irina was already prising her fingers loose.

Riiiiiiiiippppppppppppppp! Irina tore the magazine in half. 'There,' she said with satisfaction. 'It not exist any more. It happened. It sucked. Now, get over it!'

Irina could earn a fortune in Hollywood with her 'tough love' therapy. Under the other girl's steely glare, Hadley found herself smiling weakly. 'I guess I need to start focusing on the positives,' she offered feebly. 'Not sure what they are right now.'

'You have one day to feel sorry for yourself and eat ice cream or whatever you girls do, then it's finish. Business as usual, ja?'

Hadley took a sip of tea, even though Irina had used the icky teabags and made it way too strong. But she wasn't going to moan or ask for a slice of lemon, no sir. Irina was being uncharacteristically sweet but it couldn't last forever.

But it lasted long enough for Hadley to finish her tea

and Irina to embark on a rant about Laura and Candy that plumbed new depths of bitchery. Hadley could feel her eyelids drooping as Irina opined that 'those two spoilt bitches not last two seconds in Moscow in the middle of winter. They freeze where they stand and no one would care'.

Hadley yawned and made a noncommittal noise to show she was listening, though she didn't have one giddy clue what Irina was talking about. 'OK, I go.' Irina stood up as Hadley hunkered down under the covers. But as she got to the door, one hand reaching out for the knob, she suddenly turned. 'You tell anyone I nice to you and I give you some serious hurt.'

'Cool,' Hadley agreed. It wasn't until she heard the door close that she began to cry again.

Chapter Twenty-Four

At least her hair didn't fall out this time. It stayed stuck on Hadley's head, while the rest of her was confined to the flat.

She was never going outside again to hear people yelling new variations on how much they hated her and what a loser she was. Also, they had the paparazzi camped out on their doorstep. *Again*. At least Candy got so fed up with press representatives from at least six different countries ringing the bell 24/7 that she checked in to a hotel.

Irina and Laura weren't around much either, so Derek sent Tegan around daily to walk Mr C-C and get emergency soup supplies from Sainsbury's. It was all working out; Hadley could stay in bed or lie on the sofa, staring unblinking at the Hallmark Channel, until the day she died.

Derek had other plans. He turned up on the ninth day of her extended lie-in. One moment Hadley was watching a *Project Runway* marathon, the next Derek bounded into the room and threw a folder at her supine form.

'That's your new schedule,' he informed her calmly. 'Get washed and dressed, you've got a meeting at Canary Wharf in two hours.'

Hadley tilted her head so she could still see the TV screen. 'I'm not going,' she mumbled sullenly. 'I don't do meetings any more.'

If she'd used that tone of voice on Amber ever, it would have led to slapped faces and intensive cognitive therapy. But Derek simply hauled her up, duvet and all, and slung her over his shoulder. 'I've had a lot of time to think about where we went wrong before,' he remarked conversationally.

'Put me down!' Hadley yelped because the world didn't look any better upside down.

'You ordered and I tried to obey,' Derek continued as if Hadley's yowling and wriggling wasn't important. 'But now I'm going to be giving the orders and you're just going to do everything I tell you to, without questioning it. OK?'

'No, it's not OK,' Hadley retorted angrily, as Derek set her down by the bathroom door. 'How dare you treat me like this?'

Derek looked like he dared and didn't give a damn. 'You're angry,' he summed up with an amused smile. 'That's good. I was worried that the catatonia might be permanent. I could put you in the shower myself but I think it breaches half a dozen sexual harassment laws.' Hadley gaped at him as he pushed her through the door. 'Don't forget to wash behind your ears.'

Hadley yawned and scratched her greasy hair

ruminatively. Maybe it was easier to just do what Derek said. Saved her having to think about stuff by herself. That never seemed to end well.

Three weeks later and Hadley was still yawning. Jet lag was a killer, she thought miserably as she waited for the make-up girl to bring her two cans of icy-cold Diet Coke to place over her eyes so they'd look a little less laboratory bunny.

Derek's make-Hadley-rich strategy (codename: Operation Bling) was a thing of beauty but had a really punishing itinerary. She'd spent a day flying to Australia to shoot two more Quilty-Lux commercials back-to-back for twice the money she got last time, before flying back to London three days later so she wouldn't miss her co-hosting gig on *Life Begins at 9.30*. They'd added another nought on to their original offer and found Hadley a make-up girl with less attitude, so she signed up for the rest of the season.

'Hadley, honey, I'm sorry. Catering don't have any Diet Coke, but I'm going to the green room to hunt some down for you,' Charli, her make-up girl said breathlessly from the doorway. 'Do you want me to take your curlers out first though?'

Hadley struggled out of the depths of the make-up chair. 'It's OK, I'll go myself,' she decided. 'I'll fall asleep if I sit there much longer.'

'Maybe you should try drinking one of them after you've put it on your eyes,' Charli suggested, peering critically at Hadley's face. 'I'm going to slather you in moisturizer before you go. That flight has dried you out like an old raisin.'

Hadley stood there patiently while gunk was applied. Charli called it like she saw it, which was kinda refreshing. Most people said one thing, but meant something else completely.

And look at her, with her hair a work in progress, face smeared in gloop, stalking towards the green room. To think she never used to leave the house without frequent applications of make-up. It just went to show how much she'd grown as a person.

There was a chiller cabinet of drinks containing several cans of Diet Coke, singing their siren song right at her. But Hadley's seek and destroy mission was was distracted by . . .

'Reed,' she said as crisply as she could, wincing perceptibly as he put a hand on her shoulder.

She'd imagined this moment – meeting her absolute arch nemesis again. But she'd been fabulously dressed, possibly in Gucci couture, accessorized with some cute arm-candy like that guy from the Superman movie, and Reed was down on his luck and selling batteries from a suitcase.

In her dreams, Hadley had never thought that her face would be covered in heavy-duty moisturizer and that she'd have purple spongy rods in her hair. Or that Reed would be wearing a Christian Dior Homme suit and a carefree smile. How she hated him!

'How are you?' he asked, like he actually wanted to know the answer. 'Candy says that you've been working really hard.'

As they'd exchanged a sum total of nine words in the last three weeks ('I think you'll find that's *my* Touche Eclat actually'), Hadley suspected that Candy had passed on that little snippet with some added bile thrown in.

'Yes, I have,' she said flatly, her expression blank – a little trick she'd picked up when she was working with someone horrible (like, say, George) and she didn't want to give them any cues.

Reed was made of slightly stronger stuff. 'I came around a couple of times to see how you were – fought my way through the photographers, but there was no one in.'

It was a curveball; Reed acting like he was all concerned about her. And he was certainly tilting his head in a concerned fashion, but Hadley wasn't buying what he was selling. Nuh-huh.

'I already told you, I've been *fine*,' she insisted coldly. The blank face wasn't working so she tried a haughty glare instead.

'Well, it's good to see you again and in such a pleasant mood,' Reed drawled, reverting back to his usual snarky self because the saintly routine wasn't fooling anyone.

Hadley was saved from having to . . . she wasn't exactly sure what, but it might have involved her stiletto heel making contact with Reed's toes, by Ross Thomas, who sidled up behind her and snaked his hands around her waist. 'Don't monopolize my favourite girl,' he told Reed, who was still standing there looking like he didn't have anywhere else to be. 'Reed gave me a right bollocking for that whole Raised By Wolves thing,' he added. 'Even threatened to tell my girlfriend about our late-night poker games.'

'Really?' Hadley could feel her top lip curling and deciding to stay that way. 'Reed takes his big brother duties very seriously. Even with people he's not actually related to.'

There was an uncomfortable silence and Hadley made the welcome discovery that if she stared at Reed long enough, he began to squirm deliciously; running a finger along his shirt collar as if the temperature had suddenly gone up a few degrees.

'Have you seen those child acrobats that are on tonight's show?' Ross suddenly said, because the subject desperately needed changing. 'What horrible little bastards.'

'No one should wear that many sequins so young,' Hadley said feelingly, because, hey, she could relate. 'They're asking for gender identity issues.'

'Maybe they feel secure enough in their sexuality to want to wear sequins,' Reed ventured, with what he thought was a winning smile, which it so wasn't.

Hadley rolled her eyes. 'Yeah, whatever,' she deadpanned. 'Ross, shall we talk about the script?'

It was a good way to let Reed know that he was totally surplus to requirements. And despite his other, way obvious failings, at least he knew how to take a hint. 'OK, well I guess I'll see you after the show,' he said. Ross was his poker friend, so why was he looking at Hadley?

'You two should kiss and make up from whatever little snit you've had,' Ross said once Reed had slunk off. Hadley needed to have a word with him about co-host solidarity and sticking his nose where it wasn't wanted but Charli was bearing down on her.

'There you are,' she said in an exasperated voice, brandishing a big, round hairbrush. 'How long does it take to get two bloody cans of Diet Coke? I want your skinny arse back in the chair now.'

Hadley let herself be dragged away, Diet Coke forgotten, so she wouldn't have to think about Reed's concerned expression for a second longer.

And all the way through the show, whether she was corralling spangled, micro-gymnasts around the studio or interviewing a Spanish film star with patchy English, she was aware of Reed's eyes on her as he stood behind the cameras. His beady, piggy eyes, which weren't the least bit smouldering and anyone who thought they were needed professional help.

245

When Hadley finally got back to her dressing room, there was an overpowering scent hanging heavy in the air from the huge bunch of roses and lilies sitting on the counter. Hadley touched the delicate white and pale pink petals before her fingers closed around a card buried deep in the foliage.

Is there any point in saying sorry? Because I am. Let's do dinner so I can tell you in person. Reed.

Hadley scrunched the card in her fist before hurling it in the general direction of the trash can.

'Nice blooms,' Charli said, as she came up behind her and started easing down the zipper on her Cacharel dress. 'You got a secret admirer, Had?'

'You can have them if you want,' Hadley told her casually. 'They're not from anyone important and I'm beyond allergic to pollen.'

Chapter Twenty-Five

'He was just trying to say sorry,' Laura insisted, through her teeth. 'I think it was sweet. You didn't have to blow him off.'

Hadley tilted her chin down and widened her eyes. 'Stop talking to me, I'm being your best friend.'

It was hard to concentrate on being a best friend while wearing a very scratchy dress and standing on a box because Laura was freakishly tall.

Laura shut up for an entire roll of film; her cheek pressed against Hadley's as they stood with their arms lightly clasped. It was very disconcerting how Laura could hold a pose for two seconds, every inch of her screaming 'top model', then snap out of it for an instant so she could yap in Hadley's ear.

'What did he say to you exactly that's got you so wigged?' Laura pouted furiously, not because Hadley was withholding information but because the photographer had just told her to 'give it some smoulder, love'.

'I don't want to talk about it,' Hadley gritted, trying to smile in a friendly fashion at Laura, even though she was being a hugely annoying pain in the butt. 'Lots of very rude, very hurtful things. And he's Candy's brother so that's a whole million other reasons not to trust him. Don't you think he has really beady eyes?'

'No,' Laura sighed. 'I think he has gorgeous, dreamy eyes but I'm so not going there.'

'OK, shall we take a break?' the photographer called. 'I want to do something with the lights while you two change. And when you get back, I'd like less gossiping and more modelling, please.'

Hadley glared at Laura who was already striding off set. 'I need a wee like you wouldn't believe,' she called over her shoulder.

Hadley stood patiently, her arms over her head, as her dress was pulled off and then reached for a white towelling robe to protect her modesty. But Laura wriggled out of her own frock, then sat on a stool in her white lace panties, munching idly on a carrot stick.

'You should put some clothes on,' Hadley whispered, nodding significantly in the direction of the hairdresser and stylist. 'There are men about.'

Laura flashed a grin and stared down at her nipples. 'They're not men,' she declared. 'They're fashion industry professionals. It's a whole different kettle of fish.'

It was easier to stare at her own reflection in the mirror than all those acres of pale, curvy, almost-naked Laura-flesh. Hadley cautiously patted her hair; she still couldn't get used to how unbouncy it was. But Derek had insisted that things had to be done his way. And his way involved a

248

makeover, or rather a make*under*. False eyelashes, fake tan and going any lighter than honey blonde on the colour charts were strictly verboten.

'You're eighteen,' he'd pointed out sternly, in the face of Hadley's frantic whimpers. 'It's time to actually look your age, instead of a thirty-five-year-old party girl. Without all the bells and whistles, you're very pretty.' Derek meant well, but he was a terrible liar because without the best tricks of the beauty industry, Hadley was as plain as steamed potatoes. That's why Amber had started bleaching her hair aged five, dyeing her eyebrows and eyelashes when she was six, and making her see a facialist once a fortnight once she turned eight.

Hadley even wore off-the-rack now. At first she'd wanted to fire Derek for being so cruel but now all the weeklies were doing picture spreads on *Hadley's New High Street Style*. Also it was way cheaper than ready-to-wear.

'Your freckles are so cute,' Laura said, snapping Hadley back to the present, where her roommate's nipples were all she could see. 'I think they're ready for us on set.'

Laura behaved herself for the rest of the shoot, but as soon as they climbed into the back of a cab, she was off again. 'So are you and Candy ever going to make up?' she demanded. 'You should give her another chance. She feels really bad about it all.'

Candy has a funny way of showing it then. Hadley

racked her brains for one small sign that Candy was at all repentant and came up blank. 'Candy's your friend, not mine.'

It was true. Despite the house meeting ending in all-out war, Laura and Candy were still proper friends who painted each other's toenails and went shopping together. The only reason that Candy hadn't done the best friends shoot was because she was appearing in a rival magazine the same month. And Laura's friends from back home were doing exams and 'didn't have the right look for *Moda* magazine'. In fact, Hadley had been way down the list, but Derek had made her do it.

'Look, if you and Candy could stand to be in the same room then the atmosphere in the house wouldn't be such a living hell,' Laura said. 'I mean, God, you manage to get on with Irina and she's the biggest bitch in Bitchville.'

'Irina's a very misunderstood person,' Hadley said firmly. 'It's the language barrier.'

'No, I think you'll find that she's just as big a bitch in Russian.' Laura slid across the seat so she could grab Hadley's hand and do the puppy-dog eyes thing right in her face. 'Please, let Candy make it up to you? Please? For me? She's really gutted about everything. She almost nearly cried!'

Hadley considered Laura's proposal for a few long seconds, then came to a decision. 'OK, I'll accept an apology from her but I'm not having anything to do with her brother.'

Laura decided to quit while she was still barely ahead. 'Go out for sushi,' she suggested. 'You love sushi, Candy loves sushi: I hate it because it's basically raw fish; but see how much stuff you two have in common?'

The peace summit, as Laura kept calling it, took place in a Japanese restaurant by Camden Lock. Hadley wore H&M and Candy wore one of her own creations, which looked like she'd spontaneously vomited black lace down her front.

They sat opposite each other on floor cushions, across a long, low table, and Hadley couldn't help but wonder if Candy had chosen the venue because it was hard to be all dignified and aloof when you were constantly fidgeting to get comfortable. Candy snapped her chopsticks together in greeting.

'Shall we get a drink before we order?' she asked sweetly like she getting into character to play a nice girl. 'Sake?'

'Green tea,' Hadley said shortly. 'I don't drink alcohol any more.' And she never would again. She'd even thrown out her champagne-scented body buffing lotion.

Candy bit her lip as if a whole slew of words were trying to fight their way out. 'Green tea it is.'

Candy didn't seem that interested in the merits of the salmon tempura over the beef teriyaki. She was more into the idea that they could bond over their bad mothers.

'My mom's so delusional,' she confided. 'She's losing her

looks, but she still thinks she's got it going on. And she looks at me, like who are you and why are you so small? You know, she smoked all the way through her pregnancy, which explains a hell of a lot.'

Candy looked at her expectantly and Hadley realized that it was her turn to share some anecdote from her not-so-happy childhood. 'Um, there was this one time I had to ride a pony for *Hadley's House*, but when it turned up it was like a really massive horse and it kept stamping its feet and there was stuff coming out of its nose.' Hadley shuddered at the memory. 'And I was so scared that I puked up and Amber got so mad at me for holding up filming that she hauled me off to my trailer, washed out my mouth with soap and told me that if I didn't get on it, she'd sack my favourite director. He was really nice, used to sneak me Red Hots when she wasn't looking.'

'Oh my God,' Candy breathed, her eyes two perfect circles of horror. 'Why did no one report her to Child Services?'

And stupid, silly Hadley. She'd got the rules of the game all wrong. Like, they were meant to be sharing not-so-terrible stories about their childhoods and their not-so-terrible mothers and she'd misunderstood.

'It was OK,' she said brightly. 'Like, it was character building and it taught me to face my fears.' Candy didn't look at all convinced. 'Shall we order? I'm very hungry.'

Candy was still twitching but in a different way now. Not like her butt cheeks were getting numb but more as if she'd been told she had three minutes left to live. 'Let's just hang on a sec,' she yelped. 'Actually I asked two friends to join us.'

'So we can't spend an hour alone?' Hadley demanded. 'How is that making it up to me?'

'You'll thank me for this.' Candy's eyes searched the room frantically, then her face brightened as the door opened and she waved her hand wildly in the air. 'Over here, boys!'

Hadley refused to look round. She knew exactly who was coming over and when he did, she'd be able to kill Reed *and* Candy by stabbing them through the heart with her chopsticks. Maybe at the same time, because she was *that* mad.

'Girlfriend,' she heard a familiar and unexpected voice drawl. 'You're looking as lovely as ever.'

The blood in her veins suddenly decided to rush towards her head as fast as possible. Then plunge back down to her feet. Hadley looked once, just to make sure, then snatched up a chopstick. 'What the fricking hell is he doing here?' she growled.

Chapter Twenty-Six

Hadley sat rooted to the spot, almost paralysed apart from one shaky finger pointed in George and Benji's direction. 'You . . .' she choked out.

George shrugged. 'Yup, me. And I guess you're still doing the whole drama queen shtick, Hadders.'

Drama queen, was she? Hadley struggled to sit up straight and set her face to the icy composure setting. She turned to Candy. 'I could talk to him but his lawyers would take out a restraining order. Probably have me deported or thrown in jail.'

'What was I meant to do?' responded George. '*And* you sent me full-fat muffins, which was so spiteful of you . . .'

'They were meant to be fat-free. I specifically told them they had to be fat-free 'cause quite frankly, you could stand to lose a few pounds around the gut,' Hadley sniped. George was definitely her kryptonite. There wasn't another person on earth who could make her this vicious.

'I didn't think this would happen,' Benji said to Candy, twisting his hands nervously. 'It's like *Celebrity Death-match* but in a sushi bar.'

'Well, *one* of us is still a celebrity,' George said smugly, moving him straight to the top of the list of people that

Hadley would kill if she really, really had to.

'Why is he even here?' she enquired fretfully and oh no, she was leaking fluid out of her eyes again. Even tilting her head back and flapping her hands in front of her face didn't make them stop.

'He was meant to be here so you two could sort things out,' Candy said heavily, leaning over to give George a hard poke in the ribs. 'What about all that stuff you said on the phone last night?'

But George was staring transfixed at Hadley. He'd never seen her without the fake tan after all. 'She's crying,' he pointed out completely unnecessarily. 'And she's all pale and *freckly* and my God, the hair. Hadders, you look all understated and shit.'

The sobs were rising up in her throat again and George sank down on the cushions so he could wrap Hadley up in a squashy hug. 'Don't cry, Hadders. You never cry. You're tough as old boots.'

Hadley didn't feel tough as old boots, she felt soft and squidgy as a melted, no-fat, frozen yoghurt. 'I can't stand all this negative energy,' she sobbed. 'I'm meant to be figuring out who the real me is but it turns out the real me is very mopey.'

'I thought I was only one who'd noticed,' Candy murmured under her breath, as George hugged Hadley tighter. He had surprisingly strong arms.

'Look, Hadders, I had to fight fire with fire,' he

explained. 'And I had a way better press agent than you. It was nothing personal.'

Hadley fought her way free. 'But what about the restraining order and all those interviews you gave to the press about me?' she gasped indignantly. 'You never did know when to play it low key.'

'So I had my hate on? Can you blame me?' George asked, tossing his fringe back for emphasis. 'Let's face it, Hadley, you've always been jealous of me.'

All Hadley could do was gasp again. 'Not even! Why in hell would I be jealous of you?'

Candy tapped her chopsticks together for attention, not like it did any good. 'Guys, I thought you were going to air kiss and make up?'

'You were always mean to me on *Hadley's House*,' George continued. 'You totally used to misfeed me cues so I didn't steal the limelight.'

'Ha! Like, it was my fault that you couldn't take direction,' Hadley hissed. 'And don't think I don't know that your mom used to try and get it on with the studio liaison so you'd have more screen-time.'

'That's a filthy lie! Take it back!'

Hadley stuck out her tongue. 'Make me!'

'Oh, don't tempt me, little missy,' George snarled. He was so very gay and she must have just said so out loud, because the three of them were staring at her like she'd wanted to organize a lynching in Trafalgar Square.

'But you *are* gay,' Hadley pouted. 'And you totally act it. How anyone could ever have thought you were straight, I don't know.'

'You act way more gay than I do,' George burst out indignantly. 'You're as camp as a row of pink—'

'George, darling, shut the hell up.' Benji smiled at them and turned to Candy. 'Ah, silence is such a beautiful thing, isn't it?' He extended his hand out. 'Hadley, nice to meet you.'

It was just as well as that Benji was in a boy band because with his looks there weren't a lot of other options open to him. He was like a tiny, fully-poseable porcelain doll with doe-like eyes, delicate features and a crew cut that simply made him look more fragile. Like, a harsh word or a fierce gust of wind would destroy him.

'Oh, and by the way, thanks for outing me, beeyatch,' Benji added after the handshake. Obviously he was way tougher than he looked.

'It just kinda happened,' Hadley admitted with a shrug. 'I'm sorry if it caused you any inconvenience.'

'Best thing that ever happened to me,' Benji said with a grin. 'I'm even thinking about going solo.'

'Gay is the new black,' Candy noted archly. She fixed Hadley with a smug smile. 'What a good idea of mine, getting you and George back together.'

'We are not back together,' they snapped in unison.

'Oh, suck it up,' Candy suggested. 'You can take 'em out

of Hollywood, but you can't take the Hollywood out of 'em. Which is a pity.'

Hadley sat there, stiff-backed (which was hard because the floor cushion was killing her posture) eyes spitting like an angry cat, but George suddenly let out a breath and a bath-tap gurgle of a laugh. 'I can't pretend to be hard done by any longer,' he giggled. 'If I'd known what it would do to my career prospects, I'd have come out years ago. Round about the time I got caught by my High School principal indulging in locker room horseplay with the centre forward of the football team.'

George could always be relied upon for over-sharing, Hadley thought sourly as he gave her hand a conciliatory pat.

'Oh, turn that frown upside down, Hadders,' he scoffed. 'I'm sorry that things got crappy for you but . . .'

'It was my own fault,' Hadley finished his sentence. 'Because I was an overambitious, fame-hungry publicity whore who totally had it coming to her. Yeah, I already got that memo.'

Out of the corner of her eye, Hadley could see Candy mouth the words, 'total tragedy queen' at Benji, but George was snuggling up to her again like she was a life-sized cuddly toy he'd just won at the fair.

'Look, I was so mad at you but when I read *Sunday Style*, it brought it all back. I thought I knew everything that was going on behind the scenes on *Hadley's House*, but actually

I didn't know the half of it. And the people who did never said anything because you were the golden ticket,' George said quietly, his face almost handsome now the mocking expression was gone. 'It's a miracle you're even vaguely well adjusted. And will you stop looking all miserable and plagued with remorse? It's over. Pfft. Now the world knows that I'm here, I'm queer, and I'm up for the lead in Reed's movie.'

Hadley stopped looking remorseful as quickly as if someone had flicked the off-switch on the tears button in her head. 'Say what?' she rasped, and pushed George away, because, hello, could you say limpet? She narrowed her eyes at Candy. 'Oh, when were you planning to bring this up?'

'Reed loves George, but not in a gay way.' Candy tapped the menu with one finger. 'Can we order soon? Watching you two throw down has really made me work up an appetite.'

Chapter Twenty-Seven

H adley wasn't sure what was meant to happen after that. Like, maybe she and George could be civil to each other if their paths crossed again, which wasn't that likely as she refused to go anywhere that the general public might be lurking. But it simply wasn't the case. George was determined to cling to her side like extra-sticky glue.

She couldn't work out if it was guilt, boredom, or the unthinkable – that he actually *liked* her, but whatever it was, he was constantly on the phone or taking her out to strictly VIP parties where she sipped lime and soda water cocktails and tried not to watch him and Benji making out. Which shouldn't have been hot but kinda was in a *Brokeback Mountain* sort of way.

But mostly she helped George work on his audition piece for Reed, as the role of a runaway teen who turns to drugs and hustling to support his childhood sweetheart as they try to carve out a living on London's mean streets.

'No one will ever love you more than me,' Hadley whispered, tears streaming down her face. The living room was strewn with pages of script and she and George had been at this for hours. 'We're here and it's now and the future is for ever. We just have to reach out and take it, Jake. Grab it with both hands.'

Hadley wanted to write Reed's script off as pretentious, arthouse drivel but she was in the moment. She was *so* very in the moment. And right now, she was Lisa Caruso, cast adrift in a cruel, uncaring world, dabbling in drugs and prostitution, and her boyfriend was dying in her arms.

George sat up. 'Jeez, you're really getting into this.'

She ignored his attempts to kill the mood. Why couldn't he just hurry up and die already so she could go to the bathroom and have a good, uninterrupted weep. 'I'm acting. Maybe you should try it,' she advised.

'Oh, whatever,' George said, flopping back down, his head in her lap. 'The future . . . people like us don't get to have a future.'

'See, that's where you're wrong,' she gulped round the lump in her throat. 'You can't leave me, not when . . .'

She paused because George was flailing about on the carpet like he was having a fit.

'I'm in my death throes,' he explained helpfully. 'I'm great at dying.'

'But you've just been knifed several times by a drug runner that you totally screwed over. Do you think you'd have that much energy if you were bleeding to death from multiple stab wounds?' Hadley waved the script in George's face. 'It doesn't say anything in here about you spazzing out all over the place.'

'It doesn't say I don't.' George paused mid-flail. 'I'm inside Jake's head and I think he'd cling on to life as hard as he could.'

'But that's not what he says . . .' Hadley's argument that Jake was giving up because he was a big, fat loser with bad decision-making skills was interrupted by a slight cough from the doorway where Candy and Reed were watching them with matching amused expressions. The sneer was genetic? Freaky!

'Reed, how much did you see?' George asked in a teasing way, which was totally inappropriate, just like the way he was fluttering his eyelashes.

'Enough. I think we saw enough. Right, Candy?'

'Hell, yeah,' Candy muttered. 'We thought you were in full-blown anaphylaxis.'

It was quite the diss but George was sitting up eagerly. 'I'm so glad you're here,' he gushed, every molecule in his body straining towards Reed. 'I'd love to talk about Jake's motivation.'

Reed had crouched down to tickle Mr C-C behind his ears, which was wrong on so many levels.

'Well, it's giving you an unfair advantage,' Reed said smoothly, though Hadley noticed that his ears were bright red. Interesting. Even more interesting was the way he was staring at her as she knelt in the middle of the floor. 'Hey, Hadley,' he said softly.

Candy really couldn't be relied upon to stop her beady-eyed half-brother trying to interact with her roommates. She was more preoccupied with leafing through the stack of magazines on the coffee table. 'Which bastard stole my copy of *Vogue Italia*?' she demanded. 'I bet it was Irina!'

It was time to make herself scarce because what with George's drooling, Candy's growling and Reed's staring, Hadley was starting to feel majorly uncomfortable. Besides, Candy's *Vogue Italia* was super soggy because she'd dropped it in the bath last night and she needed to hide the evidence.

Hadley got to her feet, twisted round to glance at her back and mock-shuddered. 'Ewwww!' she wailed, loud enough that Candy covered her ears in protest. 'I have carpet fluff all over me.'

It was a flimsy excuse, but hey, people expected her to be shallow. And now she had a pretext to scurry out of the room, stopping only to scoop up Mr C-C en route. Her hand brushed against Reed's as she picked up a floppy, blissed-out three pounds of Mexican Hairless. Reed's little finger hooked around hers for a moment, a moment long enough for Hadley to catch her breath.

'Don't go,' Reed whispered so only she could hear but Hadley was already averting her eyes and scurrying out of the room.

Chapter Twenty-Eight

'So, I was thinking about acting. People say I have a really nice speaking voice and has Benji said anything to you about if he's going solo?'

Hadley stifled a yawn, and tried to discreetly peek at her Gucci watch. 'He doesn't really confide in me,' she hedged, tilting her glass of cranberry juice so it turned a fiery red in the glow of the candlelight. Barry Barnett was enough to make anyone fall off the wagon. But she was still sober and going to have serious words with Benji and George for setting her up with this out and out loser.

'He's got an out of control crush on you, Hadders,' they'd said.

'You have so much in common. You both like Prada and dolphins,' they'd said.

'You can't let one bad experience with a boy turn you into a celibate freak. Anyway, Barry isn't clever enough to send text messages, let alone take pictures on his phone,' they'd said.

'Make sure you go to a private members club,' Derek had said, because Hadley ran everything past him now. 'I'm not sure he's right for your image and I don't want any photos leaking out.'

So, here she was on a blind date with Benji's band-mate and wondering if it was possible to die from terminal boredom. Barry was easy on the eye with his rippling arm-bumps (shown off in a tight white tank top), brilliant white smile and silky soft, brown hair, which flopped beguilingly. But, man, he was absolute hell on the ears.

'. . . and he went and got a personal manager and why would he do that if he was going to stay with the band?' Barry asked, but didn't wait for Hadley's answer before continuing in the same nasal monotone. 'It's all right for him, he's the androgynous one. He's got transferable skills; but ever since we did the video where I was a boxer, people think I'm a thug.'

'Right,' Hadley sighed as Barry paused to take in some much needed air. 'It's getting kinda late, do you think we should . . .'

'And also I think I could play older, even though I look boyish, but I have an edge too. Like, I could be a gangster – but with a heart of gold . . .'

Lord, when would it end? Hadley shut her eyes then opened them on Ross's grinning face.

'Why, Miss Harlow, are you on a *date*?' Ross made it sound as though Hadley was engaged in sordid behaviour under the table. As if !

'This is Barry,' Hadley gestured at her companion, who was looking miffed at being cut off mid-flow. 'And this is Ross and Alicia.' She beamed at Ross's girlfriend because she was super-sweet and way generous with her Selfridges discount card. 'And this is some other people.' Looming behind Ross and Alicia were Reed and, quelle surprise, a straggly-haired girl with a sulky face.

'Budge up then, mate,' Ross ordered Barry, who was forced to shift along the banquette. 'Couldn't get a table. What a bunch of tossers.'

'He even tried the whole "do you know who I am" routine,' Alicia said dryly, sliding in next to Hadley. She cast a professional eye over Hadley's outfit of TopShop tunic over jeans. 'Love the ensemble. Oooh, are your shoes from Gina?'

Alicia was the accessories editor on *Polka Dot* magazine so they always had a lot to talk about. Like bags and shoes and jewellery and scarves and 'it's a bluey green, or maybe more of a greeny blue. Kind of teal but with a hint of turquoise', Alicia was saying about her new bag when Hadley realized that something really interesting was happening across the table.

Barry was happily jawing on to the straggly-haired girl who seemed to be hanging on to his every mind-numbing word. And Ross and Reed (it sounded like a sitcom double act) were in a little huddle. Reed was talking a lot, using his elegant fingers to make point after point, while Ross nodded along. Hadley wondered what they could be talking about so intensely, when Reed suddenly looked up, right at her and then spread his hands, as if he was in deep despair.

Probably trying to find a way to tell George that his deathbed scene needed a little work, Hadley thought, as she turned back to Alicia.

Barry was the first to call it a night, with a long, garbled explanation about dance rehearsals that no one paid any attention to apart from the straggly-haired girl, who clung to his arm and asked if he'd drop her off first.

And then there were four.

'That guy,' Ross said, gesturing over his shoulder at Barry. 'You can do better than that. Bloody hell, even Raised By Wolves would be a step up.'

'I was forced on a blind date,' Hadley protested. 'He did nothing but talk about himself. And people accuse *me* of being self-involved. Like, not even.'

'Who accuses you of being self-involved?' Reed asked. Hadley could have smacked the indignant look right off his face. He was, like, the prime suspect.

She settled for a lemon-sour, 'Well, your sister for one.' And all of a sudden Ross and Alicia really had to go 'because we promised we'd drop in at this launch and it'll be way too boring for you two.' There was a flurry of coats, the cheque was paid and they were hurrying off before Hadley could even ask Alicia if they were still on for a seaweed-wrap body exfoliation on Friday.

And then there were two.

Hadley could simply stand up and leave but Reed was

already sitting down next to her, although there was a perfectly good seat on the other side of the table.

'Did you get the flowers I sent you?' he asked, staring at her face like he had to take an exam on it in the morning.

'Yes,' she said shortly. 'I gave them to my make-up girl.'

Reed considered that for a moment, before he shrugged. 'You're really determined to hate me, aren't you? Why don't you just get out all those nasty things you've been calling me in your head and we can draw a line under it and move on?'

There had been a lot of nasty things. Like, really a lot. 'Creepy-voiced, rodent-limbed jerk-face' being a personal favourite, but Hadley couldn't bring herself to say it out loud. 'OK, it means something that you said sorry 'cause usually people don't but the stuff you said to me, it was unforgivable.'

Reed ran his fingers through his already rumpled hair, making it even tuftier. 'I read that *Sunday Style* piece and I felt like an absolute shit. It's kind of hard to reconcile the girl from that article with the girl I know who comes out with bizarro statements every time she opens her mouth.'

'I do not,' Hadley snapped, and he had the nerve to laugh in the face of her most haughty disdain.

'I've just listened to you argue that the death sentence should be reinstated for people who don't wear antiperspirant.'

Hadley took an angry swig of cranberry juice, which did

269

nothing to calm the twisty knot in her stomach. 'I happen to feel very strongly about personal hygiene issues.'

'You're the strangest girl I've ever met,' Reed said, his voice low and intimate, then promptly changed the subject. 'So let's talk about your read-through. With George,' he prompted, at Hadley's blank expression.

'Oh, that. You need to talk to him about his motivation 'cause he's playing Jake like he's got to save the world and win the girl all in the space of ninety minutes.' Hadley's brow wrinkled in consternation. 'Not that I'm down on George and not that I care. Your script? Way overwritten.'

Reed flinched for one beautiful moment because you never told writer/directors that their scripts were anything other than 'a shoo-in for a Best Screenwriting Oscar'. 'Oh,' he said. 'Because you seemed like you were into it.'

Hadley allowed herself a mild eye-roll. 'I was *acting*,' she explained kindly. 'Been doing it professionally since I was three.'

'You know, when I wrote the script, I saw Lisa as this hard-as-nails survivor,' Reed said, ignoring Hadley's dig, even though it should have wounded him. 'She's the real driving force in the relationship. She's tough and impenetrable; but you gave her heart and soul. Will you audition for me?'

Now it was Hadley's turn to stare at Reed, who didn't look like he was being funny. Well, not funny ha ha anyway. And although Derek was meant to be handling these discussions, she decided to make an executive decision. 'I don't audition,' she said grandly. Which wasn't strictly true. She never *used* to audition, but only this morning she'd read for the part of a sea captain's flighty young mistress in a TV series about pirates. She'd looked surprisingly good in a bonnet.

Reed wasn't the least bit phased. 'Well, would you meet with my producer?'

'You'd have to talk to my agent,' Hadley admitted unwillingly, until she got it.

'Oh! Oh, you . . .' There were no words, so she settled for hitting Reed on the arm with her clutch bag.

'What the hell did you do that for?' he demanded, rubbing the spot like a weeny suede pouch had inflicted that much damage.

'This is all part of the big, grand apology. You offer me the chance to audition for your movie and I'll be so overcome with gratitude that I forgive you even though you were mean to me!' Hadley folded her arms tightly so she didn't slap him again.

'God, you're impossible,' Reed decided with a groan, slumping forward so he could rest his chin on his hand. 'I think you could do something really special with the role but, hey, if you never spoke to me again, it would upset me but, newsflash, princess, I'd get over it.'

'Why?'

'Why what?'

'Why would it upset you if I never spoke to you again?' Hadley asked, because it was the sixty four thousand dollar question. 'It's not like we're friends. You're just my roommate's half-brother.'

Reed sat back and eyed her suspiciously. 'You really don't know why it would upset me?'

There didn't seem to be one good reason why the absence of Hadley's voice would cause Reed deep inner turmoil. 'Are you one of those people who have to be liked by everyone?' she asked.

'No, just some people,' Reed said so quietly that she had to strain her ears to hear him over the clink of glasses and the hum of chatter from the surrounding tables.

Hadley didn't know why he was whispering. And why he'd said 'people' like it was some kind of secret code. She wasn't that dumb. She knew about 'people' – you let them into your life and they made it hell. Or shifted closer to you so their knees bumped against yours and made goosebumps spring up along your arms.

'I have to go home now!' Hadley yelped because her thought processes were leading her nowhere good. An elbow in Reed's ribs was remarkably effective in getting him to budge so Hadley could squeeze past him.

But as she snatched up her bag, Reed was also standing up and stretching lazily. He grinned suddenly in way that made her turn the uneasy all the way up to eleven. 'We'll share a cab, OK?' he said, and didn't wait for her reply but took Hadley's arm so he could lead her through the exit.

'But I can get my own cab . . .'

Reed tutted. 'Call me overbearing, as I know you just love to do, but I'm seeing you to the door whether you like it or not.'

It was cosy in the back of the cab, almost intimate, but before Hadley could start fretting about what might happen if there was more knee-bumping, Reed was sitting a respectable distance away from her and wanting to talk. About things she really didn't want to talk about.

'So have you heard from your parents? Did they freak out when they saw the *Sunday Style* piece?'

Hadley squinted to see if Reed had a hidden microphone stashed away, but the smooth lines of his suit didn't seem to be packing any recording equipment. 'My mom wanted us to launch a joint libel action against the magazine but my agent . . . didn't think it was a very good idea.'

Derek had actually blocked Amber's number from Hadley's Sidekick and handled the call himself. Hadley had watched through the glass walls as Derek paced furiously around his office while Amber harangued him on speakerphone. Then he'd punched his desk a few times after hanging up. And her dad?

'Apparently he's accepted Jesus Christ as his personal lord and saviour,' Hadley sniffed.

Reed gave a short bark of a laugh as if he didn't think it was that funny either. 'Finding God in prison, that's original.'

Hadley was forced to agree. 'He always used to take the Lord's name in vain,' she reminisced. 'And he wouldn't even go to church at Easter or Christmas.' Yet now he'd found his way back to the path of righteousness and while he was actually 'supporting' Hadley 'in her crusade against the homosexual scourge destroying our family values', he'd been none too thrilled about her topless photos. 'I'm begging Hadley to visit me so we can pray together and get the evil out of her bones.' Hadley wondered if the born-again evangelist routine was going to impress a parole board. It sure wasn't doing anything for her.

'Oh, Hadley, why don't you have anyone to look after you?' Reed sighed and really, he had to stop being so nice. It was completely destroying her belief system.

'But I'm meant to be able to look after myself,' Hadley protested, wondering if it would be gross if she kicked off her shoes that were starting to pinch her toes. 'I can stand on my own two feet.'

'You're eighteen,' Reed pointed out, like that made any difference. 'Jesus, you're only eighteen. And I read that piece and then I realized that you've already gone through a whole lifetime of hurt.'

'Will you stop going on about that stupid article? Like,

please. And fyi, eighteen means I'm an adult,' Hadley explained tiredly.

'When I was eighteen, I was a complete mess,' Reed confessed, even as he lounged on the seat, the very epitome of hipster cool.

'You so weren't,' Hadley scoffed. 'You have, like, coolness as part of your DNA or something.'

'You wanna know a secret?' Reed grinned in an unexpected way that was almost too endearing for Hadley to handle. 'I was a geek. I was president of the chess club in High School. And I was a mathlete.'

'Oh, whatever. Like, a Seth Cohen geek and all the girls loved you even though you listened to really whiny boy-rock.' Hadley couldn't help but giggle. And then she had to giggle again until she was wheezing at the thought of a teenage Reed carrying his emo pain on his sleeve.

'I made Seth Cohen look like the most macho jock to ever pitch a home run,' Reed insisted. 'I wasn't like Candy. I didn't grow up in New York with rock stars. After my parents split up, I stayed with my dad in Long Island. I always handed in my homework assignments on time and I worked in a Subway on the weekends.'

She was beginning to see Reed in an entirely new light. Discovering his secrets; because he wasn't trying to hide them. And he was finding out about her too, because the whole way home he asked her questions and he listened. Like, *really* listened when she spoke, and it wasn't until she was in the middle of her second-best David Hasselhoff anecdote about the time they were shooting at Six Flags theme park ('and I'd had this protein shake just before I got on the rollercoaster . . .') that she realized he was staring at her mouth. Hadley surreptitiously touched the offending body part to make sure that her lipstick wasn't smeared and Reed's eyes followed the movement of her finger.

Hadley knew for a fact that her and Reed were having a moment. What she couldn't understand was why. She wasn't his type; she didn't have straggly hair, or an interest in really boring French new-wave films. Or an ounce of mystery and allure.

Maybe it was a by-product of trying to make up with her – acting as if he wanted to move a crucial three inches across the seat so all he'd have to do was pout his lips and they'd be kissing. It was all part of the get-Hadley-back-on-side service. Which was whack because he didn't even like her that much. Not really.

Hadley allowed herself one last, lingering look because up close Reed's eyes weren't actually that beady, but were slumberous orbs that were fixed on her – like staring at her face was a fine way to pass the time. Hmmm, and this close she could catch the faintest trace of his aftershave . . .

It was so time to rewind because she'd been here before. Led astray by a passably cute boy; and look how well that had turned out? 'Stop staring at me!' Hadley demanded, sliding across the seat so she could cling to the door handle. She didn't trust her treacherous body not to do something totally lame like leap into Reed's arms. 'And stop being nice to me, it's freaking me out.'

Reed stopped lounging and sat up straight so Hadley could get the benefit of his annoyed expression. 'I'm only ever going to be nice to you from now on, so you'd better get used to it,' he declared tetchily. 'And also you should know that when I make a mistake, I own up to it and then I try to make things right.'

That's what worried her. Exactly how Reed intended to make things right, because his behaviour tonight had been verging on the flirtatious and just because he'd read the *Sunday Style* piece didn't mean he had all the facts.

'I'm not easy,' she blurted out. 'Those photos that appeared . . .' Hadley shook her head because it all started flooding back. Waking up in a strange bed, being violated, victimized and the whole world thinking that she'd planned it.

'It's all right,' Reed said gently, reaching across to take her hand. 'You don't have to explain.'

'Yes, I do. People think I'm a big, old slut and I'm not. He drugged me and he *touched* me and took photos of me and everyone's seen them – seen me – and it shouldn't have been like that.' Hadley screwed her eyes shut at the horrible car crash of images flooding her mind. 'It should have been my decision who I chose to see me like that and it got taken away from me. Just like everything always does.'

She was crying again. Hadley had actually begun to enjoy crying when she was on her own and could hug a cushion and wallow in her newfound mopiness. It wasn't quite so much fun with Reed sitting next to her, watching the tears wreak havoc with her eye make-up.

'Hadley,' he said urgently, his arm curving around her shoulder.

'Been parked outside here for five minutes,' the cab driver's voice suddenly boomed over the intercom. 'Are you going or staying, mate?'

'He's going,' Hadley decided in a shrill voice, as she fumbled for the door handle again. She needed to put as much distance as possible between herself and Reed's hands. And concerned expression. And citrussy aftershave. And his mouth, oh, his mouth. 'He's so going. You're going, right?'

Reed suddenly laughed, the tension fizzing away like champagne bubbles evaporating in a glass. He leaned across and opened the door for her. 'You should try to enjoy life more,' he suggested.

Hadley scrambled out of the car with more haste than dignity. The cabbie was already pulling away from the kerb. 'I *am* enjoying life,' she insisted. 'I'm practically high on it,' but she was talking to the wind, which lifted her words and carried them into the night as the cab sped away.

Chapter Twenty-Nine

Mr C-C was scrabbling at the door as Hadley unlocked it and much as she wanted to snuggle down with a cup of chamomile tea and have a good weep, the needs of her dog came first. Sometimes being a responsible pet owner sucked.

Hadley ambled round the block, waiting patiently with her plastic bag at the ready as Mr C-C sniffed various trees and lampposts.

Finally, she was back indoors and just about to curl up on the sofa with her herbal tea and a rice-cake, but annoyingly she couldn't get her weep on. Crying was obviously like champagne; the more she did it, the more she wanted to do it. It was getting to the stage when she might have to go into rehab in order to kick her tear habit. Especially when she had to resort to such devious methods as sticking the *Dumbo* DVD on and fast forwarding to the bit where his mother was stuck in the mad elephant cage.

As soon as that trunk came snaking through the bars to cradle Dumbo, rivulets of liquid were gushing down Hadley's face like the Niagara Falls.

Mr C-C looked up in alarm as she gave a choked sob and huddled into the cushions. Not that Amber had ever been locked in a cage for being insane, but Hadley could identify.

It took a while for the doorbell to penetrate the pity party. Hadley was going to ignore it, but whoever had decided to come calling at, hello, one-thirty in the morning was obviously leaning on the bell.

Hadley shuffled towards the hall, grumbling with every step, and unlocked the door. 'I'm sure there was a house rule about booking into a hotel after midnight . . .' she began, but it was pretty incoherent with the tears and all. Besides, it wasn't one of her flatmates standing there looking a little contrite but Reed.

'I knew you'd still be upset,' he said huskily and before Hadley could point out that this wasn't the old upset but an entirely new upset, he'd taken the two steps forward that were needed to wrap her in his arms and give her a hug.

Actually it might even have been a cuddle. Hadley wasn't too sure. But there seemed to be a lot of murmuring and hair-stroking going on for simply a mere hug.

'It's OK,' Reed purred in her ear, as he guided her back into the lounge. 'I've got you.' And he certainly had got her, because she was being pulled down on to Reed's lap. She planned to struggle but it was kind of comfy once she slung her legs over the arm of the chair. Hadley could hear the steady beat of his heart as she rested her cheek against Reed's chest and let him brush her tears away with the pads of his fingers.

Hadley wanted to ask Reed why he'd come back. And she really wanted to grab the remote control and turn off the DVD player before Reed realized that she was watching Disney cartoons for no good reason. But it was just easier to snuggle harder against him until he put both arms around her really tight so nothing could get at her. After all, they'd have to go through Reed first.

'Why are you watching *Dumbo*?' he asked finally, peering over the top of her head to where Jiminy Cricket was yammering on to a bunch of crows.

Hadley 'hmmm'ed vaguely as if to suggest that the DVD player was possessed by demons who were in charge of its programming. 'It was just on,' she elaborated. 'And I couldn't turn it off.'

'Disney movies are quite interesting,' Reed said. 'You've got *Dumbo*, *Bambi* and even *The Jungle Book* based on a kind of reverse Freudian dystopia, with the absent mother and the ubiquitous surrogate father figure . . .'

Reed's voice was a pleasing, melodious hum in her ear. Hadley shut her eyes so she could concentrate on how he sounded, rather than what the fricking hell he was talking about and let herself drift away.

'You're awake,' said that same voice in her ear and Hadley rolled over to find herself staring straight at Reed. On her bed. In what the Sunday papers would call a 'compromising position'.

'You . . .' she breathed in horror.

'You were dead to the world so I carried you in here, but you're very clingy when you're asleep,' Reed said quickly, too quickly for Hadley's liking. And she was so the opposite of clingy. 'I couldn't get free so I slept on top of the covers.'

Hadley looked down and not only was she still wearing all her clothes, but someone had wrapped her in the cashmere throw from the bottom of her bed. 'Yes, but . . .'

'I was a perfect gentleman. Even when you whacked me in the eye with your elbow when you turned over.'

Hadley blinked sleepily while she processed that information, before she decided that no harm had probably been done. As long as there wasn't photographic evidence. She settled back down on her pillow with a gentle sigh, which brought her eyeball to eyeball with Reed.

They'd never been this close before. Like physically close, or even emotionally close or whatever. Despite the fine dusting of stubble, Reed had flawless skin; not an open pore or blackhead in sight. And she'd kill for lashes that long-fringed and black, which made his eyes seem even bluer. Hadley made a mental note to search online for evidence that he wore coloured contact lenses.

Obviously she still had post-traumatic stress syndrome because she absolutely could not stop staring at Reed. Mind you, he was staring right back. 'You know, you're actually really pretty. I never noticed before,' he said, which was nice of him, though technically untrue.

'I'm not,' Hadley whispered. 'I've let myself go.' It felt like the sort of conversation that should happen at a low volume.

They both watched Reed's hand lift in the air so he could bring it nearer to her face. 'Your freckles are adorable,' he noted gravely, then pulled away. 'Not sure if this is a good idea, Hadley.'

Again, the having of the moment. When did she and Reed start having these moments where it seemed like he wanted to kiss her? And he was right, there were, like, at least 547 reasons why it was a dumb idea. But then there were two reasons why it was the best idea ever.

Just once she wanted to kiss and be kissed by someone because they both wanted to, not because there was someone behind the camera telling them to, or photographers waiting to take a picture of a lingering, headline grabbing clinch.

And the second reason? Hadley could just imagine Candy's reaction if she found out and that was all the motivation she needed to close the gap and softly brush her lips against Reed's.

Hadley knew how to kiss. Or rather she knew how to kiss so it looked like you were kissing, but really you were just moving your mouths against each other, while ensuring that there were no unsightly double chins, bumped noses or, ew, spit.

But actually kissing Reed wasn't like that at all. It was wet and messy and he quickly realized that Hadley didn't have any idea of what she was doing past that first initial butterfly flutter of her lips.

He smiled against her mouth and even that felt sexy. 'Let me show you what to do,' he said.

And then he did and nothing mattered. Right then, Hadley was pretty sure that fame was fleeting and her career was simply a question mark but she didn't care. Because if she got to kiss Reed for a little while longer, then life would be sweet.

They kissed until her lips were sore and when she closed her eyes, there was this swoony feeling that she'd only ever had when she'd won her Emmy.

'Pretty girl,' Reed murmured before he took his magical mouth away. He scratched his head ruminatively. 'Well, I didn't see that one coming.'

And Hadley might have been drunk on his kisses but she was clear-headed enough to check the small print. 'In a good way or a bad way?'

Reed stroked his finger along the back of her hand. 'A good way. Mostly. You're determined to surprise me, aren't you?'

'I am? You! *You're* the surprising one, with your . . .'

Hadley pressed her fingers to her lips, which were still tingling like the time she'd had collagen filler.

'If you keep doing that, I'm going to have to kiss

you again,' Reed told her and he was leaning in close again, all ready to devastate Hadley's central nervous system with the kind of kisses a girl would remember if she lived to be ninety. Also, bits of him were touching bits of her that she really wasn't sure it was safe for him to be touching.

'You have to go!' Hadley demanded, simultaneously sitting up and giving Reed a shove hard enough that he slid off her bed and landed on the floor with a muffled grunt. 'Now!'

'Yeah, it's probably best not to rush things. It's all happening a bit soon,' Reed muttered, almost to himself. 'We're not a natural fit, though that's not necessarily a bad thing really, even—'

Hadley had never realized how much Reed could yammer. 'We're not a natural anything,' she exclaimed. 'And make sure there are no photographers around before you leave.'

Reed scrambled to his feet, trying to tug out the creases on his black shirt, which was crumpled beyond the ability of all but a really good laundry service.

'You need to work on your tender goodbyes,' he said dryly, snagging his jacket from the end of the bed.

'I liked the kissing,' Hadley assured him, then wished she hadn't because did that make her sound slutty? 'But we didn't even clean our teeth and I have stuff to do today . . .' she tailed off and studied her fingernails intently.

285

'I'm going,' Reed clarified. 'And I'll see you soon. At your audition.'

Hadley's head shot up so she could glare at Reed who was looking alarmingly similar to Candy, what with the annoying smirk. 'I already told you, I don't do auditions,' Hadley protested stridently, but she was talking to Reed's back as he exited the room with a cheery wave.

Chapter Thirty

The screen test was held in a studio in East London two days later. Derek had proved very unwieldly about the whole issue. Grumbling at the injustice of it all, Hadley followed the detailed instructions on the call sheet that Derek had sent over and turned up in her plainest top, scruffiest jeans, face scrubbed free of make-up and hair pinned back.

She looked like the poster girl for washed-out street urchin.

She was shown into the rehearsal room by the straggly-haired girl from the other night, who introduced herself as Reed's PA (he had a PA, what was up with that?). Hadley stood at the doorway for a second, taking in the huge white space; sunlight streaming in from the large windows so there'd be nowhere to hide.

'Hadley, glad you could make it. Let me introduce you to everyone,' Reed said, getting up from his chair. He seemed a million miles away from the man who'd given her a crash course in the finer points of making out. Also, he was wearing jeans and a cute stripy sweater. Reed didn't wear jeans and snuggly jumpers. He wore black suits with black shirts and black ties. It was quite an adjustment.

Hadley realized that she was rooted to the spot and gazing at Reed in what could be misconstrued as a dreamy way. She inched forwards with her newly modified perky smile. (Derek had told her to take it down a few notches.)

Reed put names to a frighteningly large number of people for just an audition. Hadley tried to remember that Bob was the producer and Terry was in charge of casting but really there were rules to auditions and as long as she remembered them, then everything would be just peachy.

Rule number one was to keep her handshake firm. Rule number two was to have a slightly personalized greeting for each new face. Rule number three was to not draw attention to the fact that her scruffiest jeans had cost $400 and rule number four was to not go into complete meltdown as she was kissed on the cheek by Will Vaughn, the foxiest, most hotly tipped Hollywood player since Orlando Bloom had done those films about the hobbits.

'You probably don't remember me,' Will Vaughn said coyly. 'But I spent six weeks sitting behind you at Riverdale High in *Hadley's House*.'

Damn! Hadley waited to hear that Amber had fired his ass for eating Twinkies in front of her, but he was going misty-eyed at the memory 'of my first speaking part. I had to say, "did anyone else see this shifty-looking guy hanging round the gym after the pep rally?" '

Hadley stared at him blankly because there had been so many extras in the High School scenes and they weren't allowed to approach her under pain of being ejected from the set. 'There was always some shifty-looking guy hanging round the gym,' she said finally, and, thank you Lord, Will Vaughn was smiling in agreement.

'We used to call you 'Three-takes Harlow' because you nailed your scenes so quickly.'

'What happened if you had to do four takes?' the producer suddenly piped up.

'I never had to do a fourth take,' Hadley said proudly. 'Ever.' That sounded kinda big-headed and like she was an assembly-line hack. 'Sometimes we had to do way more than three takes on the *Little Girl Lost* movies though.' And that made her sound like she belonged in TV and couldn't cut it as a film actress.

Nobody seemed to be recoiling in horror, but you could never tell with industry types. They were sneaky like that.

'Let's do Jake's death scene,' Reed said, rolling up his sleeves so Hadley had an inspiring view of his toned forearms. 'From page 113. Why don't you two guys take a minute to work out how you want to play it?'

Hadley wiped her sweating palms against her jeans. The audition was meant to be no biggie. But now she was here; kneeling on the floor with Will Vaughn's head cradled in her lap, and the crap was slowly being scared right out of her.

Apparently the new Hadley got totally bad stage fright,

which just sucked. But there was something intimate about performing for a handful of people and a camera, which left her feeling more exposed than when she was on a huge sound stage or in front of a live TV audience.

She could either channel her nerves into her character, who had to be pretty freaked out at the thought of her one true love bleeding to death, or she could choke. And the old Hadley, and the new one too for that matter, did not choke. Choking was not a viable option.

'OK, I'll cue you in,' called Reed from behind the camera. 'One, two, action!'

Hadley stroked her hands through Will's hair and willed her mouth to open.

Five minutes later, Reed told them to stop and Hadley blinked slowly as she realized that the hard floor was playing havoc with her knees and that her fingers were coated with the gunk that Will Vaughn slathered in his hair so it defied all the laws of gravity.

It was hard to gauge the reactions of her audience. The producer was scribbling notes on a pad, the casting director was staring at the two of them with absolutely no facial expression, Reed was fiddling with his camera and everyone else was smiling, but that wasn't a whole lot to go on. Hadley knew that she'd remembered her lines because no one had prompted her, but that was all she knew. She'd been out to lunch, away with the fairies, so knee deep in character that when she looked down at her jeans she still expected to see them splattered in blood.

'I gather you won't do nudity, right?' asked one of the suits. 'Partial nudity?'

The next person who saw her naked breasts would be the guy she was in a long-term, committed relationship with. 'You'd really have to talk to my agent about that,' Hadley said sweetly. And if Derek thought she was going to flash her nipples for the role then he really needed to have the thinking part of his brain retuned.

'OK, great,' Reed said distractedly, still frowning at the camera monitor. He glanced up and gave Hadley one of those slow smiles that would turn her into gloop if she wasn't made of sterner stuff. 'I'll see you soon, OK?'

Will Vaughn walked out with her 'cause he was an old-fashioned Southern boy whose momma done raised him right. 'You were awesome,' he assured Hadley. 'Totally blew everyone away. I hope we get to work together on this.'

'When do you think we'll hear about callbacks?' Hadley asked as they lingered at the front door.

'I've already got the part. The contract's been signed.' Will nibbled his fingertip anxiously. 'At least, I thought it had been signed. My agent said they were overnighting it. Why? What have you heard?'

Urgh. Paranoid actors were the worst and she ought to know. Hadley patted Will on the arm. 'Nothing. Just one of my friends was up for the role and I mean, like, that's how

I got my audition. Reed saw me helping him with a read through.'

'Well, I hope *you* get the part. I hate the two other actresses up for it,' Will confessed, snaking a packet of cigarettes out of his pocket. 'One of them cheated on my best friend and the other one has really bad breath. Like, she's too good to go to a dentist.'

It was weird. Six months away from LA and Hadley had forgotten how bitchy everyone was. She kinda missed it.

'Well, it was great to meet you,' she said, reaching up for the standard air kiss. 'Or, like, meet you again. Sorry for not remembering you.'

'Don't sweat it, baby. And I'll put a good word in for you. I'm the name attached to this project – it gives me a certain power. Laters, Hadley.'

Chapter Thirty-One

It wasn't like Hadley expected Reed to call and profess his undying love or offer her the part. Or, like, both. Except she had and he hadn't.

A week went by. Then another one. She hung out with Irina and was introduced formally to Javier, which actually meant that she sat on the sofa while they bitched at each other for an hour.

Laura had jetted in for three hours. It was long enough that Hadley could have shared about the Reed kissage but Laura would have told Candy. Which should have made it all Romeo-and-Juliet-like, but it didn't. It was just super-annoying. Especially as Candy herself was hanging about like a little black cloud which usually meant that Reed came around, but obviously both Hadley's kisses and screen test were too sloppy to keep his interest. No wonder that her whole world felt grey and damp.

Though actually it *was* grey and damp. Summer in London had been way too short and now it rained all the time. Hadley peered out of the lounge windows one Saturday morning as she waited for Tegan to deliver her weekly provisions, and sighed. The rain was a metaphor for her soul or something.

Hadley's reverie was interrupted by her beeping phone; Tegan announced her presence by hacking up a lung.

'I can't go to Sainsbury's for you,' she coughed down the phone. 'I've got a really bad cold.'

'You poor thing,' Hadley cooed, because she was really good at doing sympathy. 'I hope you're tucked up in bed.'

'I feel like ten shades of crap,' Tegan confessed as Hadley winced. Tegan was a nice girl but she did like to over-share.

'So can someone else from Fierce get my shopping, please?' Hadley asked, eyeing the sheeting streams of rain with distaste. 'Or, like, order it on the Interweb? Will they deliver in the next hour 'cause I'm almost out of soya and linseed bread?'

There was a pause while Tegan had a choking fit. Hadley hoped her germs couldn't pass down the phone line. 'Derek says you should do your own shopping now,' Tegan informed her. 'He says you have to look the British public in the face and also he wants to see you at the office at four pm.'

'I can't go out, it's raining!' Hadley didn't have to fake her outrage. 'And why do I have to look the British public in the face when they hate me? And what does Derek want on a Saturday afternoon?'

'Hadley, talking really makes me throat hurt,' Tegan wheezed. 'Wear a baseball cap or something.' And with that pithy piece of advice, she had the nerve to hang up. Hadley would definitely be having words with Derek about her.

As it was she pulled on her Miu Miu coat, because there was no more lean steak mince left for Mr C-C, and gingerly opened the front door.

Mr C-C wasn't in the fairest of dispositions either. He took one look at the soaked pavement and promptly sat down on the mat. 'No way, mister,' Hadley tutted as she clipped his leash on. 'You are going for a walk and you can damn well like it.'

Once they got to the supermarket, he practically jumped into his Louis Vuitton carrier because although the English were meant to be a nation of dog lovers, they sure didn't love them when they were in their shops.

As Hadley perused the soups for one that was low-fat that she hadn't tried yet, she saw two shop assistants pretending not to stare at her. They weren't doing a very good job of it. Hadley grabbed the nearest carton (tomato and coriander *again*) and beat a hasty retreat before they called Security to have her and Mr C-C thrown out of the store.

She'd just got to the end of the aisle when they cornered her. Hadley gave Mr C-C a warning jiggle and made her eyes go big. 'Is there a problem?' she enquired demurely, pushing her sunglasses up her nose.

The woman closest was running her eyes enviously over Hadley's coat but her attention snapped back to her face. 'Oh, you're Hadley Harlow, aren't you?' she said uncertainly and when Hadley nodded, she took a deep breath. 'We used to see you in here all the time.'

With your small, yappy dog and would you mind leaving and never coming back, you gay-bashing, drunken slut. Hadley waited for the inevitable, but it never came. Instead, the other woman dared to pat her arm.

'Saw you on the telly with that horrible rock band,' she confided. 'Thought you handled yourself really well. I'd have peed my pants, I don't mind telling you.'

Hadley did mind being told that but she pinned on a slightly lop-sided smile. 'Thanks, that's really good to know.'

'We knew all that stuff in the papers couldn't be true because you were so sweet and funny. Was it all rehearsed?'

It felt like the Raised By Wolves disaster and the hairy unmentionables that had got waved in her face had happened years ago to someone else. 'Well, some of it was but if I'd known that some smelly rock star was going to get his *thing* out, I'd never have done the show,' Hadley told them, as they listened, rapt. 'It was totally traumatizing. I'm gonna be in therapy for years.'

Both women shook their heads and tutted. 'It was disgusting, you poor thing. So, would you mind signing a quick autograph?'

It had been so long since anyone had asked for her autograph that Hadley had trouble making her letters as swirly as they used to be. '*To Pat and Jean, thanks for all your support and the great soups you sell, Lots of love, Hadley Harlow*' she scrawled.

By the time she left, weighed down with cartons of soup because Pat and Jean had explained that she could buy two and get one free, the smile on her face wasn't faked any more. The three minutes that it took to walk back to the flat stretched into fifteen as she was stopped five more times by people commiserating with her about her awful parents and the dreadful treatment she'd had at the meaty hands of Raised By Wolves. She'd even got a couple of wolf whistles from passing van drivers, including a bellowed, 'I think you're bloody gorgeous!'

The public loved her. They really loved her. Hadley wasn't exactly sure why, but the public were fickle like that. It was best to just enjoy it while it lasted.

Hadley enjoyed it all the way to Fierce's offices. The sun had put in an appearance so she'd caught the bus, though the driver had got really snippy with her for trying to pay with a ten-pound note. A really nice girl had paid her fare and they'd talked all the way to Tottenham Court Road about TopShop. As far as Hadley was concerned, that pretty much made her an honorary Londoner.

'Hey Derek,' she chirped, breezing into his office without knocking. 'I had an awesome journey into town. I got the bus all by myself!'

'Um, that's great, Hadley.' Derek didn't seem quite as enthusiastic about her news as he should have been, but then there was a polite cough from the other side of the room.

'Hi Hadley,' Reed said calmly, as if it hadn't been days and days since he last saw her and he wasn't a cad who got his kicks from seducing young girls and then leaving them high and dry.

'What's he doing here?' Hadley turned to Derek because he wasn't wearing black and didn't have stubble that tickled her face when he kissed her. Not that Derek ever *kissed* her (air kisses didn't count), but it was way easier to look at him and his sheepish expression.

'The three of us need to sit down and have a chat,' Derek supplied, pulling out a chair for Hadley.

It was hard to sit down next to Reed and not look at him. Instead, Hadley stared at the cuff of his shirt, resting on his bony wrist, and tried not to reach out and touch it.

'I want to offer you the part of Lisa in the film,' Reed said, his voice soft, as if they were talking intimately, just the two of them. 'You blew everyone away at the audition and I've spoken to the money people, showed them the footage we shot, and they think you and Will would be a real box office draw.'

Hadley hadn't been expecting that. She'd been expecting a 'maybe' and many long and drawn out negotiations that might have ended in a tentative 'yes'. 'Oh . . .'

'But until we've got a contract that I'm happy with, nothing is going to be signed,' Derek snapped, cutting right across her. 'For starters, there will be no nudity. No partial nudity. No nipples, no pubic hair, no butt cleavage. Eight weeks' shoot time . . .'

'But you have to allow for reshoots.' Reed held up his hand in protest. 'Two weeks for reshoots is practically industry standard. Anyway, you need to take this stuff up with my producers.'

'Hey, guys, I'm not sure how I feel about this,' Hadley said but she could have been made from thin air for all the notice Derek and Reed took.

'Everyone knows that this project is your baby,' Derek sneered at Reed in a way that had to be fake. It was very unbecoming. 'You call the shots.'

Hadley's head went back and forth as Derek and Reed argued about box office percentages and principal photography dates and a whole load of other stuff that didn't need to be dealt with right now. Like, they were playing at being hotshot Hollywood players.

'We're shooting one week in North Carolina so you'll have to clear her schedule,' Reed snapped at Derek, who snapped right back, 'I don't care how little money you have, she's not flying coach.'

Her. She. Maybe Hadley really had become invisible since she entered the room because neither one of them had even said her name. Or listened to what she had to say. Wow, it was just like old times.

'Time out, guys!' Hadley had to shout so loud she was sure she'd strangted her vocal chords. 'It's cute and all the way you're acting out scenes from *Entourage*, but I don't want to do it.'

Derek patted her hand in a conciliatory manner. 'Don't want to do what, sweetie?'

Now it was easier to look at Reed, just to make sure that he got the message. 'I don't want to do the movie.'

Reed and Derek moved seamlessly from playing hardball to good cop, bad cop. Derek cajoled and cooed and held her hand, while Reed's voice got clipped and crisper until he was spitting out words like they were bullets, while his eyes got so cold that Hadley was amazed they didn't freeze over.

'It's not about the money or the partial nudity,' Hadley repeated for the seventeenth time – she'd been silently counting in her head. 'I just don't want to do it.'

'But Hadley, we talked about how you weren't going to do that thing any more where you said that you didn't want to do things.'

'No, we talked about how when I say I don't want to do things, I really don't want to do them,' Hadley explained because it was really simple and there was no reason for Reed to squinch up his face as if his brain was about to burst out of his ears.

'What is the problem?' he bit out, raking his fingers through his hair. 'What the hell is the problem?'

It really looked as if another time-out was needed. Derek obviously thought so too, as he nervously patted

Reed on the shoulder. 'Can you give Hadley and I five minutes?'

Reed stood up, all the better to simultaneously loom and do his Wrath Of God stare on Hadley so she squirmed in her chair. 'Twenty-four hours,' he announced curtly. 'Tomorrow, Garden Café in Regents Park at three. And don't bring your agent.'

Chapter Thirty-Two

After yesterday's deluge, the air had a crispness to it that was a sure sign that winter was getting ready for its starring role.

As Hadley walked through Regents Park towards the zoo she kicked up piles of russet and golden brown leaves, even as she wrapped her coat tighter around her. She'd never get used to how there were, like, four distinct seasons here. In LA, it got a little overcast and rainy at the end of the year, but sunshine was in big supply. In London, it was cold enough that her nose had turned a fetching shade of red. Not only was that too cold to even think about, it was downright un-American.

Reed was waiting for her in the Garden Café. Hadley breathed a sigh of relief as she opened the door and was hit by a warm gust of air scented with the aroma of ground coffee and home-baking.

'Hey,' she said, pulling out the chair opposite and tugging off her gloves. 'Sorry I'm late. I got all turned around by the Rose—'

'What's going on?' Reed asked without preamble, his face as dark and cloudy as the sky outside. 'Do you want more money? Do you want me to kiss your ass a bit more?

Why have you turned down the part?'

Hadley hadn't expected Reed to start getting pissy with her before she'd even taken her shades off. 'I'd love a cup of tea, thanks,' she said calmly, because it was important to establish that she wasn't being browbeaten by Reed in angry-director mode. 'Lapsang Souchong, no milk and a slice of lemon on the saucer.'

Reed's lips flat-lined but he gestured for a waiter and ordered, his voice spitting out Hadley's specific instructions in an ironic tone. 'And I'll have a filter coffee and the hot crumpets.'

'What are *crumpets*?' Hadley asked, her curiosity piqued, as whatever they were they sounded very rude, but Reed just handed back the menu and folded his arms. Really, he shouldn't wear head to toe black because it made him look way forbidding and scary.

'The point,' he bit out. 'Get to it.'

Hadley forced herself to meet Reed's eyes and wished they wouldn't glint like that. 'Well, there's two points, really.'

'Hadley . . .' And he really, really shouldn't growl.

'First point is George,' she said simply because that was all that needed to be said.

'What about George?' Or not.

'Will Vaughn has already been cast but George hasn't even auditioned yet and we've only just re-established our friendship.' She was gabbling, her words coming out in a sticky rush of not making sense. 'He's only just starting to trust me again.'

'George is a big boy,' Reed said. 'He'll get over it. I need a name attached to the movie. He's not a name.'

Reed really should be more savvy about actors and their fragile egos. 'But he hasn't even had an audition and he'll think I deliberately sabotaged him again.'

'Let me get this straight.' Reed smiled in a way that wasn't half as pretty as the other smiles in his repertoire. 'You're turning down what could be a career-altering opportunity in case George has a hissy fit?'

'Well, yeah.' Hadley frowned. 'And it's not like Candy is going to be all hearts and flowers if I take the role either. She'll be mad at you. Probably madder than George would be at me.'

A little muscle in Reed's cheek twitched twice when she mentioned Candy's name. Hadley wanted to press her finger against it and woah! Where did *that* thought come from?

'This film has been the most important thing in my life for the last three years,' Reed told her throatily. 'And now that I have the chance to make it *exactly* how I want to, my bratty sister and your gay best friend aren't going to stop me. You're perfect for the part of Lisa, don't you get that?'

'Oh, I love her. Like, when I read the script, she makes my heart break a little bit because she's so tough but deep down inside she's all mushy,' Hadley assured him. 'But

George plus Candy equals nothing good.'

The waiter came over with a laden tray and Hadley gratefully curled her hands round her teacup because there was still that tic in Reed's cheek that she wanted to prod. She looked at Reed's hot buttered crumpets with interest, especially as he was liberally smearing one with strawberry jam. He wasn't going to keep his body lean and mean if he persisted with such unhealthy eating habits.

'You're starting to drool,' Reed commented, cutting a crumpet in half and handing it to her in a napkin.

'But I can't! Fat and sugar and refined wheat . . .'

'Just eat the damn thing already!'

Hadley nibbled around the edge and had to stop a tiny moan of greed from leaking out. The actual crumpet was kind of bland but the melted butter and sticky sweetness of the jam more than made up for it. 'You know, one morning you'll wake up ginormously fat and then what will you do?'

Reed grinned around a mouthful of crumpet. 'More of me to love.'

He had one tiny blob or jam clinging to his bottom lip and even when Hadley carefully dabbed at the same spot on her own lip with the napkin, he didn't take the hint.

'You've got . . . oh, here.' She reached over and rubbed the offending mark clean with her thumb, closing her eyes as Reed nipped at her hand and her tummy dipped all the way to her feet. 'Made you look about six,' she sniped, because her face was burning and he was smiling knowingly.

'So, Candy and George was your first point?' he asked, changing the subject because it needed to be changed, stat. 'And the second point I already know. Just not sure of one thing: is it because I kissed you, or because I haven't kissed you again?'

'You didn't even call!' Hadley gasped indignantly, pushing away her crumpet. 'Like, even if you wanted to keep a professional distance, you could have called.' She lowered her voice. 'Did it suck really badly? You can tell me, I need to know so I can improve on my performance.'

'Did what suck really badly?' Reed asked.

'Kissing me.' Hadley had to restrain herself from whapping him over the head with her napkin because he was so dense.

The smile that Reed gave her was predatory and sweet all rolled into one and tied with a bow. 'Parts of it did, but I rather liked those parts.'

Huh? 'Oh!' OK, she could be dense too. 'Then why didn't you call?'

'I was in LA and then I was in North Carolina and I knew it would get weird over the phone and I wanted to make a casting decision based on your audition, not because I was missing you,' Reed said and now his smile was a hundred per cent sweet as he stroked her cheek.

'You missed me? Like, really?' Hadley allowed herself ten

seconds to revel in the cheek-stroking and Reed's tender look before she pulled away. 'Actually the kissing wasn't my second point. Didn't factor in to my decision at all.'

Reed shut his eyes, then opened them again so that all Hadley could see was blue. 'What was the second point?' he asked politely, like he wasn't just trying to humour her.

'Well, it's like yesterday this girl on the bus asked me where I got the jacket I was wearing in *Heat* magazine. And then we had a chat about Ross Thomas and how he's all flirty but really he's with Alicia . . .'

Reed did that thing again, where he listened patiently even though she wasn't getting to the punchline any time soon.

'And, like, six months ago, when anyone stopped me it was because they thought I was dead or I was in rehab or recovering from an OD. None of which were true,' she hastily added.

'Well, the fact that you're breathing puts paid to the death rumours,' Reed said dryly. 'So, your fanbase . . .'

'Has shrunk and now they mostly know me from *Life Begins at 9.30* and it's just I'm liking only being a little bit famous instead of a lot famous. I'm making enough money that I'll be able to buy somewhere to live and OK, it won't be a mansion in Malibu but it's just me now and I don't need that many extra rooms . . .' Hadley gave a frustrated sigh. She shouldn't try to explain stuff. It worked much better when Tegan drafted her press statements.

'You're worried that if you do the movie and it's a hit – which it will be – it will start all over again?' Reed said, and no one had ever looked at her like that. Like, they loved to look at her like that. 'What happened to that girl who used to think that fame was the only thing that mattered?'

'She grew up,' Hadley said ruefully. 'There are lots of things more important than fame, like friends and having a proper life and TopShop and . . .'

'Oh God, you're amazing, Hadley,' Reed exclaimed. 'You *do* say ridiculous things, you really do. It's adorable. You're adorable.'

'You're just saying that so—'

'Come on, let's get out of here. I want to show you the boating lake,' Reed said, standing up and holding out his hand.

The actual boats were tucked away for winter, but they walked along the edge of the water, gloved hands clasped together. It would have been romantic if Hadley could stop flinching from the arctic gusts of wind biting at her face.

'You're going to be in my film,' Reed suddenly said, coming to a halt. 'You're perfect for it and I'm way more stubborn than you. I'll handle George. I'll even handle Candy and she's got a really mean right hook.'

George would love to be handled by Reed, Hadley thought, squeezing his fingers. There was a lot of that going round. 'If, and it's a ginormous if, I decide to do the movie,

309

you'll have to tell him that you and Derek forced me into it,' she decided. 'And that I cried and drank full-fat Coke because I was so upset. It's the only thing he'd believe.'

'So, my super powers of persuasion have worked?' Reed asked lightly. 'You'll be my leading lady?'

The look Reed was giving her spoke volumes. More volumes than a really big bookshop. 'I don't know if I can handle the fame thing on my own. If I even want to.'

Reed's woolly hands cupped her face. They were pretty itchy, but it didn't seem like the right time to tell him that. 'But you're not on your own. You have people in your life who care about you, Hadley. It's about time you started to realize that,' he said with his mouth, which was coming closer and closer. And all Hadley could think was that the other kiss hadn't just been an early morning, pity-fluke. And then she stopped thinking about anything except Reed's hands twisting in her hair, the faint scratch of his stubble on her face and his mouth doing things to hers which should definitely have a PG13 warning slapped on them.

Things were definitely moving to an R-rating when it began to rain, which was one heck of a buzz-kill.

Hadley lifted her head, which meant she had to stop kissing Reed. 'Wet,' she pointed out indistinctly.

'Just ignore it.' Reed tried to tug her back into his arms, but Hadley twisted away.

'My hair will go all frizzy! And there might be a

photographer lurking in the bushes, then you've had it.'

'Oh, whatever,' Reed sneered. 'Like anyone would want to take a picture of *that*.'

And kissing Reed was the only way of getting him to stop teasing her. So she did.

Hadley floated back to Camden on a fuzzy, glowy cloud of almost happiness. She might even have been *completely* happy except her feet were soaked and she'd ruined her Prada boots by splashing in puddles.

She and Reed had walked through London for hours. In the rain. Which would have been romantic if it hadn't been so soggy. And over dim sum in a Chinese restaurant in Soho, she'd ninety-nine per cent promised to do the movie or Untitled Reed Barrett Project, as it was currently known.

Irina was camped out on the sofa watching the Fashion Channel and eating her way through a family-sized bag of Doritos dipped into a jar of peanut butter.

'Yo,' she said by way of greeting. 'I walked your dog, so I have your Chloe bag now, ja?'

'Ja,' Hadley agreed because the heavy padlock on her Chloe bag was totally giving her carpal tunnel syndrome. 'You know, you're not doing your cholesterol levels any favours.'

Hadley flopped down next to Irina and hugged her knees to her chest.

Irina flicked her a glance. 'You look like you on drugs.'

'I *am* on drugs. Like, if love is a drug.' She just had to tell someone, even if Irina wasn't the most care-and-share type person of her acquaintance. 'I'm going to be second lead in Reed's new movie and I think that we might be in love with each other.'

There! She'd said it. She'd admitted that she was only second lead, though to be fair, Will Vaughn was more high profile than her at the moment. But the love thing had popped out of its own accord.

Hadley's expression was serious enough that Irina actually dropped the remote control. 'For real?'

'Completely for real,' Hadley breathed, her eyes wide. 'But you mustn't tell anyone about any of it. Especially if that anyone is Candy.'

A slow, sly smile crept on to Irina's face. 'Well, I like your evil plan to get one over on that bitch.'

'This isn't about Candy. Though she'll throw the world's biggest hissy fit when she finds out, which is like a free gift with purchase really.' Hadley's face was aching from all the smiling. But the day just kept getting better and better.

'What the hell are you looking so smug about?' Candy demanded, struggling through the door with her suitcase. 'Did you get another toilet tissue commercial?'

Hadley could see Irina's jaw clenching, all ready to spit out a few words to rock Candy's mean-spirited world. A quick, surreptitious pinch of her thigh put paid to that.

'You wouldn't understand,' she told Candy kindly. 'I'm just, like, growing as a person and the universe is rewarding me in a really special way.'

Candy's face was enough to turn even soy milk sour. 'Like I even care,' she scoffed. 'I'm going to bed because I just can't handle you two right now.'

Hadley settled back on the sofa and shared a beatific smile with Irina. Plus, she'd totally managed to snag the remote control so they could watch a rerun of *Hadley's House* on cable rather than lots of girls with zero body fat marching down the catwalk. Good times, man, good times.

Chapter Thirty-Three

'Five minutes, Miss Harlow,' someone called through the door of her trailer. *Her trailer.* She had a trailer. Or it was more like a really small mobile home, but it was still a trailer with her name on the door. And it was still a movie set, even if she was only getting second billing.

Hadley concentrated on smoothing down her thermals and then pulling up her jeans before she scrutinized her butt in the full-length mirror. There was four inches of snow outside and she was due to spend most of the day lying in a sleeping bag on top of it. The insurance people had even insisted that she'd had a flu jab so she didn't hold up filming by going all croaky and stuff.

It was funny but she didn't even feel that cold. Not just because the portable heater was going full blast, but because she was burning up from the buzz she always got on the first day of a new film. It had been a while but Hadley recognized the churny, sicky, giddy feeling in her stomach.

She sat down on a chair so she could pull on a pair of greying Converses and admire her little collage of congratulations cards. One from Laura, telling her to give Will Vaughn an extra snog on her behalf. One from Irina, which Hadley hadn't even been able to decipher, not because it was in Russian but because the handwriting looked like it belonged to someone with no arms. There'd even been a card from Benji and George, all the way from LA where Benji was launching his solo career and George was shooting a pilot for a new TV show. '*Break a leg, bitch*' it proclaimed, so Hadley guessed that George was still a little upset.

He'd told Reed that he didn't really feel that the part was suitable what with all the drug-taking and prostitution, but Hadley had sensed the whiff of serious sour grapes. He must have drunk from the same glass as Candy, who'd been like a force ten hurricane crossed with the Wicked Witch of the West ever since she found out.

Not like she'd even found out everything there was to find out. And it wasn't as if officially there was anything Candy needed to find out. Hadley had always thought that when you had a boyfriend, there'd be a discussion. Maybe he'd say, 'I'm your boyfriend and you're my girlfriend.' Just to get it out there in the open, but Reed never did. He'd just say, 'Am I seeing you later?' Or 'Shall we go to Wagamama for lunch?' then hold her hand as they walked along Arlington Road, though that could have been to help steer her around the hobos that hung around the drop-in centre. Either way, it was very boyfriendly behaviour.

It was something that she'd have to ask Alicia about.

Laura still had the whole boy embargo thing going on; Irina wouldn't even talk about Javier most of the time and Candy? Ha ha ha!

It was kind of a mom-conversation if she'd had a mom who wasn't Amber. The minute the news of her film role had hit *Variety* and *The Hollywood Reporter*, the phone-lines between London and LA had started buzzing. Amber had even sent a gift basket from Hadley's favourite LA spa retreat.

So she was kinda talking to Amber again, but only on speaker phone with Derek present. Hadley still didn't know how she felt about it but at least she had photos of the twins to stick on her wall. Little Kai had a really mutinous look in his eyes, which didn't bode well for the future. But it was Rocky that she felt sorry for. Poor kid was definitely going to be booked in for some hairline threading before his third birthday. Still, being a sister was cool as long as you didn't get all stalkery about it like certain people she could mention whose name just happened to be Candy Careless.

Hadley took one last sip of cooling tea, careful not to dislodge the cold sore that the make-up team had carefully applied and stood up. She couldn't wait to get on set. Well, as soon as her knees stopped banging together and she lost the going-to-puke-any-second-now feeling. She gripped on to the side of the dressing table as a wave of panic threatened to rock her off her feet.

'Princess, I thought I'd escort you to the set,' Reed came through the door and stared at her anxiously. 'You all right?'

'I'm going to explode from nerves and I've told you a million times not to call me that,' Hadley snapped, as she tried to talk and do her deep breathing exercises simultaneously.

'You'll be fine,' Reed said smoothly. 'You're a professional. The minute you get on set, you'll forget everything except your motivation – and your lines,' he added hopefully.

'But what if I don't?' Hadley wailed. 'And what if no one takes me seriously as an actress?'

Reed practically rubbed his hands in glee. Nobody, not even him, looked good with that much smugness emanating from every pore. 'I'll fire them,' he announced proudly. 'I can do that. I even have a megaphone to shout orders through.'

It took a moment to penetrate the foggy mist where her brain used to be, but Hadley remembered that the day wasn't meant to be just about her. She was beyond evolved now. No, it was Reed's big day as a first-time director, on his first movie, which he'd written, co-produced and sweated over. Why he'd decided to work that hard when he was so handsome she still hadn't figured out.

'Congrats on the megaphone,' Hadley panted, practically pretzelling herself in half as she struggled to breathe. 'And the whole director thing. But, fyi, don't fire anyone on the first day because everyone else will hate you. Do you think I'm having a heart attack?'

Reed crouched down so he could peer at her face, which had to be all red and scrunched up by now. He didn't seem that repulsed. 'Generally, I think people who are having heart attacks are too busy having them to ask if they're having them.' He straightened up and patted her back in a pretty damn perfunctory manner. 'Come on, you can't be late on the first day.'

There was a major head-rush as Hadley regarded her trailer from the right way up. Reed was holding out his hand and tapping his foot impatiently, but she breezed past him.

'I don't want people to think that I got the part because I'm sleeping with you,' she explained. 'So ixnay on the hand-holding.'

'But you're not sleeping with me,' Reed pointed out silkily, and there was absolutely nothing in his tone of voice or facial expression to let Hadley know how he felt about that. 'I hope that you're not going to be this crabby all the time. It's a two-month shoot.'

'I am crabby, aren't I?' Hadley halted two steps from the door so she could tug on Reed's big puffy anorak sleeve. He was going to be toasty warm in that. 'There's so much riding on this. And it turns out that I don't like the pressure like I used to.'

'You'll be fine,' Reed said, cupping her face like he could see the real Hadley through the cold sores and the heavy panstick and the fake cuts and bruises. 'Good luck, princess.'

Hadley decided to take the high road and not yell at him again. 'Good luck to you too, Mr Hotshot Movie Director.' They shared one of those smiles that Hadley didn't know she could do, until Reed had taught her. It was another moment and she loved it when they had those. Then something occurred to her.

'Do you promise that I'll get to wear something pretty at least once in the film? Maybe a little Marc Jacobs number and we go easy on the teen prostitute make-up?'

Reed opened the door of the trailer, and ushered her out. 'You'll have to get your people to call my people, Miss Harlow,' he said in a faux LA accent, which sounded absolutely nothing like the real thing.

And she had a tart retort all good to go but then she heard that hum of expectation as she carefully edged down the trailer steps. Hadley stood motionless for a second, watching the bustle as the film set came to life; extras milling about, the camera dolly being wheeled into place, a coterie of people gathering around the camera monitor, even the runners handing out cups of coffee and last-minute script edits.

It felt a lot like coming home. She belonged here and anyone who thought that she didn't could just get over

320

themselves. Hadley slipped her hand into Reed's, who gave her fingers a comforting squeeze, and walked on to set.

She was *so* ready for her close-up.

Film and TV glossary

So what the heck does all this industry lingo actually mean, huh?

Agent
The person who looks after all the business dealings of the talent, from helping to select projects and roles, to negotiating how much money they get.

Craft Services
Craft Services on a film or TV set keep everything running smoothly for the crew members, but generally Craft Services means the catering provided. This is usually a permanent buffet (as well as hot meals), featuring the kind of sugary snacks and carb-laden yummies that most actors shun.

Development
When a film or TV project is in development, it means that there's a lot of behind-the-scenes stuff going on to try and help it get made – from making the script word-perfect to trying to rustle up funding. About ninety-nine per cent of projects in development never see the light of day!

Director

The head honcho who's in charge of making the film and translating the pages of the script into what we see on the cinema screen. All the big creative decisions like casting, costumes and even the music rest on their shoulders.

Equity Card

Equity is the British actors' union which regulates the industry and decides how much regular film and TV workers get paid. (Though if you're a big star, or even a little star, you get paid a lot more than the standard Equity day rate.) It's very hard to work in film and TV without an Equity card.

Greenlight

This means that a project that *was* in development has been given the go-ahead by a studio, or 'greenlighted', as they say in the business called show.

Green room

The green room on a live TV show or in a theatre is the space where the stars and hangers-on can chill out and have a quiet drink, before, during, and after the show. Weirdly, the room doesn't actually have to be green.

Jumping the shark

Is that moment when you realize that a formerly good TV

show has suddenly got rubbish. The term comes from an episode of the long-running Seventies show *Happy Days*, when in a desperate attempt to actually have something exciting happen, the character Fonzie jumped over a shark on a pair of water skis. (See *www.jumptheshark.com*)

Independent Film

A film like *Little Miss Sunshine* that's made without pots of money and without much interference from a major studio.

TV Pilot

A test episode made to screen to TV networks and production companies who'll hopefully like it and stump up the cash to develop and shoot a whole series. Pilot season is the busiest time in the TV actor's calendar as they try out for lots of shows in the hope of landing one that will actually get picked up.

Producer

The power behind the scenes on a movie. The producer is responsible for finding the money, hiring the crew and arranging for the actual distribution of the film so it finds its way on to the cinema screens.

Publicist

Although agents can handle press enquiries, most

celebrities also have their own personal publicists, who organize interviews, photo shoots and TV appearances. Sometimes they'll even leak stories to the press on their client's behalf so the celebrity can get their side of a story into the papers without looking desperate enough to have done an interview. When two celebs split up and a close friend is quoted as saying, 'Well, she's absolutely devastated', it's safe to assume that the close friend is actually the publicist.

Screen Test
An audition which is performed in front of a camera so the director can see what the actor looks like on screen and possibly send the film to other people like the producers or the studio before a final casting decision is made. Established actors and actresses usually refuse to audition or screen test because it's totally beneath them.

Syndication
When a TV network sells a programme to a television station and agrees how many times it will be shown. All the US shows we see in the UK (like *Lost* and *Ugly Betty*) have been syndicated over here. Actors pick up syndication fees every time one of their shows is sold to a foreign territory or gets re-aired/repeated.

Talent

Another way of describing an actress/model/whatever. As in, 'I'm handling the talent for this movie.'